THE SAFE HOUSE

SAM BARON

Storm
PUBLISHING

To request permissions, contact the publisher at rights@stormpublishing.co

Ebook ISBN: 978-1-80508-422-8
Paperback ISBN: 978-1-80508-424-2

Cover design: Henry Steadman
Cover images: Shutterstock

Published by Storm Publishing.
For further information, visit:
www.stormpublishing.co

ALSO BY SAM BARON

FBI Agent Susan Parker

The Therapy Room
The Murder Club

for
May
&
Sheila,

my
alpha
&
my
omega

and

for
Leia

my
tau

"It is justice, not charity, that is wanting in the world!"

—Mary Wollstonecraft,
A Vindication of the Rights of Woman

ONE

He descends into darkness.

The stench rises to greet him.

It is the smell of huddled masses, tired and poor, yearning to breathe free.

The rough wooden door, misaligned and leaning off its hinges, grinds against the dirt as he forces it open.

He raises his smartphone, shining a light on the under-ground chamber.

Two dozen pairs of eyes gleam up at him.

Frightened faces thinned by deprivation and trauma, and the exhaustion of the long journey from their countries to this one.

The children murmur fearfully, clutching at their mothers.

The mothers hold their children close, but offer no words of comfort.

After a lifetime of suffering, they have none left to give.

He turns the cellphone light on himself, illuminating his face.

At once, the mood in the sanctuary changes.

"It is the saint, the farishta, the angel of mercy," the refugees say to each other in their diverse tongues. "We have nothing to fear from him. Without his help, we would be in the clutches of the traffickers or the American police."

"I have brought you food and water," he says, holding out the sack.

A chorus of thanks and blessings rises from the weary flock.

The sack is taken from his hands and passed around, grubby hands tearing off chunks of stale bread and devouring it greedily. It returns to him within minutes, empty.

"El Santo, when will we be relocated?" asks a middle-aged man with a wife, three young children, and an ailing mother.

The question is echoed by several voices, some in their own languages.

He holds up his palm, asking for silence.

"Soon, very soon. Rest assured, I am doing everything in my power. It is not easy going up against the might and power of the United States."

A chorus of agreement.

"Even now, I have just come from a lengthy interrogation by agents of ICE."

Muttered curses, quickly sketched crosses, prayer beads and icons clutched. Every immigrant and refugee knows to dread the US Immigration and Customs Enforcement agency. They have all heard the stories from relatives, friends, friends of distant friends.

"You are a bhagwan," says one South Asian refugee mother, raising her joined palms in supplication. She speaks in her own language; her teenage son translates. "We are blessed to have found our way to you."

He joins his own palms in response. "I am no god. I'm just an American who remembers what so many of my countrymen seem to have forgotten. That this country was built on the backs of immigrants, slaves and indigenous peoples. Without them, there would be no America. You have as much right to be here as I do, and I will make sure you find your way in this land. I have people working to create new identities, new documents, for all of you. Once those papers are ready, we will relocate each person to our allies who will help you integrate into the local community, find jobs, and make a home for yourselves. By this time next year, you will be free to walk the streets and exercise your rights like any other American!"

He continues for a few minutes more, as his captive audience listens, wonderstruck.

By the time he is done, their eyes are full of tears of hope, their heads full of dreams of the new life awaiting them.

With regret, he concludes, "Now, I must leave you again. The next time I return, it will be to take you from this grotto to your new homes. Stay strong, stay patient, you do not have much longer to wait now. God be with you, my friends."

The clamor of gratitude and emotion is loud and heartfelt.

He pulls shut the groaning door, leaving them in darkness once again.

Then he takes the heavy padlock from the pocket of his cassock, fixes it to the latch, and locks it with the key.

He drops the key in the dirt.

There is no further use for it.

He climbs the uneven steps to the surface.

He takes a moment to savor the clean, sweet air of the open countryside.

The California night is brilliant with stars, the spring air bracing.

Somewhere in the nearby hills, coyotes howl their nightly laments.

Something scurries by in the underbrush.

The delicate, sweet fragrance of orange blossoms drifts to him on the night breeze.

The man, known as the Saint and by many other names,

checks the explosive charges he planted earlier before he went down to the sanctuary.

He makes sure they are buried deeply enough.

Satisfied, he walks back to the detonator that he had set up earlier beside his pickup truck.

He takes a moment to say a final, silent prayer for all the souls he is about to consign.

Then he turns the detonator key.

The sound of the charges imploding is muffled, a reverberation he feels through the soles of his feet and in his bones.

In a state which experiences over ten thousand earthquakes a year, about twenty-seven a day on average, it feels like just another minor tremor.

For a moment, there is no indication that anything has happened.

Then, with a slow, muted rumbling, a large rectangular section of the ground collapses.

Dozens of tons of earth descend with crushing force, filling the underground sanctuary, burying its occupants, one and all.

He imagines the huddled refugees in the darkness below, their terrified upraised faces, their dirt-choked screams.

Those not killed instantly by the weight of the collapsing earth and rocks will die quickly of asphyxiation.

Their terror will be short-lived.

Their lifelong suffering ended at last.

Their relocation accomplished, as promised.

They are now permanent residents of these United States.

He bows his head one last time, shedding a final tear for these lost souls who have finally found their way home.

Then he takes off the cassock, throws it in the bed of the vehicle, dons the battered Stetson, climbs into the truck, and drives away into the night.

The truck radio is tuned to an all-night country music station.

A familiar hit from a few years ago comes on as he drives, the gravelly voiced crooner singing of cold winter nights and unfaithful lovers.

He starts to hum along, unaware that he's doing so.

Already, he has shed the persona he had donned for the immigrants, like the cassock in the back of the truck.

He is no longer the priest, the saint, the angel.

Once again, he is becoming the man that his family, colleagues and community recognize.

The Saint is gone for now, and will stay gone for a while.

Until the next time.

When the next batch of immigrants arrives.

TWO

My life is in ruins.

I'm Susan Parker, Special Agent-in-Charge at the FBI's Los Angeles Field Office, and I'm standing outside the smoldering wreck of my family home.

It was a modest house, a modern California single-family, two-bedroom, two-bath cottage on a quiet side street within a football's throw of Centurion High. My late husband Amit and I bought it eight years ago, not long after we learned that I was pregnant. We scraped together every dime to make the down payment, took out a mortgage we could barely afford at the time, and moved to Santa Carina Valley in July, four months before Natalie was born.

I remember standing on this concrete driveway, thinking, *My first house!* I remember how proud I felt that day, heart swollen with anticipation at all the birthdays, anniversaries, holidays, and family occasions we would celebrate under that gray-tiled roof. I was positively giddy with excitement.

I kissed Amit, he kissed me back, it was a beautiful summer day, and a hummingbird circled us briefly before dancing away. We were young, still in our mid-twenties, very much in love, recently married, newly pregnant, our lives stretching ahead of us like a sun-drenched California highway waiting to carry us into a brilliant future.

Fast forward eight years.

That future lies in ruins.

Amit is dead and has been gone for over a year although it still feels like yesterday.

Natalie, God bless her, is the light of my life and the center of my universe; she'll turn eight this November.

It's late August again, and my lovely, love-filled little family dream home is a burned-out hulk.

The charred skeleton of the frame lies in broken angles, the hollowed-out interior a blackened heap of ash and debris.

Everything we owned, everything we possessed, is in there, burned to ashes.

It makes me angry.

Angry enough that I'd like to shoot someone. The Clothesline Killer in particular, the guy who did this two months ago. A serial killer who fixated on me in a hunter-prey relationship that turned deadly for my family. But that's no longer an option.

My sislaw, Lata, is talking to the person from the insurance company, a prissy guy in a suit too dark for this hot August morning, who keeps dabbing at his damp forehead and talking on his cellphone. The vibe I'm getting from him is not positive at all.

I was talking to him until a few minutes ago, when Lata saw my questions getting a little too intense and quietly suggested I go over and check out the vegetable garden. She just wanted me to cool off before I lost it. We don't really have a vegetable garden, just a few tomato, green chili, cucumber, and strawberry plants.

And marigolds.

Marigolds are a must for any Hindu ritual and Lata and my in-laws are Hindus. I'm not because though I'm also from India,

my family were Christians from Goa, hence the surname
Parker. But since my family is long since gone, I generally go
along with whatever Lata wants to do. She's not particularly
religious, neither am I, so mostly it involves celebrating festivals
from both cultures to expose my daughter Natalie to the diver-
sity of our blended fam.

I'm rambling now.

I tend to do that when I'm emotionally unanchored.

This house and its contents were everything that I owned in
the world. That we owned. As it is, I could only just manage the
mortgage payments thanks to Lata chipping in. With her out of
the Marines and spending so much time helping to care for
Natalie, our earning capacity has diminished rather than grown
this past year and a half. All our equity was tied up in this
property.

Now, it's all gone, and we have nothing to start over with.
Without this insurance payout, we're basically homeless and
broke.

Finally, Lata finishes talking to the insurance guy, who puts
away his clipboard and leaves, still dabbing his forehead and
talking on his cellphone as he drives off.

Lata doesn't look happy.

I go over to her.

"So? When are they coughing up the dough?" I ask
anxiously.

Lata makes a placating gesture with her palm. "They just
need to sort out a few more legalities."

I clench my fist in frustration. That's the same tripe the
company has been feeding us for the past two months. I
suppress my natural tendency to sound off about insurance
companies and indicate the burned house instead.

"I did this."

Lata shakes her head. "The Clothesline Killer did this."

"I'm the reason he came here."

"You were doing your job," she says.

"I'm failing at my job. FBI agents are supposed to protect and serve American citizens, not put their own family in harm's way or get their homes burned down."

"You're a hunter. Sometimes, the prey turns on you, fights back to avoid getting caught. That's not your fault."

"Why are you making excuses for me?" I demand.

"Because you always do this."

"Do what?"

"Find a way to blame yourself for all the world's problems. If I only had a dime for all your imaginary failings, Suse!"

I point at the shambles of our house. The house that Lata moved into after her brother's death, helping me not only with Natalie and the mortgage, but in getting my own life back on track. Before that, she'd only rented, so this is the closest thing to owning a house she's ever experienced as well.

"This is very real, Lata. Our house burned down!"

"Yes, Suse, but we're alive and safe. Natalie, you, me. Focus on that."

She's right. I do tend to be a doomsayer. And when it comes to myself, I'm my own worst critic.

I soften my voice. "I'm trying, Lata. I really am. But it's now been almost three months and the insurance company is still making noises and avoiding cutting a check. We're literally living off the charity of your family."

"That's what family is for," Lata says.

"Yes, but what if the insurance doesn't pay out? How do we buy a new place? How do we survive? All our equity, my life savings and Amit's life savings, and yours... it was all tied up in that pile of ashes. This is a goddamn disaster."

"We've survived bigger disasters," she says.

She means Amit's death. And she's right. When it happened, I thought that would break me. It *did* break me. I'm not the Susan I was before Amit died, I can never be that

Susan again. But I did survive, impossible as it seemed at the time.

She takes off her shades, her angular face softened by those brown eyes that are so eerily exactly like her brother's. For an instant, it's like Amit himself is looking at me.

"It's just a house, Suse," she says gently. "Things. Stuff. Not..."

She pauses and looks away.

Not a person. A person you love.

That's what she's unable to say out loud.

"All that stuff, it's replaceable," she says quietly now. "We can buy new things, a new house. We'll get past this, we always do. Now, bring it in here."

She pulls me in for a hug.

I hug her back, grateful for her.

When we separate a moment later, I feel better. They say even holding hands with another human being, especially someone close, calms the brain's anxiety center. If I'm a mess now, then without Lata I'd be a walking disaster.

And she's right, of course. She always is.

We will get through this somehow, impossible as it seems now.

We *must*.

For Natalie's sake as well as our own, but especially for Natalie.

Lost in my thoughts, I see a large white panel van turn into my lane and slow as it approaches the house.

My pulse quickens.

What's it doing here?

Then I relax a little. I know that van. It's the mobile unit my team and I use while on a case. I recognize the tacky paint from the times we've stenciled or stuck on phony names and logos to pass the van off as a plumbing service or electrician.

Special Agent Ramon Diaz waves to me as he steps out of

the van. I can't recall ever seeing Ramon look hassled, but he definitely looks hassled now. He appears positively distressed.

"Ramon," I say, "what's up?"

"Susan," he says in a tone which tells me instantly that this is serious. Ramon *never* calls me by my name. "I need you to come with me right now."

THREE

"Where are we going?" I ask Ramon.

Ramon doesn't respond. He's intent on driving. He hasn't said a word since I got in the van with him.

We're on Canyon Road, heading northwest, driving through a wooded neighborhood with walled-off residences. We passed Natalie's old preschool a mile or two back, but beyond that, there's nothing out here except undeveloped land.

I notice that Ramon isn't using an app to navigate. Clearly, he's been this way before.

It's just the two of us right now. The van is large enough to accommodate my entire team—five of us, plus Detective Naved Seth, our local liaison with Santa Carina Valley Police Department. Ramon hasn't mentioned if the others are coming and whatever this is, it isn't an official investigation.

I look at Ramon again. He's usually an easy person to read but right now, I can't tell what's going through his mind. That concerns me.

A former gang member in his teen years, Ramon still has the full body tattoos to prove it. Although he had all the gang markings removed when he quit that life, he could still pass as a banger. A product of the rough streets of East LA, he started his career in law enforcement as an undercover narcotics cop for the LAPD. Finding it hard putting away people from his old neighborhoods and wanting to go after bigger fish, he applied for and was accepted by the FBI around seven years ago.

We met when I was still a junior agent, he a rookie. Two years ago, when I made SAC and was allowed to hand-pick my team, he was at the top of my list. His light-hearted attitude and sense of humor, lightning-fast reflexes, brilliant computer skills, and relentless work ethic make him one of the finest FBI agents I've had the pleasure of working with.

In all these years, I've never seen him so disturbed.

"What's going on, Ramon?" I ask him now. "Talk to me."

He shakes his head and jerks his chin forward in a gesture that I interpret to mean, *let's just get there and I'll explain.* Fair enough.

Most days, I wouldn't be able to get Ramon to shut up even if I asked him nicely. Whatever this emergency is, it's got him rattled.

"Okay," I say. And settle in for the rest of the ride.

My phone buzzes.

I check the screen before answering.

CBI, New Delhi calling.

I frown. The CBI is India's equivalent of the FBI, a federal organization that investigates crimes at a national level. It's the official Indian point of contact for foreign law enforcement agencies like Interpol. This isn't the first time I've heard from them but why are they calling me now?

"Good morning," I say politely, "this is Special Agent in Charge Susan Parker. Who's calling?"

The person at the other end makes an apologetic noise. "Good morning, ma'am. I am Amrit Pal Prasad, Additional

Superintendent of Police with Central Bureau of Investigation, calling from New Delhi."

"Yes, Mr. Prasad, what is this regarding?"

"Miss... er... it is Miss Parker, am I right?" he asks.

"Call me Susan."

"Thank you, Susan. Amrit, please."

"Amrit, how may I be of assistance?"

"Susan, I think my junior colleague, Inspector Mahak Arora has been in touch with you?"

"Yes, I recall her calling me."

"Thanks for confirmation. Do you recall when was the last time you spoke to her?"

I watch a group of high-school teens go by, some skateboarding, others walking, all in an energetic, boisterous mood. They're carrying towels and neon pool noodles and are probably heading for the community pool just two streets over.

"It was some months ago," I say.

I can actually remember the exact moment when she called. It was April of this year, four months ago. I had just left the FBI field office at 11000 Wilshire Blvd in downtown Los Angeles after a committee hearing and was on my way to join Lata and Natalie at an amusement park for the day. I'm not sure of the exact day but I remember the thought that struck me the moment I saw the caller ID: *This is something to do with Amit's death.*

All those feelings come rushing back again now, leaving me with a tingling, unnerved sensation.

"By referring to her call log, I believe it would most likely have been April of this year," he says.

"That sounds about right, Amrit."

"Did she say which case she wished to speak with you about?" he says.

"She did not," I say.

"Did she mention any specific details about the case?"

"Only that it concerned a series of murders in India as well as in the US that might be connected. No names, or dates, or other details."

"I see. And she would have said that she was coming to the US and wished to speak with you personally, am I right?"

"She did. She told me she was flying to Washington, DC, the following week and wasn't sure how long she might be there. She expected to come to California once she was done in DC and would get in touch with me when she was here," I say.

I'm starting to feel like I'm under interrogation. There's a pedantic tone to this guy's questions that feels like he's reading off a checklist. A faint beep every thirty seconds or so tells me the call is being recorded, even though he didn't ask my permission to do so.

"And when did she get in touch with you after that?" he asks.

I frown. "She didn't."

There's a pause, then he says, "Please to repeat?"

"Inspector Mahak Arora never contacted me again. No calls, texts, emails, nothing. I did wonder about it but she hadn't given me any details, so I had no idea what case she planned to discuss. Eventually, I figured she probably didn't need to interview me after all and had returned home to India."

A moment of silence.

"Amrit?" I ask. "Are you there?"

"Ma'am, are you quite sure you had no personal contact with Inspector Mahak Arora? She did not come to meet you in person, perhaps? At the FBI field office in Los Angeles? Maybe even at your residence?"

I glance at my burned ruin of a 'residence'. "She did not. No contact, no in-person meeting, nothing. What is this about, Amrit?"

"Susan, thank you for your time, I will be in touch. Is this the best number to reach you?"

"Yes. Is Inspector Arora all right? She did make it back to India, didn't she?"

He doesn't answer immediately, though I can hear him breathing.

"Amrit?"

"Thank you for your time. We will revert."

And with that, he's gone.

I look at my smartphone.

CBI, New Delhi call ended.

What the hell was that about?

I look out the window to get my bearings.

Santa Carina Valley, like most suburban towns in LA County, sprawls across only a few dozen square miles in the rolling hills of Southern California. Drive south out of SCV and you'll hit the tangle of perpetually gridlocked freeways leading eventually to the San Fernando Valley and Los Angeles. Keep driving in any other direction and you'll find yourself in ranch country or undeveloped wilderness.

That appears to be exactly where we're headed.

I can see that Ramon clearly doesn't want to engage until we reach our destination, so I glance at my phone. There's a text from Lata.

Everything ok?

I'm fine, en route to a scene.

I don't know for a fact that we're on our way to a crime scene but what else could it be?

We've just passed a subdevelopment of under-construction new suburban houses, and now we're out in the wild. The road is still excellent. We Californians don't pay the nation's highest state taxes for nothing. But on either side, all I can see are hills and valleys.

This is quite literally the great wild west of yesteryear. Countless early Hollywood westerns were shot in these rolling hills and valleys in or about Santa Carina, standing in for every place from Texas to Arizona as required.

About fifteen minutes later, just as I'm getting antsy again, we finally turn off the road onto open countryside. The van jostles and rattles and I feel the suspension protesting as Ramon floors it like a 4WD across stone and brush without slowing. The only thing visible for miles around is open scrubland.

Just when I'm about to ask him where the hell we're going, the van skitters around a pile of rocks and Ramon brakes abruptly.

He's out of the van before the dust can settle.

I take a second to glance at the other vehicles parked around haphazardly. They look like they've only just got here, too, since they haven't accumulated much dust yet.

There are people, mostly Hispanic from my initial impression, all standing around gazing at the ground, many with kerchiefs or bandannas clutched to their mouths and cheeks, looking like they've just witnessed a tragedy.

What's going on here? What is everyone standing around looking at?

It can't be a crime scene, not officially at least, because there's no sign of any first responders. No ambulances, fire trucks, local PD, FBI, Border Patrol, nothing.

I know Ramon wouldn't bring me into a dangerous situation without giving me sufficient warning, and securing backup, but I've learned you can never be too careful.

Discreetly, I check that my service weapon, a Glock, is secure in my hip holster, and my backup weapon, a Sig Sauer, in the shoulder holster.

FOUR

Ramon is talking softly to a couple, an older man and woman. Like all the other people standing around, kneeling, sitting in the dirt, they look Hispanic, and from their clothes and appearance, they're working class. Straw hats, faded jackets, threadbare tee shirts, coarse dungarees, brown faces deeply lined from sun exposure and decades of manual labor.

They're all gathered in a large irregular pattern around a patch of sunken earth. At first glance, it resembles a sinkhole I once saw appear in an LA street during a flash flood. On closer inspection, I see that chunks and slabs of rock and dirt have burst upwards before falling back in. The entire patch is depressed by around two feet below surface level. I squat down on my haunches, examining it closely.

Are those wooden beams and pillars under the piles of dust and crumbled rock?

"CD," says a woman's voice.

A young Hispanic woman with a buzzcut and bright, alert, kohl-lined eyes meets my gaze squarely. She has the look of someone who has seen violence and meted it out as well, but is still able to maintain a calm, relaxed demeanor. I've seen that look before from my sislaw, Lata.

"Controlled demolition?" I say, slipping off my sunglasses to get a better look at her—and allow her to see me more clearly as well. I don't sense any hostility from her. My gun hand has already relaxed.

She nods, pointing at the sunken patch. "From the way it presents, I'd say they used C4."

"Plastic explosive?" I say. "That's heavy-duty stuff. Military access only."

She squats down beside me, and points to various spots in the depression. She explains how the way the ground collapsed would present differently if the person had used other demolition options, or if it had been the result of a natural event like an earthquake.

As she talks, I use the opportunity to size her up discreetly. She gives the impression of being very competent, someone accustomed to shouldering responsibilities and giving orders, but also trained to respect the chain of command. I'm barely a hair over five foot six but she's several inches shorter than me, small built but with a compact, dense physique that I'm pretty sure is packed with coiled energy. Panther strength, Lata calls it, and it's hard-won through a combination of intense deep core workouts and actual physical combat experience. Way beyond my fitness level.

I'd be willing to bet that in a knock-down fight, this young woman would beat the shit out of me without even working up a sweat.

When we stand up again, I say, "Gunny?"

Her brown eyes widen with surprise. "Gunnery Sergeant Paula Contreras, USMC," she says.

I take the offered hand. "Special Agent in Charge Susan Parker."

In response to the unasked question in her eyes, I add, "My sislaw's in the Corps. I know the look and the way you explained that was just so... gunny."

She nods. "That obvious, huh? Where's your sislaw stationed?"

I name Lata's unit and last deployment and that gets a bigger reaction. "She mustered out, but she still keeps in touch and consults from time to time."

Her face lights up. "Respect! Never deployed with them but heard the stories. Those guys kick ass. Your sislaw must be one tough devil bitch."

Ramon approaches us. His muscular shoulders are hunched over, like he's absorbed some of the emotional weight that the others are carrying.

He nods at Paula who acknowledges it without making eye contact.

"Susan's the best. If there's anyone who can get to the bastards who did this, she can," he says.

Paula glances at me again with a shrewd, assessing look.

I ask Ramon, "What exactly are we talking about here?"

He and Paula both look at me.

"Jefe," Ramon says softly, then moves his head to indicate the depression. "This is why I brought you here. I wanted you to see with your own eyes. I know how important it is to you to see the scene untouched."

I frown, glancing at him, then at Paula, then at the patch of sunken earth. It's still just a patch of dirt, unless I'm missing something. "There was something down there, wasn't there? Some kind of underground bunker, maybe?"

As we've been talking, the other people have begun gravitating toward us, in ones and twos and groups. They cluster around us now, their tear-streaked faces staring at me with an expression that I've seen too often before.

Ramon and Paula stare at me, too, not saying anything.

I look around at the others, seeing the pain and grief in their eyes.

"What was down there in that bunker?" I say.

By now, the feeling I had earlier when I arrived has grown to cover my heart. Cold tendrils of ice creep across my chest, chilling my bones.

An old man in a straw hat and bandanna speaks. He has on a jacket with the name of a landscaping service stitched on the back. His voice is hoarse with grief.

"It was a safe house," he says. "The border coyotes would bring our people here to wait till it was safe for them to be taken elsewhere. We stayed here for four days ourselves before we were brought to Arizona. That was twenty-three years ago."

I stare down at the sunken patch of earth, this time looking more closely at the disrupted sods and shattered slabs of stone, the dusty bones of wooden pillars and beams sticking up at grotesque angles. I can't imagine spending even an hour in that underground room, let alone four entire days.

The chill deepens, filling me with deep, awful dread.

My gaze returns time and again to those little stick-like things poking up out of the debris. They're so heavily lathed in dirt and concrete dust that I failed to recognize them for what they were at first sight.

I now see that they are human limbs.

Arms mostly.

Belonging to women and children, judging from their size.

Clawing their way upwards, toward light and air.

Reaching for a sky they can never touch.

This wasn't just a demolition of a bunker out in the middle of nowhere.

It was mass murder.

And from the appearance of the bodies and the relative lack of decomposition, this happened very recently. Within the last twenty-four hours most likely, as the bodies have barely begun to decay.

"Who was down there?" I ask in a voice that echoes my fear of what the answer might be.

The old landscaper's eyes are sorrowful and bleak.

"Our families," he says.

FIVE

I'm angry, frustrated, thirsty, and increasingly filled with despair for the world.

I've spent the past hour on the phone, trying to call everyone from Chief McDougall of the Santa Carina Valley Police Department to the California State Police, and I'm getting nowhere. The instant they realize that the dead are illegal immigrants who were smuggled in across the border by unknown, dubious parties, they turn and head for the hills. They see a situation fraught with complicated political implications during an election year and they all start posturing and passing the buck on jurisdiction. It's a potential political time bomb that could blow back on anyone who steps in and none of them want to stick their necks out.

At my wits' end, I finally call Deputy Director Zimal Bukhari, who's been my immediate supervisor for the past several months.

Bukhari took over from my old boss, Deputy Director Connor Gantry. She's a breath of fresh air compared to him.

She listens to me explain the situation then asks in her usual quiet but precise way: "What is it you expect me to do, Susan?"

For a moment, I'm speechless. My first instinct is to say, "Your job, ma'am." But that's the tired, frustrated me reacting. Bukhari is one of the good ones, as they say, and she's only trying to talk sense into me. I take a breath to calm myself and look around at the activity that's sprung up in the past hour or so.

One of Ramon's cousins, a hefty young man with a hard hat and safety jacket, is instructing the operator of an excavator as they attempt to remove the tons of dirt and debris under which the victims are buried. A convoy of construction vehicles and workers arrived a little while ago, friends of Ramon and the other surviving relatives. They are attempting to excavate the bodies without damaging the corpses, not an easy task.

There is still no police presence on the crime scene, neither local, state nor federal.

Finally, I say, "I guess I'm looking to help these people any way we can."

Not unkindly, Bukhari replies, "You're a smart woman, Susan. You know what would happen if I were to send out a team. Once the machinery of the Bureau moves into action, nobody can stop it. It's a Jagannath."

I don't miss her use of the Hindu god's name instead of the western equivalent 'juggernaut', which comes from the same root. It conveys the sheer unstoppability of the Hindu deity Jagannath once his army gets rolling. Bukhari constantly surprises me with her zeitgeisty awareness, another reason I like her.

"There must be *something* we can do, ma'am. We can't sit on our hands while everyone else keeps passing the buck. In the past hour, Agent Diaz and I have called every possible person from Chief McDougall at the SCVPD to CHP to California State Police, the mayor, local politicians, you name it."

"And what did they say?" Bukhari asks in a knowing tone.

"Nobody wants to have anything to do with this. One knucklehead even started to patch in Border Patrol and ICE."

"And what did you say to that?" Bukhari asks with a grin in her voice. She hasn't known me long, but she knows me well enough to know what I would say.

"I hung up on him. These people aren't the ones we need to apprehend. They're the grieving relatives of the victims. They deserve justice. It's the monsters who did this to their relatives that we need to go after. Whoever that unsub or unsubs may be, they committed mass murder on American soil. Isn't it our job to investigate it?"

She's silent for a long moment. I hold my breath.

"Okay," she says at last. "Give me some time. I'll call you back."

I feel my parched lips crack a smile.

"Thank you, ma'am!" I say.

Ramon turns his head to give me a tentative look.

I shoot him a thumbs up.

He closes his eyes, and I can see his lips silently mouth, "*Madre de dios.*"

We settle in the open doorway of the mobile unit van, Ramon, Paula, and I, sipping bottled water and sodas and watching the frenzy of activity. We offered to help but those working the site said that too many hands would only cause confusion. The best way we could help was by trying to kick-start the engine of law enforcement to bring the perpetrators of this evil to justice.

An excavator is doing the heavy lifting part, bringing up the remains of the underground shelter and its occupants.

The yellow bucket of the excavator jerks its way up, carrying a load of debris and human bodies. Dirt streams through its tines.

My stomach drops as I look at the lifeless child, not much older than my own daughter Natalie, sightless eyes filled with dirt staring at a world they will never see again. As the bucket descends, caring hands take hold of her and lift her out of the dirt and debris, cradling her gently.

A woman old enough to be her abuelita, one fist clutching a rosary, closes the child's eyes and bends low to kiss the little face, back heaving. Her tears wash runnels through the caked mud on her granddaughter's face.

All around the site, similar scenes play out as relatives and loved ones of the deceased reclaim the bodies, venting their sorrow. The sound of plaintive wailing cuts through the whine and grind of heavy equipment.

As I told Bukhari, I have made calls. So has Ramon.

We were both met with reluctance, confusion, dissembling, delays, and denial.

There are jurisdiction issues. Legal complications. The dead were illegal immigrants who breached border security. They could have been criminals—drug runners or mules, cartel workers, I'm told. The phone lines are crackling as every law enforcement agency and politician with local interests talks to each other, to their lawyers, to their superiors in Sacramento or Washington, DC.

People are trying to untangle the spider web of bureaucracy to determine who takes the responsibility of handling the corpses and investigating the deaths. Buck-passing at its bureaucratic best. Eventually, some will step up and do something, if only to milk the tragedy for its political value.

It's only a few minutes later when my phone buzzes and Bukhari speaks to me briefly. When I hang up, I'm not sure how to feel exactly.

"No go?" Ramon asks, reading my face.

I take a breath and release it.

I explain what Bukhari summarized.

She admits that the FBI also don't want to step into the "hot mess" the situation could potentially become unless ordered to by someone in the DOJ, the Department of Justice, under whose authority the Bureau officially falls. However, she understands that I'm already emotionally invested in the case now, and that my team and I would like to proceed with it in our own personal capacity. To that end, she offers to cover for us by creating a fiction of a "training exercise" that we are currently on, granting us a few days to investigate. All without official Bureau support and backing, of course.

Bluntly put, we're on our own.

Ramon nods, and it breaks my heart to see how easily he accepts the fact that the very institution he works for, has risked his life and limb for, has served for so many years, is unable to help his people right when they need it most.

Bukhari is right.

Bringing in the Bureau means we would have to inform other federal authorities.

That could lead to ICE, DHS, Border Patrol, all swooping in and scooping up these people, many of whom are either illegal immigrants or quasi-legal at best.

What good would that serve?

The last thing these people need is for their own immigration status to come under scrutiny, possibly to be arrested and held, pending deportation.

I can't put them through that.

Whatever their origins, they are American residents now.

They have lives, families, jobs, community ties, connections to the local towns and cities where they live. Several of them have been accompanied by friends, spouses, even a boss or a foreman in some instances: they are part of the fabric of American society, just as I am, despite being born in Goa, India, almost thirty-four years ago.

My blood boils as I watch the line of bodies extending. A dozen, fifteen, it keeps lengthening. What monster would do this to people—to families—who had suffered so much already and came here seeking a better life?

Paula says something in Spanish to Ramon who answers her before turning to me.

I raise my eyebrows.

"Paula says we will do it ourselves, as we always do," Ramon translates. "We may be poor, marginalized, but we are not helpless. We are a country within this country. We will not let this go unpunished. If even the FBI does not help us, we will take the matter into our own hands."

I shake my head. "Don't lose hope. The FBI can't help us officially. But that doesn't mean they aren't going to help at all."

She frowns, intrigued by my answer. I ask her to give me a little more time.

Soon enough, I'm able to show her what I mean.

The rumble of arriving vehicles alerts us.

Car doors slam, disgorging familiar faces.

Special Agent Kayla Givens, ebony comb pinning her big hair, comes over and gives Ramon a hug.

"I'm so sorry this happened," Kayla says.

Ramon thanks her and they hug.

Special Agents Brine Thomas and David Moskovitch go next, offering commiserations.

My attention shifts to the large white doublewide trailer rumbling to a halt. I glimpse Special Agent Marisol Mancini's model-perfect features in the specially modified driver's cockpit. I nod to her as she parks the mobile forensics unit.

The last vehicle is a yellow Camry driven by a man several years older than me. Detective Naved Seth of the Santa Carina Valley Police Department emerges and walks toward me, nodding by way of greeting. He exchanges words with Ramon, too.

Moments later, the door of the white trailer opens and a ramp unfolds mechanically. Special Agent Marisol Mancini,

FBI Chief of Evidence Investigation and temporary medical examiner of Santa Carina Valley, rolls down on her wheelchair, coming straight to me. She's one of the Bureau's leading forensic experts.

She speaks crisply in a cigarette-rasp voice. "So, Susan, we are here. What is it you want for us to do?"

I look around at my team.

Ramon, Kayla, David, Brine, Naved, and now Marisol.

Intrigued by the new arrivals, the relatives of the survivors have joined us. The construction vehicles have fallen silent, too, the last of the victims unearthed and laid out. The workers stand behind the mourners, curious. We are all gathered around near the line of bodies.

I go to the old abuelita who lost her beloved granddaughter. Her wizened face looks up at me. I ask Ramon to translate for me as I bend down and speak, addressing her but directing my words to everyone.

"This is my team," I tell her. "The best in the FBI. We have caught many killers before. Once we set our sights on a suspect, we never back off until we find them. Whoever did this"—I point to the sunken remains of the underground safe house and the line of wrapped bodies—"we will hunt them down and make certain that they are brought to justice. Your granddaughter and all these others whose lives were unjustly taken from them will have justice. I give you my word."

Her eyes fill with tears, and she squeezes my hand between her own. Then she touches her rosary and says something in Spanish.

"'Blessed are they who observe justice, who do righteousness at all times,'" Ramon translates.

I thank the old lady.

The crowd disperses slowly, busying themselves with the grim task of arranging funerals for the dead. There are still complications to be sorted out, death certificates, burial licenses, a tangle of bureaucratic form-filling, but even in America, there are ways to get things done without going through official channels.

I check my team, their faces serious. For once, there's no friendly banter, no quips or wisecracks. This one is different. In a sense, it might be our toughest case yet. I can see it on every face. They want to get the monster who did this, no matter what it takes. They don't need motivating. That line of bodies, some of them small enough to be carried in one arm, is all the motivation we need.

"Let's get this son of a bitch," I say.

SIX

The man known as the Saint watches the FBI woman and her people at work.

Of all the names he's been called, he likes farishta the best. It means angel in Farsi and reminds him of his two tours overseas, each of which included multiple dark ops missions to root out rebels. But the majority of his flock calls him the Saint, since the immigrants seeking sanctuary in America tend to come mainly from South Asia these days rather than the Middle East, and they understand the concept of a saint better than that of an angel.

So be it. The Saint he is.

He is sitting cross-legged in his hidey hole, a flat-bottom dugout three feet below the surface, only his head sticking out. There's room enough for him to stretch out and lie in it; it would render him invisible to anyone even a few meters away. He's sitting because he wants to see what's going on. The safe house is only thirty meters away, close enough that he doesn't need the sniper scope. The rifle itself is still in its case in the trunk of his truck which he parked a mile away off the road and left covered. He isn't expecting trouble and doesn't plan to cause any, for now at least.

He is in a ghillie suit, and he knows that as long as he sits still and doesn't make eye contact, he'll be pretty much invisible to the folks he's spying on. Greenhorns always underestimate the part about not making eye contact with the target, but the Saint knows from experience that it's a real thing. Something in our hindbrain starts buzzing when anyone stares directly at us for too long, even if we can't see the person or animal who's staring.

The Saint was once tracked by a mountain lion for almost five miles before he finally spotted it watching from behind a rock. Its color blended in with the rock so perfectly, it was like the rock itself was watching. But as soon as he matched gazes, it felt like an electric shock to his nervous system. The lion instantly broke off contact and wandered away, glancing back one last time as if to say, *I almost had you.*

In your dreams, kitty.

The woman in charge is a brunette in jeans and a tee shirt. She's an FBI agent. He knows this because she's wearing a gray Quantico sweatshirt with the famous initials on the front. But even without the shirt, he'd have figured it out from her handguns, one in a shoulder holster, the other in a waist holster. They're both Bureau-authorized firearms. And then there's the way she and her team talk to each other. That familiar dead serious attitude and stiff way of speaking and going about their work, like they all have sticks up their butts.

The FBI woman interests him.

He points the scope of his Mk 12 rifle at her, tracking until she is in the crosshairs of his sights.

She has a certain look about her that tells him that she's used those handguns and isn't afraid of using them again.

He's seen that look before.

It's the look of a soldier who has seen more than her share of the darkness and lived to tell the tale.

That earns his respect. It takes a veteran to know one.

He takes a moment to study her, trying to get a sense of her as a person as well as a leader.

She's pretty, with an athletic figure and, judging from the way she moves, can handle herself when shit goes down. She has that way of stepping on the balls of her feet even though she's wearing heeled boots, which makes her ponytail bounce and swing with every step. There's an energy about her. A natural perkiness. Not in a schoolgirl way, but like a soccer mom who means business.

Not a woman to take lightly.

The earpiece in his left ear crackles with a dispatch. He's been monitoring the law enforcement channels since his sensors got tripped a few hours ago.

He was at work at the time but still at his desk, not yet rolling because it was a paperwork catch-up kind of day. It took him just a few seconds on his phone to wake the drone he'd left in the hidey hole and send it up. It shot back video footage of the kill site and the people moving around it.

That was all he needed to see. He pulled his jacket off the back of his chair and drove out here, making sure to take a side route to avoid running into one of their vehicles.

Since then, he's been listening in on the radio, but there's been no chatter that suggests either the locals or the feds are sending people in. Ditto for the local news and social media updates.

Back at his own workplace before he left, he was keeping his ears open in case word had gotten out. Nada. Nobody mentioned anything about a demolished underground safe house with a couple dozen immigrants found dead. And that was the kind of thing people *would* talk about. Especially in a burgh like SCV and an office like the one he worked in.

The fact that word hadn't gotten out, and that the state and federal authorities weren't moving in told him that the situation was too politically messy, tangled and sticky for anyone who was someone to want to make the first move. Especially in an election year.

Even the social media influencers who ought to have gotten wind of it were staying clear.

None of those considerations or complications seem to bother this young FBI firecracker.

He watches as she gives instructions to her people. They're clearly used to taking orders from her, which means she's probably a senior agent or a special agent in charge. They're not rookies themselves: they strike him as a competent, smart, and tough-looking group that operates smoothly and does the job with practiced efficiency. He's guessing that they've weathered a few firestorms together.

The FBI woman says something to the Hispanic guy on her team. The Saint watches her closely, catching the occasional word on the wind. Something about the bodies.

The Hispanic guy goes off to take care of whatever chore she just gave him. Another dude comes over to her, asking questions. Now, this guy he definitely recognizes. He's seen Detective Naved Seth around the valley a time or two and knows him by face and reputation. NYPD transfer, joined the SCV police department late last year. Detective Seth has a rep for being a closer and a bulldog. He's probably the FBI woman's local PD liaison. Which makes them partners.

After a few minutes, the Saint switches his attention back to the kill site. The forensics woman in the wheelchair is still gathering evidence.

He tracks and refocuses on the brunette in charge. After watching her for several more minutes, he's reasonably certain that he knows her from somewhere. Somewhere local.

It takes him several more minutes, but he figures maybe she

has a son or daughter; he might have seen her picking the kid up after drama class at the elementary school. That's possible. The Saint has two teenage sons. Both attend after-school clubs. Drama for his thirteen-year-old, digital filmmaking for his fifteen-year-old. Maybe her kid's a teenager, too, in which case he or she might even know Derek and Trey.

He makes a note to check it out.

He's going to be keeping an eye on her.

Just in case.

SEVEN

I've divvied up the interviews with the family members of the deceased. They arrive in a steady stream, wracked with grief. By midday, there are over three dozen of them in all. It's a while before they're in any shape to talk to us and since most have come from out of town, we need to get their interviews on record as soon as possible. We're doing this one off the books, so we have no official authority to compel them to stay back.

The final count of the dead is twenty-nine. Almost half that number, fourteen, are minors. One of the biggest motivations for immigrants to cross borders illegally is to seek a better life for their kids. It hurts me to imagine the hope and dreams these little minds carried with them when coming to the great US of A. All destroyed by the cruelty of a mass murderer. Looking at those little shapes in the body bags breaks my heart.

I owe it to these twenty-nine dead to bring the killer to justice.

Because of the myriad other aspects of the case I have to deal with, I can't do all the interviews myself or even sit in on all of them. If this were a Bureau case and we were doing it by the book, I would have done just that.

But the Bureau way would require strict protocol, coordination with the Office of General Counsel, bussing the relatives to a secure facility with video and audio recording capabilities, among other things. It would take days. These people are still mostly living hand-to-mouth. They can't afford to miss work for several days.

We have only this one day to get them all down. They are all understandably nervous being around so many federal agents. It's only because Ramon is one of us that they even agree, reluctantly in most cases, to talk to us at all. Even then, they only agree to audio recordings, no video and no pictures. This last one sticks in Agent David Muskovitch's gullet: as the seniormost agent on my team as well as a lawyer, he's a stickler for procedure. But I override his objections. I'd rather have their statements without pictures or video, than not have it at all.

I decide that we'll split up into pairs for the interviews: Brine and Kayla, David and Ramon, Naved and me.

The first is with Paula Contreras, the Marine who introduced herself to me when I arrived. Her cousins are with her, but they elect to let Paula speak for them all.

Paula's the most composed of them all, summarizing her background quickly and efficiently, with minimal emotion and comment.

"I came from Panama via Mexico with my sister and brother fifteen years ago," she says. "I was the middle one. My elder sister, Rachel, was seventeen at the time, I was fourteen, Max was twelve. A coyote brought us across the US border and put us on a truck that brought us up here to this same safe house."

She pauses to look at the sunken ground. "We spent five days there. He came on the second day with food and water. He let us out in pairs to, you know, relieve ourselves. Warned us not to try to go out without him. He came again on the third day. And then finally on the fifth night, he put us in a van and drove us somewhere not far away, where he opened the van doors and told us to get in the house quickly. It was a quiet house in a regular neighborhood. We stayed there for a month, I think, maybe five or six weeks, then he put us into foster homes. After that, we were pretty much on our own."

"When you say 'he'," I ask, "whom do you mean exactly?"

"The Saint," she says promptly. "We were told to expect him."

"Could you describe him, please?" I say.

"He's a priest, average height and build, maybe in his seventies now and mostly bald and he's gotten real lean and his cheeks are kinda sunken, but back then he had a little more weight and a high hairline but he still had some hair, turning gray. Brown eyes, I guess. White Hispanic. He talks with a bit of an accent when he speaks English."

Naved asks, "When you say, 'now', you mean you're still in touch with him?"

"Sorta. I saw him maybe two or three years ago, before I shipped off for my first tour. I wanted to let him know. Asked for his blessings. He was happy for me. I think he'd been diagnosed with something, that's what my sister said anyway, but he wouldn't talk about it. If I had to guess, I'd say cancer. That would explain the hair loss. You know. Chemo."

Naved and I exchange a glance.

"Can you tell us where to find this priest? The Saint," I say.

"And his full name?" adds Naved.

"Sure. Everyone knows him as Father Santos. I never thought to ask for a first name. When we used to talk about him, we just called him 'the Saint'." She gives us the name of a church on the outskirts of Santa Carina Valley. "He was still there when I met him last."

"Thanks. And contact details for your sister and brother, too?" Naved asks. "We'd like to get in touch with them, if that's okay."

"My sister's still deployed," Paula says. "Jerusalem. US Embassy." She gives us a number we can call. "That's her DRC, Nathan Lindgren."

I nod. Amit used to go through the Deployment Readiness Coordinator to schedule his weekly video calls with Lata when she was deployed in Afghanistan.

"And your brother?" I ask.

She looks at me. "He was Navy Seal, on a mission off Somalia last year when he went MIA. He's PD."

"Missing in action, presumed deceased?" I say.

She nods.

"I'm sorry," I say gently.

We ask her more questions, trying to get further details but those are the most useful things we were able to glean.

The next interview is with a South Asian father-son pair.

Husain Abidi and his son Ahmed Abidi are Rohingyas, one of several persecuted minorities in Myanmar. The Abidi family fled Rakhine, the most impoverished state in the China-controlled nation, and sought asylum in Bangladesh. From there, they found their way into India, and joined the steady stream of marginalized people seeking a more permanent home and better prospects. Like many South Asian refugees and immigrants, they came to the United States via Mexico hoping to find work as migrant farm labor, since farming is the only real skill they possess.

Husain and Ahmed came through about seventeen months ago. Once the father and son found paying work, they sent for the rest of the family. Ahmed's wife Nargis, their two daughters, and Ahmed's brother Sarhad and his family were expected to follow.

They now account for six of the victims extracted from the safe house, all lying in body bags.

Husain's English is rudimentary, and we make no progress

for several minutes. Nobody at the site speaks Rohingya or Burmese.

Naved tries switching to Urdu, and I can see by the way both men respond that they're surprised and relieved. They manage to communicate well enough for us to ask some basic questions. Naved offers to translate but I suggest it might be best if he questions them then summarizes for me.

Naved does just that then turns to me. "They describe him as a priest in a cassock, average height and build. They didn't get a good look at his face or his hair, but their impression is that he's a White man. The only thing is, they don't agree on how old he was. The father says he was a middle-aged man, but the son insists he was young, almost his own age. I tried pressing the point but they're both adamant in their own impressions."

I look at the son, Ahmed. He said he was only twenty-two at the start of the interview, but he looks several years older. The father is in his early forties but could pass for ten or even twenty years older. Poor nutrition, long travel, and a hardscrabble youth have taken their toll.

Ahmed says something to Husain who replies in an argumentative tone. They go back and forth for a minute. Somewhere in the son's arguments, I catch the words "pickup truck" and "ringtone".

Naved shakes his head. "They're both still insisting they're right. Twenties and forties, they can't decide. Other than that, they don't really know much more. Everything was handled by an intermediary, a broker. To them, Father Santos was just another in a long chain of men."

"What was Ahmed saying about a pickup truck and a ringtone?" I ask.

Naved speaks to the son who answers, addressing his responses to me directly. Husain interrupts his son more than once, and Ahmed finally stops speaking and averts his eyes.

Naved shakes his head. "It's a bit vague. He thinks the guy

drove a pickup truck and used a particular new song as a ringtone. That's why he's sure he was a younger man. The father says that Ahmed was feverish during the days they were in the safe house and was probably hallucinating. They were both down here almost the entire time, so he couldn't possibly have heard the man's ringtone or seen a truck. Even Ahmed seems a bit confused."

"Okay," I say, "thank them and let's move on."

The third interview is with the old abuelita whose granddaughter was killed in the safe house.

I ask Paula Contreras to act as an interpreter. Panamanian Spanish is different to Mexican Spanish, but because she's spent more than half her life in the States, Paula has smoothed out her accent to speak it as the locals do. After all, forty percent of California is Hispanic, the single largest ethnic group, so Spanish is the lengua publica. I keep meaning to learn the language, too: it's been on my to-do list for years.

The old abuelita's name is Maria Francesca Flores, and the dead granddaughter was Consuelo Carina Flores, her son's only child. She speaks for a long time about her family's sad history and how her son and his wife struggled to have children for years. None of us have the heart to interrupt her.

She recalls the priest, Father Santos, that they all refer to as the Saint. She remembers him as a kind, gentle soul. She can't imagine that he would ever do something like this. He was dedicated to helping his people and doing good. She says it was an open secret in the local community that he helped people like her. He drove around in a pickup truck and there was always a stock of food and water in the back, ready to be handed out to whoever needed it.

He helped run what some referred to as the 'secret railroad', a loosely connected network of good Samaritans who helped refugees and immigrants coming up out of Mexico. She says he once told her that he himself had traveled from Mexico in his youth, and this was his way of giving back what he had once received. She speaks highly of him, singing his praises.

Then she says something that makes me sit up.

"Ask her to clarify that part again," I tell Paula. "The part about him being a soldier. Did she mean that literally or as a metaphor?"

Paula translates and the old abuelita nods. Her withered fingers haven't ceased working her rosary throughout the interview, and they're at it even now, counting off each bead, and I imagine her silently reciting the catechisms in her head.

"She says she has forgotten now because time has taken much of her memory," Paula tells Naved and me, "but she thinks perhaps he was a soldier himself once."

The old lady gestures at Paula.

"Like me," Paula says.

I frown. "Does she mean he was a Marine?"

"No, I think she just means that he served."

Paula asks a few more questions. The old lady answers patiently but I can see her energy is depleted. We need to wrap this up soon.

"She doesn't know," Paula says at last, "or if she ever knew, then she doesn't remember now, but she's always thought of him as a soldier of God. She doesn't believe that he could have killed her granddaughter and the others. He saves lives, he doesn't take them. Of that part, she's absolutely certain."

We continue for a few minutes more but that's pretty much all we can get out of her.

Our final interview is with Ramon himself. Naved and I have to wait for David and Ramon to finish their interviews. We avoid talking too much about our impressions, maybe because we're both a little overwhelmed by the sheer number of fatalities and the amount of work we have ahead of us.

I peek in on Marisol Mancini as she works in her mobile van, but she has nothing significant to report just yet.

It's late afternoon by the time we reconvene with Ramon. David sits in with us, and midway through the interview, Brine and Kayla finish up their interviews and join us as well.

I lay my hand gently on his tattooed forearm. "I can't imagine how hard this must be for you, Ramon. And it must feel weird being on the other end of one of these interviews."

"Not really, boss. I mean, I got called in for questioning a lot during my gang days. You know all about that."

"Sure, but that was as a suspect. Now you're a witness. It's different. We need your help, Ramon. I need you to dig deep and tell us anything that you can recall about the Saint, about the victims, the secret railroad, or anything else. I don't need to tell you how sometimes even the most insignificant detail can make a huge difference."

He nods slowly, rubbing a spot on his chest with his thumb. It's an unconscious gesture and one he does often, even more so when he's working on the weight bench. That's where he was shot when he was much younger and ran with a notorious East LA gang for a brief while.

When he begins to talk, his normally effusive, gung-ho personality is subdued. Ramon might be all tattoos, gym bod, and crewcut hair but as all my team members and I know, that's Ramon's outer persona, a persona he built to help him fit in with the rough crowd he ran with back in the day, when growing up. There's a softer, gentler, sensitive, poetry loving, art-appreciating Ramon Diaz that most people never get to see.

One of those bodies back there is that of Ronaldo Diaz. He wasn't Ramon's biological father; he was more than that. He was the man who saved Ramon when a cartel sicario massacred his entire family. Ramon was eleven, an orphan, and if the cartel found out he had survived, they would have hunted him down like a dog. Ronaldo passed him off as his sister's son from Chiapas, raised him like a son, and gave him his own name.

When Ramon passed puberty and grew into a replica of his

dead father, Ronaldo decided it was time to get out of Dodge. He brought him illegally into America. They crossed the Rio Grande together when Ramon was fourteen, and made a life in Chino, California. When Ronaldo was deported several years ago, scooped up in a random raid by ICE, Ramon struggled to survive. Forced to fend for himself in one of the shadiest neighborhoods of East LA, he fell in with a gang, went through a difficult year or two, then turned undercover informant for a DEA agent.

Ramon's intel led to the arrest of some big-ticket OGs, and the DEA agent got a promotion and was able to wrangle a work permit for eighteen-year-old Ramon, which Ramon worked hard to turn into a Permanent Resident card and eventually, citizenship. He recently got word from Ronaldo that he was coming back into the US illegally to take care of some unfinished business and that he would be getting assistance from an ally this side of the border who was known as El Santo by their people.

That is pretty much all he has to offer. He never met the Saint himself. When he crossed over a decade and a half ago, it was by a different route. He can't think of anyone who would have wanted to kill Ronaldo, though he admits, in response to a question from Naved, that it's possible that the cartel could have finally caught up with the man.

When he finishes, he looks at me. Ramon is a tough guy, he's seen things that I can't begin to imagine, both as a child in Mexico and in East LA when he was running with the gang. But right now, he has a face of glass. I can see right through to the grief that's wracking his soul. "I don't care who did this, Susan. When I find out who it was, I'm going to put the puta down myself. None of you are going to talk me down with noises about justice and due process. This was the work of a monster, and he doesn't deserve anything except a bullet in the face."

EIGHT

By the time we're done for the day, I'm exhausted, parched, very irritable and cranky, and badly in need of a shower. Ramon's construction site buddies were considerate enough to bring a port-a-potty with them, which saved us having to walk out into the arroyo to pee behind the chapparal. They also managed to organize a taco truck to feed all of us.

Since I rode in with Ramon this morning, I don't have my Prius. Naved offers to drop me home in the evening and I accept, thankful that I won't have to endure a long rideshare trip alone. Despite our exhaustion, there's a mountain of work to be done and only a handful of us to do it. The basic rules of crime investigation won't bend for us: the first day or two of an investigation are the most crucial and we need to make the most of every waking minute.

It's been a long, grueling day and I miss my shower and my bathroom, with all my stuff lined up in neat rows, beside Natalie's bath toys and bubble bath. It makes me hurt to think of all that now reduced to a pile of blackened plastic in the charred skeleton of our family home. We're staying at my father-in-law's condo in Bel Air for the time being.

The drive to Bel Air adds an extra hour and nine minutes and by the time I reach, I'm barely functional. The day's difficult work has taken a greater emotional toll on me than a physical one.

"This guy," I say to Naved as he negotiates the usual snarled traffic on the freeway. "The Saint. What's your take on him?"

Naved is silent for a moment, thinking. "There's a lot of contradictions I can't resolve. He's young, he's old. He's a priest, he's a soldier. He's a saint, he's a mass murderer."

"So you're assuming he was the killer?" I say.

"He's all we have right now," Naved replies wearily.

"I'm not so sure about that. I mean, you heard Ramon and Maria, the abuelita, and from what Kayla and Brine and David said, the other witnesses pretty much corroborate that he was a force of good."

I go on as he takes the ramp to get off the freeway.

"The Saint was rumored to have a network of safe houses along the immigrant labor route, and one was in Santa Carina Valley, where Ronaldo intended to lay low until it was safe to emerge. He expected to make contact with Ramon sometime this week. That was the last time Ramon heard from him. Ramon feels it's possible that the cartel finally caught up with Ronaldo and that they're the ones responsible for the safe house explosion. It's just like them, take out the whole safe house, don't give a damn about the collateral damage," I say. "It's a plausible explanation. If this was the cartel, it would explain the scorched earth method. Blow up the safe house, kill everyone in it, send a powerful message."

Naved clears his throat as he pulls up at a red light. "Don't shoot the messenger but you know we have to consider the possibility that Ronaldo might have been involved in more things than he told Ramon."

I frown. "Are you saying Ronaldo might be partly responsible for the safe house deaths? That's crazy, Naved. How do you even get to that from what we have so far?"

"I'm not saying that's what happened, Susan. I'm just pointing out that we can't put white hats on anyone until we know more. You're the one always reminding me that we shouldn't write off anyone as a suspect."

I sigh. "You're right. We should consider the possibility that Ronaldo's past caught up with him. Except... that's such a terrible thing. It would destroy Ramon."

"I know," Naved says gently, "that's why I'm only speaking about it here, to you. I won't air it out loud or put it down in the case notes for now. I hope we can eliminate the possibility quickly and get to the real killer."

I rub my face. "If it's not the Saint, then we're pretty much out of luck. I wouldn't know where the hell to even start."

Naved slows his Camry as we approach the gated entryway to the condominium complex.

I use the keypad to enter the condo number and wait for the electronic gate to send a message to the owner, asking for authorization. My father-in-law Kundan responds seconds later, sending a six-digit code to my phone. I enter the code and the gate tilts up to allow us to enter.

I direct Naved to park in one of the guest spots allotted to residents. Getting out, we walk past some of the most expensive cars you can think of, all in the low to medium six-figure price range. A few of them are in the visitor guest spots. Probably a dinner party or soiree at one of the tony condos.

That assumption is confirmed a moment later when we find the elevator lobby packed with a crowd of several couples, and at least one trio that looks like a throuple, all decked out in designer couture and accessories that probably cost several times the value of my car and house combined.

I'm itching to continue our discussion but we both know better than to talk around civilians.

The fancy elevator arrives quickly but is rapidly filled and it looks like Naved and I will have to wait for the third trip to get aboard.

Great. I ignore the side eyes and wrinkled noses as the Bel Air crowd takes note of my grungy, dusty state and shuffles to keep a distance. I don't blame them. I probably reek from the long day spent in the sun, handling grimy evidence and enduring the punishing August sunshine, but it was an honest day's work and I'll be damned if I let a bunch of one-percenters intimidate me.

As we wait in the brightly lit, polished granite elevator bay, Naved asks casually, "How are things between you guys now?"

He doesn't have to name them for me to know he means Aishwarya and Sujit.

Naved is aware of my complicated relationship with my mother-in-law Aishwarya Kapoor nee Chopra, and her brother Sujit Chopra.

When Naved and I met on our first case together in November last year, an unexpected connection surfaced, linking it to the death of my husband Amit a year earlier. It came as a shock and almost derailed me at the time. Naved offered to take over the task of looking into the connection to help me stay focused on the case at hand. He continued his private, off-the-books digging even while working on our next case in April this year, and he found evidence that Amit had reached out to his uncle, Sujit, shortly before his death.

"I haven't really spoken to him since," I say.

Naved raises his eyebrows to indicate the condo upstairs. "And the dragon?"

I grimace.

Naved is well aware that there's no love lost between my mother-in-law and myself, so I say with complete honesty, "She's still the queen of monsters-in-law, but I think we've come to an accommodation."

He frowns, inviting me to say more.

"I pretend she doesn't exist, she does the same," I sigh. "The only reason I moved in here at Kundan's invitation is because Aishwarya doesn't live here. If I had to see my monster-in-law at the beginning and end of every day, I would rather live in a tent!"

Naved chuckles softly, shaking his head at my response.

I shrug.

"What can I say? I hate being part of a classic Indian mother-in-law versus daughter-in-law feud, but it is what it is. At least I have a great father-in-law. Kundan is the only reason I even make an effort anymore. He's the best grandfather ever and Natalie loves him to the moon and back. If not for him, I swear, I would have broken off all contact with Aishwarya years ago."

Naved nods. "I can totally understand. From what I've seen and heard, she's quite a character."

"Let's not even talk about her. I'll lose my appetite," I joke weakly.

I can't wait to see Natalie and hug her close. An image of the dead little girl at the safe house plays over and over in my mind.

Even the ten-second elevator ride seems interminable. I need a hot shower and to change clothes.

"I'll go grab myself a quick shower," I tell Naved as the elevator slows at our floor. "You go ahead and order us something. I don't care what it is as long as it's chicken and spicy."

The elevator doors open and I step out, almost colliding with the last person on earth I expected to be here tonight, the monster-in-law herself, Aishwarya.

NINE

"Susie! How lovely you're here. Everybody, this is my famous daughter-in-law, the FBI agent."

Aishwarya's spontaneous outburst turns several heads and I suddenly find myself being scrutinized by a roomful of designer-clad upper-crusters. Several of them are the same people who were waiting with us in the elevator lobby downstairs. They take in my dusty, disheveled state with the air of a pack of pampered purebreeds presented with a scrappy street dog.

Lata takes me aside and whispers: "I'm so sorry. She just turned up out of the blue. Didn't even let Dad know she was going to throw this sudden shindig."

Typical Aishwarya. I shrug it off, too tired to deal with my mother-in-law right now. "Nats?"

"Dad took her to the arcade to get her away from all this. He just texted me to say that they were going for a new high score on Super Mario. They're heading for churros and ice cream afterwards. Not to worry, Kundan will have her home safe and sound by her bedtime. He knows it's a school night."

A pang of disappointment fills me. The one night I really

needed to spend some time with my daughter. I feel an irrational blast of anger at Aishwarya for coming in and disturbing our already precarious lives. I know she didn't do it for that reason, but she does enjoy being a force of disruption.

After a few barely polite nods and a generic muttering that I hope passes for a greeting, I try to sidestep Aishwarya and head to the guest suite that Lata, Natalie and I are occupying temporarily.

Aishwarya smiles at me with the glazed look she gets when she's had a few. "Do join us," she says, then gets a stronger whiff of my naturally acquired new fragrance. "But you probably want to shower and change first."

I don't bother to reply. Every word either of us utters brings us a step closer to one of our blowouts. All I want to do is get by her so I can go into that spare bedroom suite and shut the door, but Aishwarya being Aishwarya, she remains firmly planted in my way. Her eyes are scanning Naved now. The intensity of her scrutiny could easily replace a TSA baggage scanner.

"Who's your friend?" she asks, with an odd tone. I know that tone, unfortunately, just as I know most of Aishwarya's typical put-down phrases.

Naved smiles politely. "Detective Naved Seth, SCVPD. I'm Susan's liaison and partner," he says. "You have a very beautiful house, ma'am."

Aishwarya ignores the compliment. "Why, this is turning out to be a cop convention! You know, your boss is around here somewhere. So is yours, Susie. Isn't that lovely?"

"Peachy keen," I say. "Let me just grab a quick shower."

Connor Gantry and McDougall are both here? The thought of making small talk with them makes my head hurt.

Aishwarya continues blocking my way for several more seconds before finally giving me a pointed smile that leaves no doubt who's the boss. Then she suddenly loses all interest in Naved and me and glides away, saying something she probably considers sparklingly witty to her guests, but which sounds just plain boujee to my ears.

I drag Naved to the suite. A couple standing right outside the door look amused as we go in, but I really don't care what they're thinking. I shut the door behind us and lock it, exhaling loudly.

"Fuck," I say. "Fuck fuck fuck."

Lata and I have a house rule against profanity. A necessary caution when you're the mother of a seven-year-old who has the retention of a sponge and can read lips across a room. But Natalie isn't around, and Aishwarya always gets my blood pressure spiking. Every frigging time.

"Sit anywhere," I tell Naved as I check my phone, scrolling through my missed calls and messages. Several of them are from Lata, and there's one missed call, one voicemail, and a text message all from Kundan.

"They tried to warn me," I tell Naved. "Apparently, Aishwarya flew in unexpectedly to host a casual dinner party for some of her friends who are part of a super PAC she's putting together to fund the governor's re-election campaign. It's one of those impromptu things."

"She's... Imax 70mm," Naved says.

"In Dolby sound," I agree. I drop the phone on the bed. "I'm hitting the shower. You order us some grub."

"Won't she be expecting us to join her for dinner?" Naved asks as I go into the bathroom and start peeling off my shirt.

"You bet she will," I say, poking my head out to grin at him. "And I'm happy to disappoint her."

When I step out of the shower, I hear voices through the closed door.

Lata waves at me when I come out. I wrap a towel around my head, feeling much cleaner and fresher in a pair of baggy jeans and a shapeless tee shirt, my comfort wear.

"Naved was just telling me about the safe house murders," Lata says. "So horrible. I hope you catch the asshole."

I sigh. "It's not going to be easy. We have zero support from the authorities on this one. We're literally doing this on our own time. The only reason we're even able to work on the case is thanks to Deputy Director Zimal Bukhari. She's showing us as attending an off-site training exercise at an undisclosed location, so we don't lose our jobs for going AWOL."

"That's unbelievable," Lata says. "Someone commits mass murder on American soil, and nobody cares because they were just poor immigrants trying to get to a better life."

Naved gets up, waving his phone as he goes out. "Food's here. I'll go down and get it from the delivery guy."

Lata looks at me. "You ordered in? Mom's hired some fancy caterer that charges, like, three hundred dollars per plate!"

I shrug. "She can eat mine."

We both realize what I just said and burst out laughing.

We're still laughing when Naved slips back in, carrying a bag with a franchise logo. "I don't think your mother-in-law is very happy about this. She actually gasped when she saw me bringing this in."

"You should have invited her to join us," I suggest.

Lata wags her finger. "Now you're just being mean!"

The guest suite is designed exactly like one in a five-star hotel. We move to the living room area and start taking out boxes of food and plastic flatware.

As I open the little white cardboard boxes, releasing the familiar aroma of Chinese comfort food, I say, "Naved, what did you mean about Ronaldo being involved in other things? Like what?"

"Look, I didn't want to say anything in front of Ramon," Naved says, "but you do know that Ronaldo Diaz was once a collector for the cartel, right?"

I unwrap a pair of chopsticks and dig into the crispy pork.

The first bite makes my mouth explode with juices. God, I am so hungry.

"That was a long time ago," I say between chews. "He was forced into it because of family debt, but was actively trying to get out when he went to Ramon's family home to collect money from them. When they came up short, the sicarios massacred the entire family. Ronaldo saw young Ramon and made him hide to escape the sicarios. He covered for him, pretending that the room was empty, and came back later that night, to get Ramon. They both went on the run together."

Naved helps himself to a forkful of noodles, using the plastic flatware because he says he's clumsy with chopsticks. "Exactly, and we all know that the cartel never forgets and never forgives. So, when Ronaldo was deported back to Mexico almost eight years ago, it doesn't make sense that the cartel never tracked him down and killed him. At least when he was in the US, it's possible—unlikely but possible—that he could have evaded their wrath by changing his identity and appearance, but back home? Impossible."

I eat a chili shrimp, then another one, then a piece of cashew chicken, thinking it over. "I hear what you're saying but he survived almost eight years down there."

"That's exactly what I mean. A few weeks maybe, even several months, but eight years? That's not even a miracle, it's just unbelievable." Naved cracks open a can of soda and takes a sip. "It's not credible that the cartel would let him live. So long as he was in the US under a different identity, they could claim he was dead, but for him to be walking about as large as day on home turf? That's like a slap in the cartel's face. They'd never have let that pass."

"So you're saying that the only way he could have survived those eight years was by rejoining the cartel?" I say skeptically. "That sounds far-fetched. Why would they ever trust him again?"

Naved shrugs. "Maybe he had information to trade. Contacts in the States that he developed while he was here. Could be any number of reasons. From what I understand, he never stole from the cartel or worked against them. His only sin was helping Ramon get out of the country and quitting his job without permission. Maybe he was more useful to them alive than dead."

We toss ideas to and fro as we eat. I can't say that I like questioning the integrity of the man Ramon practically worshipped but our job is to go where the evidence takes us and Naved does have a point.

Sipping my soda, I ask, "What about this Saint everyone was talking about? He was the main contact here in Southern California. Everyone said that the safe house was his."

Naved spreads his hands. "Exactly. Why would he suddenly start killing immigrants after helping dozens of them in the past? Why destroy his own safe house when it would be obvious that the evidence would point to him? It doesn't add up."

"Still, we need to track this guy down and put him in a room. He had to have been involved. If your theory about Ronaldo is right, then maybe he was working for the cartel, too."

"That doesn't track," Naved says. "The cartel doesn't run coyotes. Too much risk and exposure, too little profit. They have their own conduit, a network of mules that bring in their poison. They know better than to use these poor bastards." He takes a sip. "But I agree, we need to find him and talk to him. He might know something."

"Natalie and Kundan are back," Lata says as she enters the room. "I came to check if you guys are done."

"Just cracking open our cookies," I say, holding one out to Naved who grins and waves it away.

"Come on," I say. "Don't you want to know what the future has in store for you?"

"No!" he says, intensely enough that it comes off as funny. But he laughs at himself, and cracks open his cookie anyway.

"'Expect the unexpected'," he says. "Whatever the hell that means."

I open mine, popping half the cookie into my mouth and crunching it up as I read the tiny slip of paper. "'Fortune favors the bold'."

Lata quips: "I think that means if you eat greasy Chinese food, you deserve a bland, generalized prediction!"

"Har har hardy har," I say, rolling my eyes. "Thanks for the vote of confidence."

Naved stands up, stretching and yawning. "I should get going. I have a long drive back. See you tomorrow?"

"I'll walk you out," I say.

I dust off the crumbs from the fortune cookie and we go out of the suite, Lata following. The living room and dining area are no longer packed with Bel Air's finest. People in crisp white uniforms are finishing the after-party cleanup. We pass the lounge area on our way to the elevator.

"SAC Parker," says a familiar voice. "Trying to make a quick getaway? That's mighty sneaky of you."

TEN

Deputy Director Connor Gantry is seated on a chaise lounge, a glass in hand. Beside him are Chief McDougall and Sujit Chopra. Aishwarya, Kundan, and my daughter Natalie are with them, too. Everyone except Natalie has a drink in their hands or in front of them.

I knew that my in-laws know my former boss and the local police chief personally, and Aishwarya is on the same charitable and cultural committees as both of them, but it's still unnerving to see them sitting in the house I'm currently living in.

At the sight of my daughter, I lift Natalie off her chair and give her the biggest hug possible.

She hugs me back, then laughs as she signs: "Mom, you're crushing me!"

"Sorry, honey," I sign back, laughing as well. "I'm just happy to see you. Did you have a good day, sweetie?"

"It was awesome," she signs back. "I won at Super Mario! It was a new high score. Except, I think Dadu might have let me win. Mom, please tell him that he doesn't have to do that anymore. I'm almost eight now. I'm not going to sulk and cry if I lose once in a while."

Behind me, Kundan starts signing, and I tap Natalie's shoulder to alert her.

"She won fair and square, Susan," Kundan says. "Pinky swear!"

I laugh. "Let's just call it a tie, how about that?"

Natalie nods her head vigorously, then unleashes a huge yawn, followed by another.

"I think someone needs to go beddy-bye," I say gently, stroking her hair.

She presses her cheek against my side.

Naved gestures, indicating that he's going to leave and that I should stay with Natalie.

I'm about to nod yes when Chief McDougall says, "Not so fast, Seth. I'd like a word with you, if you have a minute to spare. I know you must be real tired after your inter-agency task force training exercise today, but you can spare a minute for the man who signs your paychecks. Come over here and park your butt on this chair."

Deputy Director Gantry says to me, "You too, Parker. You can put your daughter to bed, then come back here. We're waiting so don't take too long."

What the hell is this? An interrogation?

I take Natalie into the suite, help her change into her pajamas, then stand at the door and watch her brush her teeth. All the while, she signs, catching me up with her day. Dadu's the best, seems to be the recurring refrain.

I feel a twinge of something.

Regret for not having been there with her to share her joy? Guilt at missing what turned out to be a perfect day, one of only so many that she would experience as a kid? Jealous of my father-in-law for being able to make her so happy when it should have been me doing the happy-making?

All of the above.

She gets into bed, yawning again, and asks for a story.

Natalie has to be able to see my lips, or my hands, when I'm telling her a story. Within the first thirty seconds, her eyes are drooping, and before a minute's up, she's slipped deep into dreamland.

I continue talking for a couple more minutes, just in case. After that, I trail off, leaving the impromptu story unfinished, and just watch her sleep. Unable to resist, I stroke her hair back from her face, caressing her head. It felt like a miracle when I first held her, damp and warm, her tiny heart against mine, beat-matching. I remember Amit's face watching us, glowing with the purest joy possible. I never saw that particular expression before or after. It was the closest he ever got to nirvana, I think. Or so I'd like to believe.

We miss you still, Amit, I mouth silently. *Always will.*

The tableau in the lounge hasn't changed.

Except now Naved is sitting on a couch before Gantry and McDougall, and has a glass beside him with an inch of what looks like Scotch in it. He isn't drinking, just staring blankly ahead.

I take a seat beside him.

Gantry and McDougall are sitting on armchairs beside each other, like a two-man bench of judges presiding over us.

Behind them, Sujit and Aishwarya are comfortably settled in identical matching Queen Anne armchairs.

Lata is the odd one out.

She's sitting by the bar on one of Aishwarya's vintage stools, a can of Coors in one hand. Her body language tells me she's not happy about this ambush, didn't know it was going down, and is very much against it.

I give her a look that's equivalent to a smile of reassurance. I know my sislaw well enough to realize she'd never go along with anything that would make me uncomfortable. Whatever this bullshit is, it's all Aishwarya's doing. It stinks of her signature brand of toxic perfume.

Kundan is nowhere to be seen. I'm guessing he decided to remove himself from a situation he doesn't approve of, to avoid a confrontation with his wife and brother-in-law, neither of whom he's particularly fond of. The feeling is mutual.

"You two went off the reservation today," Gantry says.

Neither Naved nor I say anything. We've been on the other side of this kind of set-up often enough to know that unless you're asked a direct question, you don't volunteer a response. Depending on the question, maybe not even then.

McDougall leans forward, his breath reeking so strongly of Irish whiskey, I can smell it from four feet away.

"The hell you think you were doing out there, Seth?" he growls.

Naved stirs, looking at his boss.

"Sir?" he asks.

"You heard me, detective."

"Sir, are you referring to our trip to the crime scene? I was just—"

McDougall doesn't give Naved a chance to finish. His large face is flushed from drink and anger as he growls, "Cut the bullshit. That's not a crime scene. A bunch of wetbacks who entered the country illegally happened to pick the wrong place to hide, and the roof caved in on their greasy skulls. The only crime involved was the one they committed when they violated our border."

Naved doesn't respond to that one.

Aishwarya leans over and says something to Sujit which both brother and sister seem to find amusing. Lata, who's the only one close enough to overhear, glares at the back of her mother's head.

Smooth as a two-man band, Gantry picks up the beat, pointing to me. "That goes for you, too, Parker. The deaths of those illegals is no concern of the Bureau. You need to wipe this off the bottom of your shoe and get back to hunting down the real scumbags out there."

I say quietly to Gantry, "Aren't you currently on leave, sir?"

He wrinkles his nose.

"That's a misunderstanding," he says curtly, suddenly sounding defensive. "It's going to be sorted out shortly."

"If that's all, sir, we were about to head out," I say, standing up without waiting for a response. Naved takes the hint, rising and following me out.

"Let the dead stay buried, you hear?" McD calls out after us. "Our job is to keep America safe from scum like that. Good riddance, I say!"

ELEVEN

The instant the elevator doors shut, I turn to my partner.

"I'm so sorry that happened, Naved," I say. "You didn't deserve to be interrogated like that."

"Neither did you," he replies. "It's not your fault, Susan. You looked as surprised as I was. I'm guessing you didn't know they were going to be there."

"I didn't even know Aishwarya was going to be there. Lata said she was in SF as usual, handling business matters with Sujit. I figure she surprised everyone by just dropping in."

I shake my head in disbelief over the encounter that just happened. "She and Kundan don't actually live together as man and wife anymore. They only maintain the appearance of a normal marriage."

Naved scrubs his face with his hands, pushing his hair back. He mutters a few curses too softly to make out. "I can understand why," he says with a laugh.

"You can say that again," I say.

The elevator opens on the underground parking level.

He looks at me as I step out with him.

"I'm heading home," he says. "Where are you going?"

"Let's get coffee. We still need to talk about the case."

Naved doesn't say anything as we walk back to the spot where he parked his car. When we're at the Camry, he pauses, then looks over the roof of the car at me.

"Maybe we should call it a day, start over fresh tomorrow?" he suggests.

I nod slowly. "You're right. It's been a day."

"Where are we meeting, by the way?"

I shrug. "I don't know. We can't use the command center, because that's the old sheriff's station, so it comes under McDougall. He made it pretty clear we won't be welcome to use any of the facilities. Hang on," I say, scrolling through our team's group chat on my phone. "I asked Brine to find us some-place temporarily. Okay, here it is. Brine says the only thing he could think of at such short notice was Toppings."

Naved frowns. "The pizza place?"

"Yeah. Why not? It doesn't get much dine-in business anyway, and we're always either eating there or ordering take-out. Besides, it's right across from the command center."

"And now, it *is* our command center!"

I laugh bitterly. "Sure. But we can make it work, right? Because the case is all that matters."

Naved nods at me, managing a weary smile. "You said it. See you there tomorrow."

"Bright and early," I call out as I walk back to the elevator bank.

The elevator door opens as I reach the lobby. Lata steps out.

"I'm glad I caught you before you left," she says. "We need to talk."

"Okay," I say, wondering what it's about, not relishing the idea of going up and encountering my monster-in-law again.

"Let's go for a drive," she says.

Lata and I walk to her Jeep and get in.

We head down to Sunset and cruise until Lata spots a Starbucks. She pulls into the drive-through lane.

"I need coffee," she says. "Do you need coffee?"

"I'm good."

She gets a triple shot of dark espresso to go, then takes Mulholland up into the hills.

She finds a spot with a view and parks.

The lights of Los Angeles lie spread before us. It's a beautiful view of a beautiful city, but like all great cities, the truth hides in the darkness between the lights.

"I'm so sorry you had to go through that," she says. "First of all, I had no clue Mom was going to drop in. She claims it was impromptu, but I know her. This is Kundan's place. They're virtually separated in all but name. She usually stays at a Beverly Hills hotel when she's here in LA. So she didn't just happen to drop by unexpectedly *and* happen to invite your ex-boss and Naved's boss just like that. She clearly had an agenda."

"I figured," I say.

"Dad, of course, had no idea either. As you know, they hardly talk anymore."

"It's fine, Lata. I'm used to your mom by now. If she hadn't pulled something like this, that would have surprised me. Besides, Kundan could hardly just throw her out."

Lata sips her coffee. "The lack of courtesy, that's what pisses me off. All she had to do was tell us she was coming by, and we could have figured something out."

I shrug because it's all I can do.

"Really, Suse, the way they *badgered* Naved and you, that shit was unacceptable."

"It's fine. Naved and I laughed about it in the elevator. That's just how they are, Gantry and McD."

"Yeah, I know, but bad enough you have to take their BS on the job. You shouldn't be ambushed at home, for no fault of yours."

"What were they really doing there?" I ask. "I mean, what's Aishwarya's intention? Because I know she always has a plan."

Lata drinks her espresso. "That's the thing I wanted to talk to you about."

I sense what's coming, and suddenly I don't want to hear it. I feel like getting out of the Jeep and walking away. Running.

But this is Lata, the closest thing I have to a life partner right now.

We're sislaws but also sisters, in the truest sense of the word. They say that if you have to take a hard blow, it's better that it comes from someone who loves you. Because it's Lata, I brace myself to receive it.

She sticks the coffee cup in the cupholder and takes my hands. Her hands are warm from holding the cup. Mine are cold, colder than they ought to be. She looks me in the eye, holding my gaze.

"The insurance company denied our claim," she says gently.

I hear myself make a sound; it comes from the bottom of my throat, but also from deep down in my heart.

It's the sound of denial.

"They said..." she starts, then shakes her head. "It's complicated, because that's how insurance companies work, deliberately burying the lede in a mountain of legalese, but basically what it comes down to is the investigation report didn't jibe with our statements about what happened that night."

I frown. "What?"

"Now, before you go off on them, let me just say that we can fight this. We have a right to appeal their decision, and even to appeal the investigation report. I looked it up. We can challenge both reports. We're getting a good lawyer to handle the case and draft our appeal. It will take a while, but it's still possible that we can get them to reverse their decision and approve our claim. I talked to the lawyer today and he's handled many cases like this. Home invasions gone wrong, house damaged, burned down, and worse. He specializes in exactly this kind of shit. He sounded very optimistic."

I struggle to speak through what feels like a throat filled with glass.

"Who..." I try to swallow, but can't. Instead, I extricate one hand from Lata's, reach down, pick up her Starbucks cup, and take a big swallow. The coffee is hot and scalds my tongue, but I don't care. I gulp down the searing liquid, trying to loosen the obstruction in my throat.

"Who's paying for the lawyer?" I ask.

Lata's eyes flick sideways. She tries to hold my gaze, but the brief flicker is involuntary. She probably isn't even aware of it. After years interrogating unsubs—unidentified subjects, which is FBI-speak for suspects and persons of interest—I know the tell. She's about to lie to me or avoid the truth.

"Let's not worry about that right now," she says. "The thing is, we will get through this. Together. We'll make them come around. I believe it will happen. And I need you to believe it, too. We'll get through it together."

I'm silent for a long moment, processing a dozen emotions, riding a rollercoaster of alternating rage, frustration, despair, grief, isolation, anger, misery, and other unnamable things.

When I trust myself to speak again, I say, "Why are you telling me this now?"

She looks confused. "I only found out this evening, just a few hours before you came home. I didn't want to tell you on the phone."

I shake my head. "It has something to do with what happened tonight, doesn't it? That's why you were sitting with Sujit and Aishwarya."

She closes her eyes.

When she opens them, I see a reflection of my own warring feelings in her eyes, too. Not quite the same but close enough.

"Yes," she says.

"Tell me."

She sighs and pulls away, taking a sip of her coffee and staring out the windshield.

The city stares back, golden and cruel as a god.

"They're the ones who suggested the lawyer," she says.

"And offered to pay for him?" I ask.

She nods.

I take the cup from her hand without asking permission and take another sip. It's not bitter enough. Black coffee ought to be bitter. As bitter as reality.

I look straight ahead as I hand her back the cup. She takes it smoothly, without fumbling, like a relay runner accepting the baton. The way we share responsibilities without needing to explain or engage in complicated negotiations. We're well coordinated, me and my sislaw.

Suddenly, I'm reluctant to look at Lata. I don't want her to see everything I'm feeling now. About her family. Her mother, her uncle.

"And what else?" I ask.

I feel her looking at me. "What do you mean?"

"There's something else, isn't there? Something you haven't told me yet. But you have to. So, tell me, Lata."

She makes a sound and I hear the break in her voice.

She hits the steering wheel of the Jeep hard with the heel of her palm. She may not be on active duty but she's still a Marine by training and mental outlook and she keeps herself in great shape. I feel the impact through the seat. The whole Jeep shivers.

"Sometimes, I just hate her so damn much," she says.

I glance at her face. I can feel the rage burning behind those still brown eyes, see it in the bunched shoulders, clenched fists, knotted abs.

"What did she do, Lata?" I say. "Tell me what she did this time?"

Lata stares ahead for the longest time then turns suddenly to face me.

There are tears in her eyes but if I were to taste them right now, I know they would taste differently from my own.

Because a daughter-in-law hating her mother-in-law, and vice versa, that's so commonplace it's almost a cliché.

But a daughter and a mother?

The most precious of relationships, yet when it goes bad, it can also be the most harrowing.

"I tried to ask her about it, but you know how slick she is at evading," Lata says, "so I can't say with one hundred percent certainty, but I'd bet my right tit that she was the one who put pressure on the fire chief to frame his fire investigation report in that particular way. Not quite blaming it on you, but also stopping short of blaming it on the Clothesline Killer, the bastard who actually broke into our home, planted the incendiary device in our garage, and burned our house down. It should have been cut and dried, a slam dunk. Instead, the report said it was 'inconclusive'. *Inconclusive!*"

She slams the steering wheel again, this time hard enough that the Jeep actually shakes from side to side.

"I'm sorry, I'm sorry, I'm sorry," she says. "I need a minute."

She pops the door open and gets out.

I do the same.

The night air feels cool and tart, with a faint fragrance of something I can't place and don't have the headspace to want to identify right now. I walk around the front of the Jeep to where Lata is standing, shaking with emotion. I reach out and put my arms on her shoulders. She feels like a coiled spring. I pull her to me, hugging her tightly.

"Why?" I ask softly.

"Why does my mother do anything? Because she can?

Because she's rich and powerful and vindictive and narcissistic? Because she and Sujit want you to fall in line, join their little group of corrupt cops, stop getting in their way like you always do. Because you're vulnerable right now, homeless with no family of your own to have your back, no money, nowhere else to go. So they believe that by getting their pet cop, McDougall, to whom the fire chief reports as you know, to make sure that the fire investigation report is inconclusive, that would give the insurance company an excuse to deny our claim."

I'm nodding along now. I already knew all this, but I needed her to say it out loud, because in my head it sounded like a crazy paranoid delusion, just another unhappy daughter-in-law blaming the classic evil mother-in-law.

"That way, we're at her mercy," I say now, following through on Lata's unfinished thought. "So she can pretend to be our white knight, swoop in and save the day. Putting me forever in her debt and forever in her pocket. FBI Agent in Charge Susan Parker, at your service, ma'am."

Lata nods. "I'm so, so sorry about all this, Suse. I wanted to yell and scream at her. To throw stuff and break things like I used to do when I was a kid and she used to pull this same uber-controlling crap on me."

"That wouldn't do any good. She'll just enjoy your loss of control and take it as a sign of her victory," I say softly, my mind spinning on a different line of thought now.

"Exactly. But it's such a shitty situation, and she's got us exactly where she wants us. That's what I think tonight was really about. She chose not to let us know she was coming over and bringing guests just to make a point. That it's her house, her rules, and her world, we just live in it. She wanted to rub it in your face. She's such a terrible person, I'm ashamed to have her as my mother."

"We don't get to choose the families we're born into," I say absently. "None of this is your fault, Lata."

She looks at me as she dabs at her cheeks with the backs of her hands. "So, what do we do now, Suse? We can take her help and play along, but you know what that will mean?"

I nod.

"I know," I say.

Then I shake my head and look at her.

"We're not going to do that," I say. "I'm not going to take her help. Not her lawyer, not her money. And as soon as I possibly can, I'm going to move us out of the condo in Bel Air and find us another place to live."

Lata nods, agreeing with everything I say, but her eyes still hold a question.

"How?" she asks.

I look out at the view. So enticing from afar, so disillusioning from up close.

"I don't know, Lata. I have absolutely no clue how right now. But I am not going to be under your mother's thumb for the rest of my life. I can't do that to Natalie, and I won't do it to myself. No matter what I have to do, I swear I'll find a way."

TWELVE

Toppings Pizza Parlor is pretty much like any other pizza joint in these post-pandemic times. Most of its business is deliveries and takeaways. Few of its patrons actually dine in.

But this is Santa Carina Valley, where there's enough space to sprawl out even if there's not enough people to fill the sprawl. The restaurant is designed to seat way more than the usual Los Angeles County pizza joint. Tables large enough to accommodate entire families sit before huge flatscreens tuned to sports channels. Sometimes, after a big home game at the local high school, the place gets packed with families and teams celebrating a win. It gets pretty rowdy on those occasions.

This being a weekday morning, it's pretty much deserted. Who goes out to eat pizza in the morning anyway?

Nobody except five FBI agents, apparently. Naved wasn't able to join us this morning. He was asked to report in to the SCVPD Office, and I have no clue as to what that's about.

We have the place pretty much to ourselves, which is why Brine suggested it. Also, the perfect food.

"We have tentative IDs on all the victims," David says. David Muskovitch is a former lawyer by profession, specializing in finance, and is our onboard expert for legal vetting and forensic accounting. "When I say tentative, I mean precisely that. These are all foreign IDs, some of them aren't even state issued. It's only due to the corroboration of their surviving relatives that we're accepting them as authentic."

"It's not like they had a choice, David," I say. "Every country doesn't have a single ID system as we do here in the States. I'm from India originally, as all of you know, and we have multiple state IDs there. PAN card, ration card, driver's license, Aadhar card, passport... Authorities demand different IDs for different purposes. And getting every new ID costs money."

David nods. "I get that, Susan. The issue here is, we have no way to confirm that these IDs are authentic. We only have the word of the relatives who we met at the site that they were who they say they were."

Ramon has been quiet since we convened. Keeping his head down, hunched over, hoodie covering his brow even though it's seventy-two outside and sunny.

He looks up now, fists clenched, eyes glaring. "What are you trying to say, that my people are lying? These weren't drug runners, bruh, they were just ordinary folk looking for a life. You trying to make out they were some kind of drug mules or something?"

David raises his palms. "Ramon, I'm just saying that we don't know for certain. I've already been told that several of these people were fleeing some kind of trouble or other back in their home countries. For all we know, they could have changed their names, forged IDs, to protect themselves. No judgment, no aspersions. I'm just pointing out—"

Ramon stands suddenly, shoving his chair back with a screech. "What, David? What *are* you saying? Huh?"

I see the staff behind the counter stop what they're doing to check us out, sensing trouble.

"Okay," I say, standing up and holding my hands out, "let's

all take a step back and breathe for a minute. Ramon, please take a seat, you're going to make the pizzaiolos nervous and we're gonna get served burned pizza. I don't want burned pizza. Do you?"

Ramon gives me a funny look but pulls his chair back and sits down. "*Pizzaiolo?* You just make that shit up, jefe?"

"It's what they're called," Brine chips in. "In Italy, a pizzaiolo is a term of respect for a master craftsman of fine pizza."

He raises a hand and calls out to the Toppings staff, "All good here, just having a convo about work, you know how stressed it gets!"

One young guy with a wooden pizza paddle laughs and says something to the other. They smile and nod and go back to work, talking among themselves. I catch one of the servers, a young woman, looking at me, and I smile and give her a small wave. She waves back shyly.

Kayla wrinkles her nose. "Never thought I'd hear the words "fine" and "pizza" together. Always a first time, I guess. My folks are from Chicago originally. We love our pie but hey, it's just pizza!"

Brine starts to voice an objection.

I raise my hands, grinning. "Okay. Let's not get off topic here. David, let's take the relatives' word for it. The IDs are good. Brine, with due respect to the Italians, here in the US of A, pizza is pizza. Moving on. Let's start with the witness statements. Ramon, were you able to do what I asked?"

Ramon gives me a look which suggests that hell would freeze over before he failed to perform any task I assigned to him.

He turns his laptop screen around so we can all see.

"I ran the audio recordings of the interviews through Carlotta," Ramon says. "She compiled it into charts so we can look at the data and find matches."

I nod. Carlotta is Ramon's pet AI project, an invaluable resource that's helped us hugely on more than one case in recent times. He keeps tweaking and updating her and it's quite incredible how much more resourceful and quick she is at processing large data dumps and helping us find patterns, in a fraction of the time it would have taken us manually.

The data Ramon shows us now is an example of just that. It would have taken hours, if not days, of inputting details from the transcripts into our Bureau computers and then involved expert analysts who would have compiled these patterns manually. Carlotta has done the whole thing overnight, and mapped out all the connections in more detail than we could possibly use.

Unfortunately, like most data dumps and AI-derived charts, there's not much that is of real use to a crime investigation. After a while spent poring over the charts and analyses, I come to the same conclusion.

"This is like looking for a needle in a haystack, when we don't even know what the needle looks like," I say at last. "All this is great to have, Ramon. Terrific work. But I don't really think there's a connection between the victims that caused their deaths. Call it my gut instinct, but I think the killer's motive was simply to kill everyone who happened to be in that safe house, regardless of their individual identities or demographic similarities."

David nods at me.

"Wrong place, wrong time," Kayla says sadly.

We're silent for a long moment. I try not to think of the sight of the old abuelita's granddaughter's corpse being hauled up out of the ground, the dirt in that little girl's hair, the sightless eyes...

All those lives, snuffed out in an instant. A terrible death. And for what?

"Motive," I say, tapping the wooden tabletop. "That's what we need to figure out here."

Ramon spreads his hands. "What else, boss? It doesn't take a Quantico profiler to figure this one out. Guy's a fucking bigot. Immigrant hater who thinks anyone with an accent who isn't white deserves to be put in the ground."

Kayla nods. "I'm with Ramon on this one. I don't think this has anything to do with anything those poor people did or who they were. I think it's just about the fact that they were all entering the country illegally. This one stinks of anti-immigrant hate crime all over."

I look around the table, inviting the others to speak up.

"That's what jumps out for me, too," Brine says.

David dips his graying head. "I think the current rhetoric, which of course isn't that current since it's been heated and reheated over the past several decades, is definitely at play here. The way the crime was carried out, the sheer heinousness of the act itself, the fact that the unsub didn't just pick out and kill them individually using knives, guns, some other means, that he didn't distinguish between them despite the wide variance in their identities and origins, it all suggests premeditated, cold-blooded, hate crime. The unsub meant to extinguish and erase them collectively. He never saw them as individuals at all. It was about what they were, rather than who they were."

I lean back, thinking that over, when I notice movement coming in my direction.

The employee who waved at me earlier comes over, accompanied by another young woman, whom we all recognize.

"Urduja! How are you doing?" I say, standing up to give her a hug.

She hugs me back. "I'm good—it's so great to see you guys again. I just started my shift. Are you working on another case? How come you didn't order in?"

We all exchange looks.

Urduja delivers pizza for Toppings and has made multiple deliveries to us when we've worked cases out of the FBI-

SCPVD joint task force office right across the street in the old sheriff's station, part of the same compound as the local courthouse and public library. She also helped us break a case recently thanks to her secret talents as an amateur sleuth. Her life ambition is to become a crime investigator.

"This one's sorta off the books," I say. "We're running this on our own time, own resources."

"But we still expect the discount!" Brine says.

Urduja laughs. "Sure. You got it. What would you like to eat?"

We place our orders. The food comes quickly, and we toss around the new theory as we eat.

"The problem with profiling this as just an anti-immigrant hate crime is that it widens the net too much. Where do we even start? With American men between eighteen and forty-five who've posted anti-immigrant posts on social media? We'll get, like, a million hits. We need something more concrete."

I take another bite of my pizza, trying to figure out how we go on from here.

Everyone reacts to someone approaching behind me. I continue chewing, assuming it must be Urduja again.

But when a familiar rasping voice sounds in my ear, I drop my slice.

"You are looking to embarrass me, I am thinking," says Marisol Mancini. "Inviting Italian to a pizzeria? What is this you are eating?"

Nobody dares reply with the obvious "It's pizza". Marisol's question is rhetorical.

She picks up a slice and sniffs at it suspiciously before trying a small bite. She chews then drops the slice back on the serving dish, dusting her hands off.

"O-kay," she says, starting to turn her wheelchair around. "I am going before I lose temper now!"

I laugh and reach out. "Marisol. Give me a break. I apologize if the pizza isn't up to your high standards but we're just regular Americans trying to grab a bite."

She swivels her wheelchair around, her beautiful face unable to conceal a faint smile. She winks at me. "I know, I know, carissima. I am just pulling the legs. Speaking of break, I do have a break for you. I find something in the forensics because, as you know, I am Marisol Mancini, magician of my craft! I think it may help with identify your unsub."

THIRTEEN

Marisol Mancini explains to us that she was able to find trace elements of a chemical on the detonator as well as other fragments recovered from the blast site. The chemical, as she first explained during her formula-packed intro which whooshed over all our heads, is a synthetic formulation created for one purpose only: to be used as a taggant.

That segues into a brief explanation of taggants.

First used as a synthetic marker to help pharmaceutical companies identify and track specific batches of various medicines as they were distributed, taggants were adopted as a tool in crime prevention, detection, and investigation. They are now an integral part of law enforcement in most developed countries and can often prove crucial in establishing guilt in criminal trials and helping courts to incarcerate violent criminals.

"So taggants," I summarize, "are basically chemicals added to specific batches of medicines, chemicals, explosives, ammunition, that can be detected and analyzed with a simple test, right? And they're used to help authorities figure out who made them, where and when they were distributed, whom they were sold to, and so on?"

Marisol Mancini nods. "Yes, this is right. How you know about explosives?"

Brine shrugs. "Military clan. Everyone in the Thomas family served."

I nod, recalling Brine's file. "Except Brine. He wanted to serve your country by joining the Bureau."

"Luckily for us," Kayla says, with only a trace of the irony she usually reserves for Brine. Being the most junior, he gets his share of genial ribbing, mostly from her, but that often covers up the fact that she really likes him.

Brine puts his hands together to make a heart symbol. Kayla makes one back.

A thought occurs to me.

"Marisol, did the detonation material also contain the taggant?" I ask.

Marisol checks her analysis. "No, it appears it is common ammonium nitrate. How do you say it, garden variety detonator, homemade."

"If he made the detonator himself, that might be another way to help us identify him. Let's make a note of that. So where do we look for this particular taggant?" I ask Marisol.

"I am thinking army supply," she says, then looks at Brine. "Yes, military boy?"

Brine nods. "Composition C, which is the generic term for this kind of plastic explosive, can only be sold by and used for military use. It's illegal for civilians to buy, sell, own, or possess. The C4 used at the safe house had to have been purchased from a batch sold by the military. That would have required an end user certificate and other paperwork. It'll be in the system."

"Okay, listen up," I say. "The safe house explosion was precision placement of charges for a perfectly executed controlled demolition. That tells us that the bomber knew what he was doing, which means he's done this before, probably a number of times. That in turn tells us that he couldn't have been a civilian. What does that say to you guys?"

Brine shrugs. "That this guy was either active serving or mustered out."

"Unless it was stolen, bruh," Ramon says.

I point at Ramon. "Very good point, Ramon. Composition C is the most popular explosive of choice for a variety of violent criminal activities. Here in the US, we know it as C4, in other countries it's RDX, but basically, they're all variants of the same compound and it's become ubiquitous. It wouldn't be impossible for a motivated individual to get their hands on a quantity of it."

"So what are you thinking?" Kayla asks, looking skeptical. "Do you think he went into a military depot and stole it? Is that even possible? I'd think the military would make it really tough for anyone to do that."

I nod in Kayla's direction. "And Kayla offers a strong counterpoint. One does not simply walk into a military ordnance depot and stroll out with a bag full of C4."

"What if he didn't use C4 at all?" David asks.

I frown at him. "Are you suggesting what I think you're suggesting?"

"What if he acquired an RDX-based alternative on the black market," David says. "It would show up pretty similar to C4, and at times, the chemical signature would be close enough to even pass for C4, am I right, Marisol?"

Marisol wrinkles her nose. "Not very close, David. They are sister chemical compounds. Not identical twins, but sibling. I would have to relook at the analysis, but it is possible."

I talk that through. "David, that's a strong angle. C4 in the form that we use here in the US is very much an American 'brand' as it were. The US military tries to control it through strict regulation but in other countries, it's so common that they don't even bother to use taggants. It's so often used in terrorist attacks and war zones around the world, often by lone wolf suicide bombers, that there's very little point trying to trace it back. Also, from what I'm aware of, the taggant adds cost that impacts competitiveness. Isn't that right, Brine?"

Brine agrees. "Cost and time. Untagged RDX, on the other hand, can probably be had as cheaply as thirty dollars a pound. It's not legal, though."

I sip my soda. "What you're saying is, if someone really wants to get their hands on this substance, it would be easier to buy it off the black market rather than go to the trouble of acquiring taggant marked military-grade C4 that would eventually be traced back to the source?"

David inclines his head. "Not easily, and certainly not legally. But as we all know, there are always ways. The dark web, using bitcoin."

Marisol chimes in: "Why did he not simply go to Walmart, Home Depot, buy fertilizer, and make his own garage bomb? Mostly domestic US bombers do this."

I sit back, considering all these options. "Exactly. Your garden variety mad bomber doesn't go to all the trouble to get tagged C4, risk it being traced back to him, and rig up a precision placed demolition when he could have simply caved in the safe house with almost any kind of bomb."

"What are you saying, Suse?" Kayla asks.

I look around the table at my team. "I think we've got ourselves something more than just a crazy bigot trying to make a statement. I'm sensing the hand of an honest to goodness artist. This is a guy who takes pride in his work. He's a person of fine taste and elegance. He doesn't just want things to go boom, he wants them to go boom in a particular way at a specific time."

"He's still a crazy bigot," Kayla says. "He killed all those innocent people and kids, the sick fuck."

I nod grimly. "Oh yes. That's what makes him so dangerous. He's a psychotic killer with a talent for explosives. But I think he's trying to express something here with the safe house bombing. And if we can figure out what he's trying to say, we'll be one step closer to catching him."

FOURTEEN

The unidentified subject is at the heart of any murder inquiry. Creating a credible profile of the unsub is probably the most important part of any investigation. In this case, we're lucky enough to have multiple witnesses who've actually met him over the years. Although, as we soon find out, lucky isn't quite the word to describe what we have.

We go to the witness statements. Marisol Mancini excuses herself to head down to the local morgue. As the acting coroner and medical examiner for Santa Carina Valley, autopsies take up a hefty chunk of her time. She has a double homicide on her table and Chief McD is pressurizing her to deliver the autopsy results by end of play. Mancini doesn't like being pressured, especially since she's FBI and only standing in as ME as a favor, but she figures the sooner she can finish the autopsies, the sooner she'll get McD off her back.

When she leaves, I check my phone, wondering what's keeping Naved. He should have been here by now. There's no text message or missed call from him so I assume he's gotten caught up in some procedural red tape back at the PD.

Ramon used Carlotta to produce transcripts of the audio

recordings of the interviews we conducted at the safe house site. We study them closely, making notes and adding them to a single file.

It's lunchtime by now and several of the other tables are occupied. A couple of the other patrons glance over at us curiously. I can only imagine how we must look, a group of suits clustered around a table covered with laptops, tablets, and documents. Hopefully, they'll mistake us for realtors meeting to negotiate commissions! Santa Carina Valley is one of the hottest destinations for Los Angeles couples looking to raise a family.

In any case, they're here for the pizza and I don't really care what they think. The case is the only thing that matters. If my house wasn't lying in ruins, I'd have gladly moved the team in there and set up a temporary command center in my living room. Whatever it takes.

"Okay, so what do we have?" I say once we've finished going over all the transcripts.

Kayla turns her tablet screen around so we can all see her notes. "Every one of the witnesses remembers the Saint. They all agree on the fact that the safe house was run by the Saint. Except for two of them, who came through Canada, all the relatives had come up through Mexico, and stayed at the same safe house when they first arrived. They had all met the Saint and agree that he was the only point of contact here. It was the same for the folks who were coming in this time."

"Okay," I say. "So far, so good. The Saint ran the safe house, he's the local contact in the secret railroad, all the new arrivals were told that he'd be the one taking care of them here. That makes him our number one suspect. How about a description, Kay?"

Kayla makes a face. "That's where things start to get a little hazy. For the most part, they all remember him as a priest. On that, we have no disagreements at all. They remember him in a cassock. Some say it was black, a couple witnesses think it might have been dark blue, one says purple, but they all admit the light was poor and they only caught glimpses of him. Almost all of them believe he was White and remember him speaking with a slight accent. The only person who actually met him after her own crossing, the abuelita whose granddaughter was killed in the safe house, insists that he was a Hispanic priest who works at a local church or mission. But that was seven years ago, and her memory is shaky. Then there's the name Santos. It came up three times, but it's hard to say if they think he was actually named Santos or because that's the word for 'Saint'. And then there are the contradictions."

I tap Kayla's note on the comment made by the younger Rohingya immigrant, taking over the narration. "This witness insists that the Saint is a young man in his twenties. His own father says he was in his forties or older. Everyone else is certain he was an older man. A few even insist he was a very old man and had the impression that he was either bald or balding under the hood of the cassock. And one person, another outlier, insists he had white hair." I look around. "Thoughts?"

David leans forward. "They were all down there in the dark for days, scared, poorly nourished, dehydrated. I think we should discount the age and physical descriptions and focus on the main points that the majority agree on."

I nod. "That he's a priest. Older man. Spoke with an accent. Might be named Santos, either first or last name."

Ramon spreads his hands. "That's it? That's like, nothing, boss."

"It's what we're sure of. We'll fill in more details as we get more info. Right now, let's stick with that," I say.

"What about the age disagreement?" Brine asks.

"I think the Rohingya boy just got it wrong," I say. "He's young, unfamiliar with American faces, I don't know, maybe he was just confused? Either way, it's clearly contrary to all the other statements."

"So then he's an older man," David says. "At least forties, likely much older."

"Yes, let's agree on that," I say.

Kayla speaks up. "Suse, what about the old abuelita's comments about him being a soldier?"

I hold out a palm, waving it from side to side. "I'd stick with the priest. It narrows our focus and gives us a starting point." I look at Ramon. "Can you check the records for—"

Ramon turns his laptop screen around, showing me. "Already done, jefe." He explains, "Carlotta sent out spiders to work the local churches as well as the archdiocese records. There are no priests named Santos in the system who are currently active. The only hit she got was for a Carlos Santos, seventy-three, deceased."

He pulls up a screen on his laptop and shows me. The death certificate shows a date more than three years ago, during the height of the pandemic.

David says, "Is it possible he changed his name? Or that Santos was just the name he gave the immigrants that he came into contact with?"

"That makes sense," I say. "He might not want them to know his real name. He must have known what he was doing was illegal and would get him arrested, and prosecuted or at the very least, deported, if anyone ever named him. He would have known the risk of at least some of the immigrants he helped being caught by ICE sooner or later. I buy the idea that he used a handle."

"Maybe that's where the nickname 'the Saint' came from?" Brine suggests tentatively.

"Or maybe they called him the Saint because that's what he seemed to them, and so they assumed his real name was also Santos?" Kayla suggests.

We toss that around for a while. Ramon tries searches with several variations of the word "Saint" in different languages, even going farther afield with loose alternatives ranging from farishta to bhagwan. Nothing throws up anything that remotely matches any priests.

"Okay," I say, feeling a little frustrated with the dead ends. "So maybe he isn't actually named anything like Saint, maybe that's just a handle that stuck. Let's look at this another way. Let's look at priests who might fit the description we have of him."

Ramon shakes his head. "That's even funkier, boss. We got contradictory descriptions."

He points out the contrasting accounts from the father and son witnesses. "One says the Saint is young, as young as the witness himself, who's twenty-two. The father says, no, he was definitely much older, closer to mid-forties. Which do we use?"

"What if we use that as a range: twenty to forty-five? No, make it eighteen to fifty. Let's keep a buffer on both ends."

He runs the search and shows us the results.

There are 1049 priests in the Los Angeles County area, which includes Santa Carina Valley. There's no town or city breakdown so there's no way to tell how many may or may not be assigned to local parishes—or were assigned in the past. We need another way to narrow down the number. Even if this was an official Bureau investigation, it would be impractical to simply go out and try to interview a thousand priests scattered across the county. A vital part of a special agent in charge's job during a major crime investigation is figuring out ways to narrow down the list of possible unsubs.

"Okay, now let's try cross-checking that with priests who served or are currently serving in the armed forces," I say.

Twenty-four priests.

"That's better," I say. "Let's get files on these twenty-four."

"Hold on," David says. "Before we start investing time in looking through files, let's check how many of those twenty-four are currently deployed."

I nod approvingly. "Good thinking."

Ramon's fingers fly over the keyboard. He stares at the screen then sighs in frustration. "Damn it!"

Ramon shoves back his chair and gets up, walking away with a heavy tread. A pair of young bespectacled men at a nearby table look up.

"Should I..." Brine asks, starting to rise.

I grab Brine's arm and pull him back down. "Give him a minute."

I turn Ramon's screen around and look at the search results.

So that's what upset him.

All twenty-four priests are currently deployed as chaplains in the US military, all of them overseas.

I show the others the result. They all look disappointed.

"So that's a bust," I say.

I glance over in the direction Ramon went.

"He'll probably just hit the restroom, pour cold water over his head," Kayla says matter-of-factly. "Maybe punch a wall or two."

I nod. When you work together as a team as closely as we have for this long, on multiple cases, you get to know a lot about each other. As agents. And as people. We have few, if any, secrets from each other.

"Let him breathe," I say.

I tap on Ramon's keyboard, digging deeper into the same search.

"Let's see where they went and when," I say.

I call up another screen, showing the start of their deployment. The most recent one was almost three months earlier.

I shake my head in frustration. "Our guy definitely set off that explosion on-site, we know that already. He had to have been physically present here in the past few days."

I feel like thumping the table, kicking over a chair, or showing my own frustration in some way. Three years ago, before I made SAC, I would probably have done just that. Now, I settle for cracking my knuckles slowly and deliberately. It's not as satisfying as a stress ball, but it does the job. David grimaces, reacting to the knuckle cracking. I don't apologize. David has his quirks, I have mine; we all do.

"So that rules out the priest theory?" Kayla asks at last.

"No," I say after a long moment's consideration. "No. It doesn't rule out anything. It just means we have to work this from the other end."

They all stare at me blankly.

Ramon comes back, his short cut hair damp. Even his eyebrows are wet. He sees everyone staring at me and frowns as he takes his seat.

I look at him, while addressing the whole team.

"Never mind the data," I say. "It's all well and good. But we know he's out there. The Saint. Let's go try and find him the old-fashioned way."

"By pounding the pavement and ringing doorbells?" David asks.

"In a sense," I say. "But not doorbells. Church bells. If he's a local priest, he's got to be affiliated to a church. So let's go knock on all the church doors in Santa Carina Valley."

Ramon's face relaxes into a grin.

"Now you're talking, boss," he says.

FIFTEEN

St. Katherine's Catholic Church is only 5.3 miles from the safe house. It's a Spanish-revival style structure on top of a hill, over-looking a pretty residential subdivision with a lovely park and playground and a Montessori preschool.

As Ramon and I wait in front of the church for the pastor, I glance down at the colorful swatch that is the local playground and park.

Before she began attending elementary school last year, Natalie would go to the preschool just across from that park. Amit and I took turns picking her up by six as that was when the after-school childcare closed.

Once in a while, our routines would magically align—a super rare occurrence—and both Amit and I would land up together. She would clap her hands with excitement at the sight of both of us, perform her signature elbow dance, and then insist on going straight to the playground. That last day, I think she spent a record hour and a half there, giving both of us precise instructions on how to play her self-created game of hide-and-go-tag.

I remember fielding calls from Gantry about a case, barking into my ear while I tried to duck under or behind colorful playground objects designed for much smaller bodies, and feeling torn between wanting to throw my phone into the bushes and give my daughter my undivided attention, and slipping away while Natalie was still counting so I could deal with the work crisis. And while facing this dilemma, I remember feeling ashamed that I would even weigh the two options.

What I wouldn't give for a chance to relive that time again.

As a family.

Ramon is looking at me. He sees something in my face and I sense he's about to ask me a question but then he glances back, sees the playground, and puts two and two together.

He reaches out, takes my hand, and gives it a squeeze. Words are unnecessary. I nod my thanks.

Two cassocked figures descend the stone steps.

"Detectives, I am Father Monroe. How may I be of assistance?"

The gray-haired Catholic priest looks from me to Ramon, as if trying to decide which of us is in charge.

I compose my face and he focuses on me.

"Father, I'm Special Agent in Charge Susan Parker. This is Special Agent Ramon Diaz."

His bushy eyebrows climb. "The FBI? I don't believe we've ever had the honor. Have we, Father Angelo?"

The younger man, the priest whom we met when we arrived and who went to fetch the pastor, looks intimidated. "No, Father Monroe. This is definitely a first."

The pastor invites us into a very pretty parlor and offers us hot beverages and lemon bundt cake. "From last Sunday's bake sale," he adds, helping himself to a thick slice. "Do try some, it's very good. Maria Quintanella, one of our parishioners, runs a baked goods delivery service from home. She made it. Started during the pandemic when she lost her husband and had to cover the mortgage and provide for herself and the children. It was so successful, she's now expanded it into a local franchise. Perhaps you've heard of it? 'Maria Bakes'? It has quite the following on Facebook."

I nibble on it as a courtesy and make the appropriate noises, eager to get down to business. Ramon is even more impatient than I am, but he's deferential, waiting for me to take the lead as usual. He's a whiz when it comes to anything to do with computers and AI, but personal interviews are not his strongest suit.

Father Monroe puts down his teacup and laces his fingers together over his cossack-covered belly, after smoothing it down.

"Please, do tell me how I may be of service, Agent Parker?"

"Father, do you have or have you ever had a priest named Father Santos at this parish?"

He regards me for a long moment without saying a word. His eyes flick from me to Ramon, stay on Ramon for a length of time, then return to study my face.

"No," he says at last, the tone curt and final.

It's a contrast to his genial, smiling manner until now. The smile is gone, too.

"Are you quite certain of that, Father?" I ask patiently.

He doesn't answer again.

"You see, I have a witness who says she met with Father Santos here at the church."

He looks into the distance, in the direction of a picture of the Sacred Heart hanging on a peach-colored wall, but not actually looking at the picture itself.

"She is mistaken," he says, again in the curt tone, unsmiling.

"I find her quite credible," I say. "She's a serving soldier in the military. She has no reason to lie to us. In fact, lying to a federal agent is a crime. It wouldn't put her behind bars, but it would definitely tarnish her military record. Possibly worse."

He closes his eyes.

I glance over at Ramon.

Ramon gives me a small nod.

He sees what I see: we've clearly hit a nerve.

Not only does Father Monroe know exactly what we're talking about, he's been dreading this very moment. All that talk about bundt cakes and bake sales was to delay the inevitable. A moment he's probably anticipated and not been looking forward to for a while now. He must be a very good priest because he's a very poor liar.

"Father..." I start to say.

He raises a hand.

"Agent Parker, I was assigned to this parish almost three years ago. At the time, I was made aware of certain... irregularities... that had been rumored about for a long time, but were never confirmed officially. You have to remember that a pastor in a relatively smaller parish like this one is given a fair amount of freedom in how he chooses to manage his flock. There are always people talking, especially in these days of social media. The days of the glory of the Roman Catholic Church are long behind us. These are the days of Answerability and Accountability. The church has had its hands full dealing with a number of crises, some of faith, others physical. However, these were not in that area. If anything, the rumors were ludicrously incredible. Far-fetched. Nobody took them seriously."

Ramon and I exchange another glance.

"Father," I say gently, "we're not here to investigate St. Katherine's. All we're interested in is trying to find Father Santos. We're hoping he might be able to answer some questions that would help us track down a murderer."

The padre blinks rapidly. "A murderer?"

"A mass murderer, in fact," I say. "Perhaps you heard about the bombing at the safe house?"

He stares blankly now. "Bombing? Safe house? I saw

nothing in the news headlines about a bombing. Did you see anything, Cecil?"

Father Angelo, who seems to have turned three shades paler during the last several minutes, shakes his head. "Not a thing, Father Monroe."

"It hasn't been reported widely," I explain. "The victims were illegal immigrants smuggled across the border and brought up here then stashed in an underground bunker until they could be provided documentation and transport to further destinations. The authorities might not have been very keen to publicize the incident."

He looks suddenly relieved. "Then you're not here to investigate St. Katherine's?" he asks tentatively.

"Well, that's a difficult question, Father. Perhaps if I could speak with Father Santos, he might be able to clear up some questions we have."

"Is that all?" he asks, leaning forward to perch on the edge of his chair. "You only came here to ask Father Santos for help with the investigation? That's it?"

Ramon and I exchange another glance.

"Yes," we both say together.

Father Monroe slaps his thighs with enthusiastic force, and springs up from his chair. "Come with me," he says.

We follow his swishing cassock through the church, out a back door onto the rear steps, down them, and into the backyard of the church, cloistered by a stand of trees that huddle around, leaning inward like a crowd of mourners around an open grave.

Several graves, actually, not open but closed now.

He walks us through the church graveyard.

We pass gravestones.

I glimpse dates as far back as the 1930s.

The dates progress as we walk farther back, to the rear of the graveyard.

Finally, Father Monroe stops before a grave and turns to face us.

Ramon and I look down.

The gravestone is clearly a more recent one.

The inscription reads: *Father Miguel Arturos Santos, SJ*.

The date is almost three years ago.

SIXTEEN

We reassemble in the parking lot of Natalie's elementary school. Ramon and I took the van to St. Katherine's while the others drove their own cars to the three other Catholic churches in Santa Carina Valley. Kayla is already in the parking lot when we pull in, David joins us a few minutes later, Brine is the last to arrive. We convene in the van, the air conditioning struggling to stave off the August heat. David wipes his damp brow with a handkerchief.

"I was in the middle of my interview with the priest at St. Margaret's," he complains mildly. "What's up?"

"What happened is that we found the Saint, bingo-bongo, on our first try," I say. "Didn't see much point in you guys continuing to chase him down."

"Great going," says Kayla, beads of sweat glistening on the scalp visible between her beaded braids. "So is he our unsub or not? Don't keep us in suspense, Suse!"

"It's a good news, bad news situation," I say. "Keep your expectations low."

I summarize what happened at St. Katherine's. When they

hear that Father Santos has been dead almost three years, all of them react.

"What about what Paula Contreras told you then?" Kayla asks. "Did she lie about that?"

"I don't think so. Paula said she met Santos about two or three years ago. It was probably just before he died."

"Are we sure that this Father Santos was the Saint?" David asks.

"I'm going to defer to Ramon on that one. Ramon?"

He sighs, rubbing his thumb over his pectorals. "Yeah. Pretty sure. It all fits. I remember him being part of a local church. Ronaldo said he met him once, don't ask me when or where exactly, he didn't say, but I think it was about ten to twelve years ago. Ronaldo asked the padre if he would hear his confession. He wanted to tell someone about all the things he had seen and been part of during his years with the cartel. He said that Santos praised him for seeking atonement, but it would be best for him to confess to his local parish priest. Santos didn't want to be seen associating with any of the people who had passed through the safe house."

"That makes sense," David says. "Based on what Father Monroe told you, the church probably had an inkling about Father Santos's involvement with the secret railroad by then, and Santos was being careful to distance himself publicly."

"How did he even get away with helping these illegal immigrants for so many years?" Brine asks. "How come nobody reported him to the authorities? I don't mean the church. We all know they protect their own unless confronted with hard evidence. By authorities, I mean CBP, DHS, or ICE."

Good question. California Border Patrol, Department of Homeland Security, and Immigration and Customs Enforcement are the three main authorities that deal with immigrants.

I ask Ramon to show us his laptop screen, as I explain: "Apparently, they did. I asked Ramon to do some research on the way here. Nothing from CBP or DHS, but ICE registered at least two official complaints over the years. Neither of them panned out because the complaints came from anonymous tipoffs, and nobody actually stepped forward to confirm or corroborate. ICE questioned Santos but he refused to cooperate so they had nothing to hold him on or pressure him with. Pretty much a dead end. Anything to add, Ramon?"

Ramon says, "Father Santos had a lot of clout locally. He stayed lowkey but in the community everyone loved and respected him. Being a Hispanic Catholic priest at a major institution like St. Katherine's is a big deal. ICE probably knew that they would be kicking a hornet's nest if they came at him without hard evidence and corroborating witnesses. They had no choice but to back off."

"Exactly," I say. "The only way they could take him down was by boxing him in with solid evidence and witnesses. Either they never got enough to do that, or they had other, bigger fish to fry."

Kayla nods. "That makes a whole lot of sense. From the anecdotal interviews we got at the safe house, it sounds like he was helping maybe a few dozen immigrants a year. That adds up to hundreds over a few decades, but it's still a drop in the ocean."

Another good point. While Santos helping hundreds, maybe even a few thousand, during his lifetime might seem like a lot, the fact is that as many as a million immigrants attempt to illegally enter the United States *every month*. It's been increasing in recent years, and a whopping percentage of that number is released into the country pending appearances in immigration court, while the repatriation process for the ones who are apprehended can take years. In any given year, there can be as many as ten *million* illegal immigrants in the US. A drop in the ocean is putting it mildly.

"So what do we conclude from this?" Brine asks.

I sigh. "We'll check it out, of course. David, make a note to speak to our contacts at Homeland, Border Patrol, ICE. We'll cover all bases but don't spend too much time on it. The conclusion is, Santos is dead and can't be our present-day Saint."

"Like I said all along," Ramon says, "no priest could have buried those people alive like that. It's ungodly."

"So maybe the bomber was never Santos in the first place?" David suggests. "Or he was someone who was working alongside Santos and took over after Santos died?"

"That makes sense," Brine says, brightening up. "We do have that father-son statement where they disagree about the Saint's age. Maybe that's because there were two different Saints on two different visits, one younger, one older."

"Another priest, you mean?" Kayla asks, sounding doubtful. "That seems like a stretch. None of the witnesses mentioned anything about there being *two* priests."

Ramon shakes his head. "Nope. I don't buy that either, Brine. The Saint was a lone wolf. Ronaldo said the dude always flew solo. It's why he was able to dodge ICE and DHS for so long. The only way they could have got him was by tailing him twenty-four-seven for months. You don't just follow a Catholic priest without strong probable cause, right?"

I nod. "No judge would sign off on *that* warrant without hard evidence which they didn't have. And the resources that would have taken, the overtime alone? No way ICE would have been able to spare the manpower and justify the cost unless they were certain of getting results. I agree with Ramon on this. Everything we've heard suggests the Saint worked alone and since Santos is dead, he obviously isn't the Saint we're looking for."

Brine's momentary burst of excitement deflates. "So, who was the priest they called the Saint?"

"If he was a priest at all," I say.

"We have witnesses who say they met a priest. They met a priest everyone called the Saint, so who the heck was he?"

Kayla raises her finger to object. "They met a *man* in a priest's cassock. It wasn't like he showed them ID or swore on a Bible."

I frown. "An imposter? I think Brine has a point here. Let's think this through. If we assume the person posing as the Saint after Santos's death was an imposter, how would this imposter know the location of the safe house? How did he know what to do, whom to contact, or be contacted by? Santos was part of a chain, the secret railroad they called it, so the imposter would have to be plugged into the same chain. And if he's been operating the past three years then what happened to all the immigrants that came through in that period? Did they pass through safely? They must have, right? He can't just have been blowing them up like he did in the safe house this time. He couldn't have gotten away with that many bodies and explosions for years. Someone would have found out, like Ramon's people did when it happened. Even illegal immigrants have someone here who's expecting them, someone who won't just stay quiet if they never show up. There's no covering up a mass murder of that size, even out in the boondocks."

We toss it around for a while longer without getting anywhere. As usual, I get so absorbed in the case that I forget where I am and what I'm actually doing here in the elementary school parking lot.

A familiar little body hurling itself at me brings me back to reality.

Natalie beams up at me, hugging my waist.

"How come you came?" she asks, signing. "Lata Auntie said you were working on a case and we might not see you for *days!*"

She stretches out the sign for 'days' making it seem like an endless age, which it is to a seven-year-old.

I nod at my sislaw who's standing a few feet away, eyebrows raised as she asks the same question silently.

I hug my daughter and kiss her on the top of my head as I reply verbally as well as in ASL. "I wanted to come by and watch you rehearse, you little star," I say warmly. "I guess I was too late. Maybe tomorrow? You've met my team, haven't you?"

"Oh yeah," Natalie says, signing to everyone in turn. "Hey, Kayla, Ramon, David, Brine. Where's Naved Uncle?"

Good question. "He'll be joining us later. How was rehearsal, sweetie?"

"Awesome, Mom! You should come tomorrow. Drama club is my favorite of all time. I want to be an actor when I grow up! Please, can I be an actor?"

I laugh. "Let's talk about it in a few years. Boy! If you're this excited, the play must be something. I've got to come by tomorrow and watch you."

Lata puts her arm around her niece, looking down at her proudly. "She really is worth watching," she tells me. "The new drama teacher is pretty good."

"He's awesome, Mom," Natalie signs enthusiastically. "And really handsome. Even Lata Auntie thinks he's 'cute'!"

Lata rolls her eyes, and I laugh again. "This I've got to see. What do you want to do now? You must be tired after a whole day of school and then drama club. You probably want to head home now."

"Actually, Mom," Natalie signs, then glances shyly at the team. "Could we go to the park?"

"Which one?" I ask.

"You know," Natalie adds. "The one we all used to go to. When I was in Montessori."

A pang of nostalgia pierces my heart. *The one we all used to go to.* She means the one next to St. Katharine's. Such a weird coincidence. I was just there a half hour ago. It's like she somehow read my mind and picked it out of my thoughts.

I'm itching to stay with my team and work the case, especially since we seem to have hit a dead end. I feel the pressure to give the team a new direction. Keeping the momentum going is crucial in the first days of a case. But when I look down at Natalie's sweet, heart-shaped face, and see Amit's eyes looking back at me, I don't have the heart to deny her.

"Sure, sweetie," I say. "Of course we can."

I tell the team I'll see them at the pizza parlor in an hour and head toward Lata's Jeep. Other parents and kids are coming out of the school auditorium now.

One of them is a heavily tattooed guy in jeans and a denim tank top that shows off his muscular physique. He has his arms on the shoulders of two young boys and is talking to them quietly. The younger boy waves to Natalie. She waves back. The dad pauses what he's saying to glance up at us and our eyes meet briefly. I vaguely recognize him, probably from similar encounters in the past. He nods in passing and I nod back, two parents acknowledging each other.

"Night, swabbie," he calls out to Lata in a gently mocking tone as he stops before a pickup truck parked one row over.

When he raises his arm to pull himself up into the truck, I see the ink on the back of his forearm. Two cannons, crisscross, with a cannonball and fire symbol.

"Night, squid," Lata calls back in a matching tone as she climbs into the Jeep.

"Who's that?" I ask as we pull out.

"That's Nate Sanderson," she says. "Former Seal."

"You two seem pally."

"Not really. We were just shooting the breeze while watching the kids rehearse," she replies. "His son's in the play with Natalie."

Lata glances at me suspiciously as she drives. She knows me well enough to read between the lines. "Hey! You're not seriously thinking Nate Sanderson could be your suspect!"

"I'm not thinking anything, I was just asking."

"Yeah, well, Nate Sanderson can't possibly be your guy, so don't even look at him funny."

"Why?" I ask, genuinely curious.

"Because Nate Sanderson is the sweetest, most tender, gentle guy around. Widowed. Single dad. Amazing man. Which is saying a hell of a lot. Especially for a seasoned vet like him. So please don't point a finger at him, or you'll be hearing from a lot of angry people who really like him, starting with me."

"Okay," I say, laughing a little at Lata's expression. "Backing off now. Just one last question."

"What?" Lata asks.

"He has this tattoo," I say, and describe it to her.

"Demolition corps," she says.

Demolition. That's explosives. Which means he has or had access to C4. Like the explosive used at the safe house.

SEVENTEEN

Susan Parker.

He knows her name now.

An FBI special agent in charge working out of the Los Angeles field office. There's a picture of her younger self on the FBI website, dating back a few years. She looks bright, chipper, happy to be a federal agent. She features in one of the background banners on the Bureau's human resources page, suggesting that they consider her a poster girl for recruitment. Figures.

He looks up from his phone screen to see the real thing, standing in the parking lot of the elementary school. She's in conversation with her daughter and another woman. Her team is there, too, standing by the mobile unit van. Looks like Agent Parker's combining work with family time. Sounds sloppy to him but that's how the new FBI rolls, apparently.

Searching online as he watches them talk, it takes him only a few seconds to learn that Parker's a widow, and that the other woman is her sister-in-law. Lata Kapoor, a former Marine. Interesting. It might be worth trying to connect with her through his vet buddies. There are a lot of vets here in SCV and they're a pretty tight community. He's betting that Kapoor and he have a bunch of friends in common.

Parker exchanges a few words with her team then heads off with her daughter and sister-in-law. The daughter looks familiar. Isn't she the one with a disability? A special needs kid, maybe? He'll have to ask around but he's pretty sure he's seen her before.

That's good. Very, very good. A widow with a disabled daughter?

That makes her vulnerable.

He doesn't like that she visited St. Katherine's. It was inevitable. They know the Saint has to be involved somehow and the old priest was the obvious person to question. But he'd hoped it would take them a while longer to track down the church and discover that Santos had been in the ground for three years.

Now that they've already turned that up, he can expect them to turn their attention elsewhere: on the taggant and the C4. That's not too great either. But it's also inevitable. That will bring them a little closer to him, but it will take some time. It had better. He has plans, and pieces to put into place before that. He hadn't expected SAC Parker to move this fast and be this driven. If it looks like she's turning into a pain in his ass, he might have to take drastic action.

Very drastic.

He watches as SAC Parker gets in the sister-in-law's Jeep Cherokee and they pull out of the school parking lot, followed by the unmarked van.

The Cherokee takes the turn on the main street and goes past him. He sees Parker turn instinctively to look back over her shoulder, as if sensing eyes on her. He knows she can't see him through the dark tinted side window of his truck, but he allows himself a grin.

Catch me if you can, Agent Parker.

EIGHTEEN

"I'll see you tonight, sweetie," I sign and say, kissing the top of Natalie's head. She's still sweaty from playing at the park, her cheeks flushed from the heat.

She nods noncommittally. She knows the odds of my reaching home by her bedtime while working a case are slim to none. And that's without taking into account the long drive from SCV to Bel Air.

I gesture to Lata to wait and walk around to the driver's side of the Cherokee.

"What's up?" she asks, indicating the parking lot of the restaurant. "Need me to park?"

"This will just take a minute," I say. "How closely do you know the veteran community here in SCV?"

She shrugs. "Reasonably well, I guess."

"If I want to try to track down someone who might be active service or a vet, and I only know this person by their skill set, what would be the best way to reach out to the community as a whole? Is there, like, a VFA or VA center? An email newsletter? A Facebook group?"

She raises her eyebrows. "All of those but Suse, are you seriously asking me for the best way to get vets to rat on one of our own? Is this about the safe house bombing? Your unsub is a vet?"

I show her my palms. "Hey, I'm just asking. We don't know anything for sure yet. You know how these things roll. Wherever the investigation goes, it goes. I have to follow the leads. I just want to know where to start."

She nods. "Fair enough. Offhand, though, I'd advise hitting one of the local bars. That's the best way to get to know a few folks quickly, maybe even make a friend or two, gain people's trust. Like I said, the community is really diverse, but if they hear that someone, especially an LEO, is looking for dirt on one of their own, they can close ranks real quick, get really defensive and hostile. Once they circle the wagons, the only way you'd get anyone to cooperate would be by waterboarding them."

I nod. "Okay, I get it. Try drinks first, then waterboarding. In that order. Do me a favor, text me the names of a few bars to start off with."

She starts the Jeep up again. "You got it. Take care, sislaw. Don't get yourself blown up!"

I wave at Natalie who waves back as the Cherokee pulls out into the street.

Urduja comes out as I'm walking to the entrance of Toppings. She's changed into street clothes and looks flushed from the heat.

"Hi, Susan, did you catch him yet?" she asks.

I can't help but smile at her youthful enthusiasm. If only it were that easy. "Working on it. You off for the day?"

"Meeting my boyfriend. He's really keen to meet you. If I'd known you were coming back, I would have told him to come on over. He takes a few shifts here, too. Makes a real mean calzone, and I know you like calzone."

"That's okay, U. You're probably going to be seeing a lot of me and the team. We're going to be using Toppings as our temporary command center for now!"

"Wow! Cool! I get to watch you work and feed you. That is so awesome," she says.

A thought strikes me.

"That is okay, isn't it? I mean, your boss won't mind us spending so much time in here?" I ask.

She shakes her head. "No way! You guys are one of our best customers. Besides, Quadros thinks you're a force for good."

I raise my eyebrows. "A force for good? He said that?"

"His words. He voted against Chief McDougall at the last election, gave his money and support to the other candidate. He also votes against McD in the city council every chance he gets. The chief holds a grudge against him for that, so none of the cops or ex-cops in SCV eat at Toppings. The same for most vets, too. That hurts his business because, you know, SCV is, like, a major retirement community for ex law enforcement and veterans. But he doesn't care. He thinks McD and his old school guys are outdated and bigoted, and he's right. He thinks the city needs a change. You should meet him, you two would get along great together."

That's a lot more info than I'd expected, or wanted, but it's not entirely unwelcome. I make a mental note. "Maybe I will. He sounds like a sensible man. Especially since he hires smart kids like you!"

She laughs. "Thanks, Susan. I've gotta run now. I told Fry I'd be there ten minutes ago!"

I wave as she gets into her little compact and zips away.

The cool air feels like a blessing as I open the door of Toppings. Before I can step in, my phone buzzes in my hand.

Law Offices of Chivers-Hall, Andrews & Associates calling

I frown and hesitate on the threshold.

Then I let go of the door, allowing it to swing shut, as I go back down the steps to the parking lot to take the call.

"Special Agent in Charge Susan Parker?" asks a crisp, businesslike male voice in an East Coast American accent.

"Who is this?" I ask cautiously.

"My name is Leland Chivers-Hall. I'm an attorney."

I glance across the street. The green turf patch outside the courthouse and public library compound is occupied by a motley group of protestors holding up handwritten signs and placards. I watch them indifferently as I try to recall if I've ever had dealings with this particular law firm, but the name doesn't ring a bell.

"What case is this regarding?" I ask cautiously.

"I'm a probate lawyer, Miss Parker, not criminal. This is not related to any FBI case."

"I don't understand."

"I can explain."

"Mr...."

"Chivers-Hall. But please call me Leland."

"Well, Mr. Chivers-Hall, maybe you should be speaking to the OGC. That's—"

"The Office of General Counsel for the FBI, yes, I'm aware. But as I said before, this is not an FBI matter."

"What is it then?" I ask. A sinking feeling hollows my belly. The last thing I need right now is a civil case brought by some irate suspect I questioned in the course of an investigation.

"It is not a civil matter either, in case you're concerned," he says, as if reading my mind. "In fact, it's not any case against you. On the contrary."

On the contrary. The hell does that mean?

When I don't reply at once, he says politely, "Miss Parker, if we could meet briefly at my offices, I could clarify things in just a few minutes. I assure you it would be well worth your time. My offices are in Sherman Oaks."

"Well, Mr. Chivers-Hall, I'm in the middle of an investigation right now. It's not very convenient for me to simply drop everything and drive all the way to Sherman Oaks."

"Yes, of course, Santa Carina Valley is a bit of a drive, especially at rush hour, I'm told," he says, "but I would reiterate, Miss Parker, the visit will be well worth your time."

"Why don't you just tell me on the phone what it is you want from me?" I say.

"I would do that if I could, but my client's instructions are explicit. I'm only to discuss the matter *in camera* with you personally."

The use of the legal phrase makes me frown again. "Who is your client, Mr. Chivers-Hall?"

"I'm afraid that, too, must remain confidential until we meet in person."

I'm getting a little irritated now. The protestors across the street are chanting some slogan in a singsong chorus. I can't hear it over the sound of traffic and am not particularly eager to know. I turn away, walking back to the restaurant's entrance.

"Is your client planning to sue me for something? If that's the case, you need to tell me, Mr. Chivers-Hall."

"Miss Parker, I assure you, this is an opportunity for you to benefit from my client, not the other way around."

"What does that mean?"

"Again, Miss Parker, I can only explain further when we—"

"—meet in person, okay, I get it. In that case, Mr. Chivers-Hall, I'm going to have to get back to you once I finish this case."

"Miss Parker, it's in your best interests to meet me at your earliest convenience. I assure you that the meeting will be entirely to your advantage."

I've had enough of this legal talkaround.

"Mr. Chivers-Hall, I'm going to have to get back to you," I say, and disconnect the phone without waiting for his response.

Whatever he's looking to sell me, I'm not buying it. I have

more on my plate right now than I can handle as it is. The last thing I need is to get sucked into some legal wrangle.

The air-conditioned interior of the restaurant is a blessed relief after the August heat.

The team is already assembled and eating.

"Hey, guys," I say, sliding in. "So, I've been thinking. The priest angle is a dead end right now. Let's not waste any more time on it."

"Makes sense since he's been dead three years," Ramon says. "But it still doesn't make sense. Someone was impersonating Father Santos these past three years."

"Sure, and we'll circle back to it. Right now, that person is a cipher, and we have no way to identify who he might be or where to start looking. So we need to put our limited resources to work on following up the lead we already have hard evidence for," I say as I pick up a chicken tender.

Kayla points a slice of pizza at me. "Taggants!"

I bop my chicken tender against her pepperoni slice. "You got it in one. Taggants. We know the unsub used this particular batch of C4. We need to use the taggants to track that batch back through the manufacture and distribution chain. That's why taggants are used in the first place. So let's use them."

Ramon nods slowly. "Okay, chief. I'll put Carlotta to work on it."

I pick up my soda and point it at Brine. "Brine, you're from a military fam. Didn't you say your uncle Ben used to be a warrant officer in charge of ordnance or something like that? Excuse me if I'm using the wrong rank. I can never keep them all straight, especially the differences in what they mean between the armed services."

"You're not far off, chief," Brine says when he finishes chewing his mouthful of calzone. "Ordnance warrant officers and ordnance enlisted are both ranks in that department. What we're looking for here are the ordnance officers. They're the guys who are in charge of acquiring, storing, managing inventory, and generally making sure the ordnance, which includes explosives, gets where it's needed and is stored securely when it isn't. My uncle Ben was an ordnance officer. I've heard some stories from him of attempted heists and even one heist that was pulled off successfully."

"Are we really thinking that this guy pulled off a heist to acquire the C4?" David asks skeptically. He picks at his garden salad. "That sounds too Quentin Tarantino!"

Brine waves a hand. "Negatory, David. I'm just saying that the ordnance depot on any base is always a target. If you ask me, our unsub here probably acquired it legitimately. It's the only way that makes sense. This stuff is very tough to get hold of."

"That's *if* he used regulated C4," David says. "If he just bought RDX off the black market through the dark web, there'd be no way of tracing that back at all."

"We could try," Ramon chips in. "But it would be like trying to track a needle in a bunch of haystacks all full of needles and no way to tell which one is ours."

I nod. "And the last thing we want is a false positive that has us breaking down someone's door only to find that all he actually did was buy some bitcoin online, not C4. Okay, so what we're looking for first are ordnance officers, right?"

Ramon does some preliminary research and shows us the results.

Kayla whistles. "Whoa! That's a whole load of possibles."

My heart sinks. "And this is for the entire United States?"

Ramon gives me an are-you-kidding look. "Just Southern California, jefe. The whole state would be three times that number."

I groan, holding my head in my hands. "How the hell are we going to check out that many possible origin sources?"

"And they're spread out across a pretty big area," Kayla points out. "We're going to need boots on the ground to help us, or it'll take us weeks to get around to questioning all these guys and auditing them while they check their inventory."

"Do we really need to do that?" David asks. "Can't we just contact them and ask them if they have any C4 missing?"

I shake my head. "No, David. Because one of those ordnance officers could be our unsub. All he'd have to do is lie to us and then get the hell out of Dodge."

"Good point. In that case, Kayla is right. We're going to need a lot of boots to cover that ground. Local PD at the very least. Maybe military intelligence?"

We're still batting the logistics of how to get the additional support we need when I see a familiar face at the door.

He enters Toppings, glances over at us, then walks past without saying anything or acknowledging me.

NINETEEN

I get up from the booth and walk over to the soda dispenser.

Naved is standing with his back to me, filling a large cup to the brim.

"Hey, you made it," I say.

His mouth is a thin horizontal line. The dark circles under his eyes look more pronounced than usual. He snaps a cap onto the soda cup. "We need to talk."

Uh-oh. That doesn't sound good.

We walk back to the table together.

Everyone greets Naved with enthusiasm. Even Ramon drags his eyes from his laptop to tap knuckles.

"Perfect timing," says Kayla. "We were just talking about how we're going to need PD support. How many pairs of boots do you think we could get to go around to army bases?"

Naved sets his soda cup on the table, then takes off his jacket.

Sweat has stained the armpits of his shirt and sketched a Rorschach pattern down his spine. He folds the jacket and lays it on his thigh as he sits down and takes a big gulp of his drink.

"None," he says to Kayla.

She blinks.

Naved looks up at me. I'm still standing, waiting for the boom to fall.

"McD's pulled me off the safe house case," he says. "He gave me busywork all day and when I went to ask him again for the third time if I could leave the station, he sat me down and gave me an ultimatum."

I slide slowly into my seat. "Let me guess. Stay off the case or he'll fire you?"

"Without saying it in so many words."

I sigh, rolling my head and shoulders to relieve the stress gathered in that area. "He knows better than to do that. In the event that he does fire you, he doesn't want to give you grounds for filing a wrongful termination lawsuit. The ACLU would be all over his ass. Let me guess, he also handed you a case. Something that's guaranteed to keep you running around in circles for a while."

Naved drinks his soda. "He put me on a robbery case. Routine smash and grab at a mini mart. The owner says there was less than ten dollars in the cash register and from what he could tell, the thieves only stole liquor, cigarettes, and some donuts."

"That's insulting," David says. "Putting one of his best homicide detectives on a case like that."

"He's clearly sending a message," Kayla says in disgust.

"Yeah," Naved says wearily. "Message received, loud and clear."

The overall mood at our table is one of stunned disbelief.

"Fucking McDougall!" Ramon says, louder than necessary.

I look around to see if anyone heard. "Let's keep the name calling lowkey."

Ramon makes a fist and brings it down with exaggerated slowness on the table. "He's a fucking asshole treating you that way, bruh," he says, less loudly this time but still too audible for my liking.

"I second that," Brine says. "This is nothing but politics, plain and simple."

"Why do people even vote for this man?" Kayla asks, glowering.

"Because he brings investment into the town," David says. "And because he and his family have been around here since the pioneers. Most of them probably just vote for him because that way they don't have to actually think of who else to vote for."

"I bet he gives kickbacks," Kayla says.

"Okay," I say. "Let's put a lid on it."

Kayla, Brine, and Ramon all look at me.

"You standing up for McD, jefe?" Ramon says.

"I'm not standing up for him, Ramon," I say. "I just think we can't afford to get into a sparring match with him right now."

"We didn't start the fight," Ramon says. "He did. We can't just take this lying down."

"I'm with Ramon all the way on this," Kayla says. "If he wants a war, then I say we go to war. We can't back down, Susan. You know this guy. He's an alphahole. If we back down before his bullying, we'll never hear the end of it. He'll bully us every chance he gets. Make our lives miserable."

I sigh. "I'm not saying we back down, or give in. I'm trying to keep our focus on the Saint. We need to crack this case. We don't have enough resources, or time, or anything to take on a war with McDougall *and* work this investigation. Especially now that our only PD liaison just got yanked from the case. Am I right, Naved? Would you say McD would agree to lending us a dozen or so uniforms to beat down the bushes for the bomber?"

Naved exhales. "Not a chance in hell."

I spread my hands, my case made.

David says mildly, "Susan does have a valid point. It could be argued that what Chief McDougall is trying to do is derail the investigation. If we let ourselves be swayed by our emotions and get down in the muck with him, there'll be nobody to catch the Saint."

"And that's exactly what McD is trying to achieve here," I say, nodding at David gratefully.

Naved clears his throat. "What Susan and David just said. McD made me spend all day today on some useless paperwork before handing me that mini mart robbery case. He was making a point. He doesn't want us to continue this investigation. He would love to shut us down. He's trying to find a way to do that without any blowback coming back to him. He gets like a dog with a bone when he makes an enemy. He won't back off. It's only a matter of time before he finds a way to shut us down completely. And if we waste time reacting to this, the Saint goes scot-free and McD wins."

Ramon slams his palm down on the tabletop, making the plates, soda cups and flatware all jump. "Fucking asshole."

Naved is sitting next to Ramon. He doesn't turn to look at him but glances at me instead, his eyes questioning. I make a very small movement with my eyes and forehead, as if to say, yeah, he's pretty overwrought.

I lean forward, trying to get us back on track. I'm already frustrated from the Santos lead not panning out and eager to keep my team working. Ramon's precarious emotional state isn't helping.

"This doesn't change anything," I say. "We still have to catch this bomber. And the taggants are the best way forward for now. You all have your assignments. Let's get to work."

Ramon folds his arms across his muscled chest and looks sullen, but doesn't offer any further argument. The others all return to their devices and resume what they were doing earlier.

Naved looks at me to make sure I'm paying attention, before

cutting sideways, in the direction of the soda dispenser. I read him loud and clear.

I get up. "I'm going to hit the head."

I go into the restroom and take a minute.

There's a poster of an old nineties movie. I take a moment to look at it, without actually seeing it. I have too much on my mind.

When I come out, Naved is standing in the hallway.

I can tell by his body language that he isn't done delivering bad news.

The same sinking feeling comes over me again.

I swallow, feeling the chicken tenders and hot salsa dip churning in my stomach.

"What's up?" I ask.

TWENTY

"Everything okay?" I ask, when Naved doesn't respond.

He's looking at a random picture on the hallway wall. It's a picture of all the Toppings employees at some kind of staff get-together. I recognize Urduja in a tank top and denim cutoffs, laughing. A tall, gangly young man has his arm around her shoulder, and is laughing with her. Naved stares at the picture without really seeing it.

The fact that he's avoiding eye contact with me makes me even more uneasy.

"Did you get a call from CBI New Delhi?" he asks me.

I frown. "How did you know?"

He sighs, rubbing his face. "I saw a note on McD's desk diary when I was in his office. He's an old school guy, still uses a planner and everything. It was in his handwriting."

My heart skips a beat. "What did the note say?"

A woman comes down the hallway, looking for the ladies' restroom. She smiles at both of us, we both nod back in acknowledgment. She goes into the ladies'. Naved waits until the door shuts behind her before continuing.

He says softly: "It just said 'CBI, New Delhi—Mahak Arora.'"

My heart kicks into next gear.

When I look up, Naved is staring at my face, studying me closely.

"You did get a call," he says.

"Some guy named Amrit Pal Prasad."

"What did he want?"

"He was quite vague. Asked me if a colleague of his had reached out to me in the past several months."

"Inspector Mahak Arora," Naved says.

"Yes."

"And did she? Reach out to you?"

"I got a call from her back in April. She said she would be coming to the US in a few weeks and wanted to meet me."

Naved sucks in a breath as if disappointed by my answer.

"Did she say what it was regarding?" Naved asks.

"Not really. Something about a case she was investigating. She was pretty cagey, just like her boss. She said she would discuss it with me in person."

"Any clues? Any hint at all?" he asks.

I'm tired of him asking questions, and impatient to get some answers myself.

"I already told you, no. What's this about, Naved? Why is CBI calling me as well as McD? You look like you know something. If you do, then 'fess up. I'm dying here!"

He walks a few steps away from me, up the hallway, pauses, turns around and walks back to me. He looks at me intently.

"I think you know already."

I frown. "If I knew, why would I be asking you?"

He stares at me. "Because it's about Amit's death, obviously."

That hits me like a kick in the guts. "Wha..."

"When you asked me last November to look into Amit's

death, I took it very seriously. I could see how badly you needed answers. Because of my caseload and liaising with you on your cases, it's been slow going and like most cold cases, it's tough catching a break when the trail's gone cold. Especially with so little evidence to start with."

"I know, Naved. I appreciate everything you've done on the case. I've already told you that a dozen times."

He goes on as if I hadn't spoken. "But I never stopped digging. Back in April, you remember I told you that I began looking into the Rao house?"

I nod. Dr. Rao's house was the site where Amit's body was discovered. It was the site of a grisly multiple murder scene and was still vacant. He was discovered there with a gun in his hand, and a single gunshot wound to the head. "You told me you learned that the corporation that owned the house was actually a shell company. The actual owners were Amit's mom and uncle, my mother-in-law and her brother."

Naved nods. "It's part of their real estate holdings, which is how they originally made their fortune in the US. What are the odds that he would choose to kill himself in a house owned by his own family? That coincidence made me look into each of them more closely. I told you in April that I found that Sujit Chopra's call records showed that he'd received a call from Amit shortly before his death and that GPS tracking placed Sujit at the Rao house at almost the exact time of death."

The woman emerges from the ladies' and stops, waiting for Naved to move aside so she can pass. I nudge Naved and he shifts an inch or two. She sidles past, giving him a dirty look.

I nod at him with more than a little irritation. "And I confronted Sujit with that information and he said Amit called him to the Rao house to talk about something, but when Sujit got there, he found Amit already dead. He was afraid the cops would implicate him, so he left and never told anyone about it."

Naved nods. "So he said. Did you believe him?"

I nod slowly. "I do, but only because I had a gun stuck in his ribs when I questioned him."

"Did you know that CBI has a file on him?"

I stare. This is news to me. "No, I had no idea."

He looks at me closely, as if searching for the lie. But I'm not lying, and I resent the fact that he's looking at me so distrustfully. "Naved, I didn't know anything about any CBI file on Sujit!"

He looks away, his jaw working. "Not just Sujit."

"You mean Aishwarya, too? That makes sense, they're business partners. What does that have to do with Amit's case. And with me?"

He looks at me intently. "The CBI investigation is into Sujit Chopra, Aishwarya Kapoor nee Chopra, Kundan Kapoor, and Amit Kapoor."

My stomach flips and the bottom drops out under me. "What? What kind of investigation? Why would they be looking into Amit, too? He had nothing to do with Aishwarya and Sujit's business. He refused to take a single cent from either of them, not even for Natalie. I've told you all this before."

He studies me the way I've seen him study so many suspects before. "Susan, the investigation wasn't into their business interests. It was a criminal investigation, involving multiple murders over several years."

My mind races. "In India?"

"The CBI only investigates crimes involving Indian citizens, just like the FBI does for American citizens," he says.

"Yes, yes, of course, but Amit migrated to the US almost twenty years ago when he came here as an undergraduate."

Naved pauses to let a trio of young men get past us and waits until they've gone into the men's restroom.

When he looks back at me, his expression is still hard and searching as any detective's would be, but there's also a touch of softness there, a hint of empathy.

"The murders took place in India over a period of time, ending roughly around twenty years ago," he says softly.

I touch my hand to my chest, feeling my heart palpitate. "Around the time Amit left Delhi."

"And they resumed after a brief gap of about a year," he continues, "here in the US, and continued until Amit's death, at which point they stopped completely."

I stare at him, wordless, stunned. I'm shattered by the implications of what he's telling me.

TWENTY-ONE

I'm still standing in the hallway, trying to deal with what Naved has just told me. He says something I don't hear and walks away. I see him go over to the table and speak briefly with my team. I see them reacting with stunned looks on their faces. Naved leaves.

Kayla comes over to me. "McD is such an asshat! I still can't believe he did that to Naved."

I nod, not trusting myself to speak.

She looks at me. "You okay, Suse?"

"I'll be fine, just give me a sec."

She looks at me as if wanting to say more, then nods. "Sure. Take all the time you need."

She returns to the table.

I take a deep breath.

Pull yourself together: your team's depending on you. There's a madman out there and you need to stop him. Afterwards, once the safe house case is over, you can try to make sense of what Naved told you. But right now, you need to do your job.

The self-motivation spiel done, I exhale slowly, and walk over to the table.

I sit down.

I pick up my soda and try to sip from it, but it's empty. I set it back down.

"Okay," I say to my team. "Let's do this. David and Ramon, you're following the materials. You use the taggant code to track down the C4. Once you have the specific locations, you double-check and confirm them before contacting each one. Look for inventory manifests and confirm them against the actual stocks in store. The obvious cause for suspicion would be a recent break-in, or pilferage, or anything out of the ordinary. Brine and Kayla, you two will follow the people. Look for individuals who were responsible for the acquisition of the C4 through the supply chain, check their backgrounds, find the end users, not just the officers who requisitioned or approved purchase of the explosive but also the actual soldiers who deployed it. Deep background searches on each one of them. Come up with a shortlist of possible suspects. Do face to face meets with each of them. Keep me informed at every stage and if anything raises even the tiniest of red flags. Are we clear?"

When I finish, there's a long moment of silence.

Everyone looks at each other.

"What?" I ask with more than a little irritation. "Speak up if you have anything to say."

Ramon looks at me. "Suse, didn't you hear what Naved said? McD just put out the word that he will not back us up even if we're under fire, need backup, or need support in any way. He's put the word out across all departments—Fire, EMTs, PD. He made us persona non grata here in SCV. We're out in the cold. What do you think that means? He's already shut us down!"

"He'd like to believe that," I say, speaking calmly but forcefully. "But he's wrong. We're not going to shut down because of his lack of support. We're going to keep doing what we're doing. We're going to find the Saint and bring him to justice. We owe it to your foster father, Ramon, and to all the other people who died with him in the safe house."

"Without police backup?" Kayla says, looking at me like I've lost my mind. "Our unsub is a bombmaker. An expert. He's got who knows how much C4 stashed away. He's almost definitely a vet or active military. He's probably got guns, ammo, mad skills. He's dangerous!"

I nod patiently. "We back each other up. We don't depend on SCVPD covering our backs. We cover each other. If we find a bomb, we call in the FBI bomb squad. Even if it's not an official case, they won't ignore a bomb or even a bomb threat."

That shuts them both up. Brine and David look uncomfortable, but don't say anything.

"Okay?" I say. "Everyone clear?"

When there's no clear response for a minute, I lean forward, lowering my voice and say, "Look, guys, I know this sounds impossible, but what other choice do we have? This son of a bitch just massacred all those people and we're the only ones who can find him and stop him from doing it again."

"You really think he's going to do it again?" Brine asks mildly. "I mean, what he did at the safe house was totally monstrous. But what are the odds that he'll blow up another safe house full of immigrants? I mean, we're not talking about a serial killer, are we?"

"You really believe that, Brine?" I say. "Didn't we learn anything at the Academy? A mad bomber is very different from a serial killer, but they have one thing in common: they're sick inside. He just got away with one of the worst mass murders in state history. That's a massive ego boost for someone with that kind of profile. He may ride high on the euphoria from his success for now, or he may feel that it gives him a license to do it again. Who knows where he might choose to plant his next bomb? Maybe he has a hard on for immigrants. Maybe he'll blow up a factory next, or a sweatshop, or any place where he thinks he can eliminate more of us. You willing to take that chance? Wait for him to blow up a school? Or a hospital? Or an immigrant-owned local business?"

Brine blinks several times. "I hadn't thought about that."

"Well, think about it now," I say, my voice rising. "Think about finding more broken bodies from the debris. Think about that abuelita's little granddaughter, staring at America with dead eyes."

Brine lowers his eyes, reacting.

"Brine, I'm sorry," I say in a more level voice. "I didn't mean to get rough with you. I'm just..."

I take a big swallow of soda from the nearest cup. It's orange soda, not diet cola, which means it's probably Ramon's. I drink it anyway. Setting it down carefully, I swipe my mouth with the back of my hand. I'm on the verge of trembling. I struggle to get control of myself.

I look around as I try to regain my composure.

The employees and customers are all looking at our table.

I attempt a weak smile. "Sorry, folks, just a little work disagreement!"

Nobody laughs or smiles, but they go back to their food. A couple of the young staffers say something to each other as they glance at me from time to time. I take a deep breath and release it slowly.

I try again, this time in something closer to my normal voice.

"Look, guys, you were all there at the safe house. You saw what this bastard is capable of. Right now, we're the only ones who are working to get him. We don't get to say we can't do this because the PD isn't going to support us anymore. Or because McD is a dick. Or because we've got too much going on in our personal lives. We don't get to make excuses. We just have to get out there, work the evidence, follow the trail, and catch this son of a bitch before he does this again. Because you know and I know that he will do it again. And he won't stop doing it until we catch him."

TWENTY-TWO

I wake up in the middle of the night to find the house on fire. Flames are licking at the walls, blackening the ceiling. Thick smoke puffs from under the closed door, causing my eyes to tear up.

The heat is unbearable as I try to feel my way over to Natalie's bedroom. The hallway opens out onto the first level and the downstairs area is a mass of rising flames. The fire snaps and crackles as it eats everything in sight.

To my shock, Natalie's bed is gone! Instead of her bedroom, I find myself in an enclosed space with only shadowy shapes and looming silhouettes at the periphery of my vision. The fire is outside, its voice now a rusty rumble as it threatens to engulf my world and everyone I love.

"Natalie!" I cry out. The tears rolling down my face sizzle as the heat evaporates them, turning them into hot steam.

Something big and fast blurs by me, too fast to see.

A loud, crumpling sound rises from somewhere just beyond my vision.

Dust billows in thick, gritty clouds, filling my nostrils and throat, making me choke.

Suddenly, a fast-moving shape looms out of the dust cloud, racing toward me.

It's a pickup truck.

Heading straight at me.

I take aim at the windshield, aiming for the place where the driver should be, and fire several times, emptying the Glock.

An explosion flares in the night.

A loud, resounding boom.

A fireball billows.

Something looms in the fire.

A dark, antlered shape with hooves and a humanoid silhouette.

It stomps toward me, bellowing in rage.

I want to shout at it that I'm a federal agent, that it must stop right there, but I'm unable to speak. My voice is mute.

As the dark antlered man-beast looms over me, roaring, I release a silent scream and—

I startle awake and sit up in bed, gasping for breath.

I struggle to regain my bearings, getting my pulse rate and breathing under control. Despite the air conditioning, the bedsheet and my pajamas are soaked with sweat.

The room is dark and silent around me.

My mind reorients itself to my current situation.

I'm in Kundan's duplex condo. I'm in the master bedroom. Natalie is in the room next door. Lata's room is just down the hall.

I rise and pad on bare feet to my daughter's room. By the glow of her nightlight, I can see Natalie's small, familiar shape under the comforter, her chest rising and falling in slow, steady waves.

Bending over her, I kiss her very softly on the back of her head, careful not to wake her. Her hair smells of the vanilla scented shampoo she loves.

I send up a silent prayer of gratitude that she's safe and sound.

Then I return to my bedroom and dial Ramon.

TWENTY-THREE

We reach the safe house just before sunrise.

I'm on the back of Ramon's Harley, helmeted and in a black leather motorcycle jacket he lent me for the ride.

I take off the helmet and place it on the back of the Harley, shaking out my hair.

Ramon puts the chopper on its stand and takes off his helmet.

We look around the site.

It looks like any other patch of dirt out here in the rolling wilderness, except for several bunches of flowers, candles, photographs, and little mementos left by the surviving family. A small shrine commemorating the shocking loss suffered by the community.

I walk around the sunken place where the safe house used to be. Everything looks so different even a few days later. I remember the horror, grief, sorrow and rage that washed through me that first day.

I relive them all, but with a sense of despondency now.

This case has been one of the most frustrating of my career.

Hamstrung by a lack of resources, the complete blackout of

official acknowledgment that this terrible crime even occurred, the fizzling out of leads that seem to go nowhere, the lack of suspects, it's now looking like an insurmountable challenge.

But I refuse to give up.

I hunker down on my haunches, reaching down to grab a fistful of dirt.

It feels cold, gritty. I feel the grit, experiencing the coarse, granular texture. This is what those people felt on their skin as they squatted in the dark, cold space that was soon to become their tomb. What thoughts went through their minds, what hopes and dreams filled their hearts in those final hours?

I try to imagine the little girl, Consuelo Carina Flores, huddling in the dark. She was almost the same age as Natalie. I shudder at the thought of my own daughter in such a place, trapped in such circumstances. My imagination recoils.

Carina. The little girl's middle name. Named for Saint Carina, just like Santa Carina Valley. She was no less a child of Santa Carina than my Natalie. And yet she died here under such horrible, miserable circumstances, in darkness and obscurity. I can't let her death be meaningless, unresolved, unavenged.

As I squat there, the sun rises slowly over the horizon.

The yellow globe, dense with early morning haze on the horizon, seems to emerge from the ground, rising in steady, burning layers to lie on the surface. Long ribbons of light stretch out toward me, over the safe house site, and I feel a finger touch of warmth on my forehead, like a benediction.

I raise my face to receive it, basking in the warmth. My eyes close, and I let my mind drift aimlessly, travel where it will.

Snatches of my dream from earlier this morning flicker behind my closed eyelids. Not the part about the fire. I don't need a therapist to tell me what *that* means. It's the part toward the end that interests me, that's what woke me up and brought me out here at this ungodly hour.

The explosion.

The cloud of dust.

I was somehow reliving the safe house explosion itself, my subconscious mind trying to imagine how it might have appeared when seen from the surface, from the killer's point of view.

I close my eyes again, trying to recall the dream again.

I'm surrounded by a cloud of dust.

There's a large, loud, unseen thing blurring past me, racing around me, just out of sight.

It's a vehicle. I knew that even in my dream.

That familiar guttural sound, a gnashing of gears, the roar of acceleration.

It's a pickup truck.

Then I hear another sound.

Music.

Was this in my dream, too?

I don't think so.

But for some reason, I'm hearing it now.

It's a song playing distantly.

A popular track.

Familiar rifts and chords, sweet vocals.

A happy-sad love song set to a dance beat.

Without opening my eyes, I call out to Ramon.

He answers me with a single word of acknowledgment: "Jefe."

"What is that song everyone's listening to these days? It's a huge hit, on the radio all the time."

He names a few tracks that are popular, mostly Taylor Swift songs.

"No, this is like a one-hit wonder by some unknown artist, a newbie. Male artist." I try to think of something more specific. A tiny snatch of lyric comes to me. "Something about love being like a monkey on his back?"

"'Love Monkey'," he offers.

I open my eyes. "That's it!"

I stand up, my knees popping.

"Ahmed Abidi, the son, talked about a pickup truck and a popular song," I say. "He could have heard the engine of the truck. Even down in the safe house, if the door was open, and the truck was parked nearby, the engine noise would be audible, wouldn't it?"

I gesture. "Out there, it's dead quiet. Sound would travel. You could probably hear a car engine for a distance. Even down under the ground, maybe?"

Ramon inclines his head, considering. "Sure. When I was with Ronaldo down there, I could hear sounds from above. Most of the time, nothing. The old priest, the Saint, would always come at night. We could always hear his truck coming."

I look at him. "So you remember him driving a pickup truck, too?"

He shrugs. "Sure."

"Why didn't you mention it during your interview?"

He sighs, shaking his head. "I should have. Anyway, that's how it was. Always at night."

"And if he was up on the surface, talking on his phone, or if he got a call, could you hear the ringtone, his conversation?"

He thinks, squinting against the rising sun. "I don't remember hearing any conversations. I don't think he ever got a call. But I think I remember a tone once. Not a call. Like for a text message."

"Okay," I say. "Okay. That's good. So what if Ahmed Abidi heard the Saint drive up in his pickup truck, get out and while he was still on the surface, he got a call and his ringtone happened to be that song, 'Love Monkey'?"

Ramon nods slowly, thinking about it. "How you so sure it's that song?"

"I'm not. But it's definitely the biggest pop hit right now, so it's plausible."

He shrugs. Sure. It's possible, chief. But how's it help us? I mean, okay, so Father Santos drove a pickup truck, but the padre is dead. Whoever this guy is, he's someone else."

"Exactly. But now we know he drives a pickup truck and has the 'Love Monkey' ringtone on his phone."

He looks unconvinced. "That's, like, a million other guys in Cali, jefe. Doesn't exactly narrow it down!"

"Granted. But what if he's not just driving any old pickup truck? What if it's the *same* truck that Father Santos drove?"

Ramon frowns. The morning sunshine bathing his inked arms and face casts him in a bronze glow, like a classical statue. "It's a stretch, isn't it?"

I use my phone to call up a number.

It rings several times.

I'm about to give up when someone answers.

"Hello?" a man's voice asks tentatively.

"Father Monroe? This is Special Agent in Charge Susan Parker. I came by to see you?"

"Ah. Yes, good morning, Agent Parker. I was just preparing for matins. If you wish to interview me again, perhaps you come by after first mass?"

"This will just take a minute, Father. Where did Father Santos stay?"

"Right here in the quarters. On the church premises. Where I am presently domiciled."

"And what happened to his belongings after he passed?"

"That was before my time. I'd have to check with Father Angelo. He was here during the transition as a novitiate to Father Santos. I would suppose that they had been given to charity. That is the usual custom when there is no family to claim them. Also, if I may be so bold as to assume, it's highly unlikely he had very much. You are familiar with the vow of poverty that we take when we enter the church?"

"Would you recall what happened to his truck?"

"His truck? You mean the old pickup truck?"

"Yes."

"Again, Father Angelo would know. Could I ask him to call you back on this number?"

"Yes, please. As quickly as possible."

"Very well, Agent Parker."

I disconnect and search my contacts for another name and number without success. "Ramon, get me the number for Maria."

"Why don't I just call her for you?" he suggests. "My Panamanian Spanish isn't as good as Paula's but it's better than trying to get her to speak English."

"Great."

He dials and speaks in Spanish. He listens then tries again, slower this time. After a moment, he taps the phone to switch to speaker mode and holds it out for me to speak.

"Good morning, Maria, this is Susan Parker. How are you doing?" I ask.

Ramon translates as best as he can.

"I am ninety-three, Susan," he translates for the old abuelita. "I just lost my most beloved granddaughter. I am not doing very well."

My heart feels for the old lady. "I am sorry to disturb you again, Maria. I need to ask you something. It will not take much time."

"If it will help you catch the monster who took sweet, innocent Consuela from us before she could even receive her First Holy Communion, then you may take all day and night asking me questions," Ramon translates, halting and correcting himself at times.

He covers the phone and interjects, "Except she didn't say 'catch', she said something that's more like 'break his balls'."

I nod. "Maria, when we talked about Father Santos, you said you remembered that he drove a pickup truck. You said he always carried food and water in the bed of the truck to hand out to anyone in need. Do you remember saying that?"

"Yes, he is Charity in human form. Always looking to help anyone in need. He is a saint. I cannot believe he would do such a terrible thing to our little Consuela and all those people. It has to be another man. A demon in human form," the old abuelita says, or at least that's the best that Ramon can manage, as he adds.

"Maria, you said you remembered him as a soldier. Soldiers often wear tattoos. Do you recall ever seeing any tattoos on his person. Anything you might have glimpsed?"

There's some to and fro on this as Ramon explains my question and fends off some queries from the old lady. He rolls his eyes. "She says how would a lady be expected to know if a man has tattoos on his person, especially a padre! She's a spicy one!"

The old abuelita speaks again and Ramon listens before adding to me, "She says she might have seen him lifting something heavy and putting it onto his truck, which made the sleeves of his cassock slip, revealing his forearms and part of his bicep. She does recall seeing some ink there. Some kind of symbol."

Ramon listens for a moment then adds, "A winged staff with a snake wrapped around it. She says she remembered asking him about it because she had seen it somewhere else before, and he said it was from a former life when he had served his country."

I release a breath I hadn't even realized I'd been holding.

"Thank you, Maria," I say. "I made you a promise that day and I want you to know that I intend to keep that promise. I will find the demon in human form who took your sweet, innocent Consuela from you, and make sure that justice is served."

After Ramon disconnects, he looks at me.

"What you on to, chief?" he asks, a bright light of hope in his eyes.

"The symbol she described is a caduceus, the universal symbol of healing. I think our Father Santos was an army medic once upon a time."

Ramon looks puzzled. "Okay. I still don't get it. He's been dead three years. He can't be our guy."

I nod. "Nope. But he's still the key to finding our key." I crook a finger. "Come on, it's light enough. I need to check something out."

TWENTY-FOUR

I pace the ground steadily in a straight line from south to north, one slow footstep at a time. Several meters away, Ramon is walking his own line. We're doing a two-man approximation of a grid search. We've been doing it for the past several minutes. I look back and see Ramon's Harley around two hundred meters away. That means we're about two hundred and fifty meters north and east of the safe house.

"How long we going to do this, boss?" Ramon asks. "Only thing I can see is dirt and more dirt."

"You know how it works, Ramon. Keep your mind open and ready to receive, like a sponge. Let your eyes do all the work. If you see anything that doesn't belong or you wouldn't expect to see out there, don't question it, just mark it with a flag and call it out."

"Okay, boss, but if it's just the two of us, we could get old doing this."

I continue walking my line, but Ramon does have a point. We've only been at this for the past hour or so, but it's a task meant for a team of several dozen people.

My peripheral vision catches something off to the right.

Even though, in theory, I'm supposed to be focusing my entire attention on just the square meter of earth in front of my feet, my natural instinct and training keeps me alert enough to be aware of my surroundings. Something that's out of place in this environment attracts my eyes, just off to my right.

I stop and look that way.

Is that...

I put down the bag of evidence flags to mark my spot on the line and walk over to the right for a closer look.

"Hey, no fair, jefe. How come you get to stroll off whenever you... What's up? You see something?"

"I think so. Come take a look."

Ramon joins me as I crouch down and peer at a rectangular depression in the ground.

"Is that what I think it is?" I ask.

"Yup," he says. "That's a sniper nest. Look. You can see the place where he lay right there. That's the mark of his rifle stand. Rested his elbows here and here."

I look back toward the safe house.

It's close enough to be able to make out the logo on the gas tank of Ramon's Harley.

"He was watching us," I say. "The other day when we were here. He watched us at work, digging out the victims, interviewing the witnesses, the whole works. I don't think he intended to use the rifle at all. He just needed the scope to let him watch us more closely."

"Son of a puta," Ramon says.

"We need to get Marisol out here, go over this nest with a fine-tooth comb. He's got to have left DNA."

"Right!"

A flash of memory from my dream returns. The vehicle blurring past me. I look around for a few minutes, and finally spot something.

"The arrogant asshole might have done us a favor," I say,

excited now. "Look at this, Ramon. It rained earlier this week. The ground must have been damp when he drove out here."

He squats beside me, careful not to disturb the tire tracks I'm pointing at. "Those are from a heavy vehicle."

"Like a pickup truck, maybe."

"The same pickup truck Father Santos drove?" Ramon says.

I smile at him. "Right."

"So this is someone who took the padre's identity?" he asks me.

"Exactly. But it's more than that. In order to become the Saint, he had to have known him well enough. I think if we find out if Father Santos had any close friends, maybe people he served with back in the day, or maybe just someone in his flock he confided in, we'll find our guy. He's someone who was close enough to Santos for the priest to have trusted him with the location of the safe house. Maybe even someone who came through the same safe house and was here because of Santos's help."

"Ungrateful SOB," Ramon says, moving around the nest.

"Watch your step there, Ramon," I caution. "There could be boot tracks, too."

"No worries, boss," he says. "Hey. I see something reflecting. You see it as well? Over there?"

I tilt my head from side to side and glimpse a tiny object in the dirt catching the slanting sunlight.

"I see it," I say. "Okay, go slowly, one step at a time and look out for evidence."

Ramon starts forward, carefully watching the ground.

He's almost at the shiny object when someone calls out in a loud yell.

"*Pare, por favor!*"

I don't need a translator to know that means *Stop, please!*

Ramon freezes, arms out.

The voice calls out again.

"Don't move a muscle, both of you. Another step and you'll blow up!"

TWENTY-FIVE

My weapon is in my hand as I turn, zeroing in on the shouter.

A slim, athletic figure in camo fatigues steps toward us. I note that they're holding something in their right hand. I take aim at the middle of their torso, targeting central body mass.

"Don't shoot, SAC Parker," she says, raising her arms. "It's me, Paula Contreras. We met the other day."

I keep the Sig trained on her. "Gunny? The hell are you doing sneaking up on federal agents?"

She points in the direction of the safe house with one hand and shows me the objects she's holding in her other hand. "I came to put down fresh flowers and this rosary," she says. "Saw you two out there, overheard your last bit of convo and put two and two together."

I frown. "What did you mean about blowing up?"

"May I put my hands down and come over to show you?" she asks.

"Anyone else with you?" I ask. "Where's your ride?"

"I came by motorcycle, too, on my own," she says. "Low rider. Left it back on the paved road. Just washed and detailed it yesterday, didn't want it getting dirty again. This fucking dust gets in everywhere."

I nod slowly. "Okay, but come slowly, no sudden movements."

She walks with steady paces out to where we're standing. I turn my body with her, keeping the Sig aimed low but held out just in case. Once she's due east of me, I'm able to see Ramon and her without needing to take my eyes off her.

"Stop there," I say.

Ramon is still frozen, legs locked in a stride. "I lower my arms now, cuz?"

"Sure," she says, "just don't take another step or shift your weight. You're almost on top of it."

"On top of what exactly?" I ask.

"I don't see anything," Ramon says, echoing my sentiment.

Paula points. "That shiny thing that attracted you? You see it there, glinting in the sunlight?"

"Sure. Looks like a silver eagle."

"If that's a silver eagle, I'm a gold nugget," Paula says. "It's a decoy, left there for anyone who comes snooping around. Old sniper trick in the wild. Ignore the coin for a second and look closer to you. See that little thing in the ground. He's covered it really well, but the wind must have eroded some of the dirt away. You can almost see—"

"I see it, I see it. For real!" Ramon says. "It's some kind of metal thing painted green, I think. I can just see a tiny corner."

"Yup. That's a Claymore. You're facing the business end. If that fucker goes off on you, about seven hundred steel balls will use you for target practice. But don't worry about them, because at that range, the one and a half pounds of C4 will be enough to rip you into body parts."

"Jesus wept," Ramon says, his tone dead sober. "Fuck I do now?"

Paula looks at me. "SAC Parker?"

"Susan," I say, lowering the Sig Sauer but not holstering it just yet.

"Susan, can I get closer to Ramon? I need to check if he's activated the Claymore."

"And if I did?" Ramon asks agitatedly.

Paula shrugs wordlessly. "If you haven't, then maybe we can all three get out of this with our body parts intact."

"If that's a Claymore, and I'm not saying it isn't," I say, "it has a lethal range of at least fifty meters. Body damage up to two hundred and fifty meters, give or take."

"Yup," Paula says. "'*Sniper's retreat, got yo' ass beat*'."

"Okay," I say, "but no funny stuff. I'm watching."

"Chill out, chief," Ramon asks. "Paula knows what she's doing."

I watch as Paula instructs Ramon. Ramon does what she says, obeying her to the letter. I try not to think about what happens if the mine goes off, about what would happen to Natalie if she loses me too right now. The thought sickens me.

When Ramon is several feet away from the deadly device, Paula finally instructs both of us to turn around and walk away.

Ramon starts walking right away, needing no further encouragement.

I pause and look at Paula. "What are you going to do?"

She looks at me, her jaw tight. She's slipped on dark sunglasses and with the sun behind her, she looks every bit the active Marine, wiry, tight-muscled, and ready to kick ass. "I'm going to set it off before someone else gets hurt."

"You can't do that. We need to seal the scene and search for evidence. If he lay down there, ate and drank anything, dropped a hair follicle or two, there's likely to be DNA. We need to gather that. It could be crucial to our case."

She looks at me for a long moment. "SAC Parker. Susan. The only way your people are going to get anything out of that hidey hole is by setting off that IED. Then you'll have a whole lot of DNA, but it sure as fuck won't just be his."

I consider for a moment.

"She's right, chief. We gotta let this one go," Ramon calls out from behind me.

I consider all my options, but finally conclude that she's right. It galls me to admit it but it's true.

I turn and walk away.

Ramon is several hundred meters away by now, almost to the end of the nearest development and the start of the paved road.

When I'm only a few meters from him, I hear a crack of gunfire, followed immediately by the resounding *thump* of an explosion followed by a skittering sound like hailstones on dry earth.

I turn, shielding my eyes instinctively, just in time to see the last debris from the Claymore coming down, raising tiny puffs of dust when they land. The nearest ones land just a couple dozen meters from where I'm standing.

TWENTY-SIX

I'm relieved when I see Paula, rising from a prone position only a few dozen meters from me. She looks in the direction of the sniper's nest, satisfied, and gestures to me. She's holding a handgun by her side.

Ramon and I walk back to her.

He bypasses me, jogging to her.

He gathers her in a big hug, talking to her in Spanish.

She nods, slaps him lightly on the cheek, and turns to look at me.

"There's no way to be a hundred percent sure, but it's my guess that he only laid one down," she says.

"How did you set it off from that distance?" I ask. "I mean, that's at least three hundred meters away, right?"

She shrugs. "Sniper training. Third best shot in my regiment."

"Nice work."

I nod, staring out at the blast area. It's small, tightly contained, but even from this distance it's obvious that any evidence we might have found is either destroyed or contaminated too badly to be of any use. "A booby trap to cover his tracks."

"And take out anyone on his six," Paula says. "It's a routine sniper thing. They cover their retreat by leaving little surprises for the enemy."

My jaw tightens with anger and frustration. "What's in those things anyway? You called it an IED."

She shrugs. "Could be. Or it could just be good old plastic."

"RDX? C4?"

"Claymores are US military so yeah, C4 mostly."

A thought bubbles up. "You said one and a half pounds. That's how much C4 one Claymore contains?" I ask.

She nods.

"Is it possible to extract the C4 from a Claymore?"

She shrugs again. "Anything's possible."

I consider that for a moment.

Ramon puts a hand on my shoulder. "You thinking what I think you thinking, boss?"

I pat his hand. "You got it, Ramon. You think you can do something with that, you and Carlotta?"

He breaks out into a grin. He's lost weight these past few days and showing his teeth gives him a wolfish intensity. "I'm all over it like brown on rice!"

"Good, you go on and get started on it. Give the rest of the team an update on what happened. I'll get Mancini to come out and check the blast site."

"What about you, jefe? You rode here with me. Your car's back at my crib."

"I'd like to talk to Paula for a bit if she can spare the time. Paula, could you give me a ride to Ramon's place when we're done?"

She nods. "Sure."

Ramon claps. "Okay then. Paula, you rock, cuz. See you ladies later."

As Ramon strides back toward his Harley, I join Paula, walking to the safe house first. She retrieves the flowers and rosary from a rock and brings them to the little shrine. I hang back, watching her kneel, join her hands, and bow her head, moving her lips softly.

The sound of Ramon's chopper starting rises, then fades as he drives away.

When she rises again to her feet, her eyes are damp and red. She slips the sunglasses on again.

I put my hand on her shoulder.

"Thank you for saving our lives, and once again, I'm so, so sorry for your loss."

She nods.

We walk back slowly to where she left her ride. It's a beautifully maintained classic model and as she said, it's clearly been recently cleaned. The chrome and metal gleam like new. The high-set handlebars have pink tassels and the seat is pink, too. Little custom touches in hot pink contrast the black beauty perfectly. The license plate on the rear is custom made and reads: *K1CK4SS*.

"That's a beautiful lady," I say, admiring it.

"She's served me well," Paula says, taking up her matching pink helmet. "Sorry I don't have a spare for you."

"It's cool," I say, getting on behind her as she starts up and rolls us out and away. "Let's go someplace we can get coffee and talk for a bit."

The ride back through Santa Carina Valley feels different somehow. The near brush with death has given me a new perspective, as it usually does. The searing SoCal sun is threatening another scorcher. This time, I actually enjoy the wind in my hair. I let my hands rest lightly on Paula's waist as we both lean into the turn onto Bouquet Road.

We pass close by the turnoff to Natalie's school and as

always, I feel a pang of emotion, wishing I was dropping her off this morning.

But experience tells me that I may have caught myself a lucky break here.

The Saint just tried to claim three more victims and if not for Paula, he would have succeeded in taking down at least two: Ramon and myself.

This was already a criminal I was determined to hunt down.

Now, it's personal.

And I think Paula might be able to help me figure out who he is.

TWENTY-SEVEN

The Saint watches as Gunny Paula Contreras roars by on her low rider. That fluorescent pink is impossible to miss even through the trees, and he side-eyes it as it goes by. He fucking hates pink.

Then he sees that SAC Susan Parker is riding pillion behind her, brunette hair streaming. How the fuck did she get here?

For a minute, he debates going after them. It's only been a few seconds since he pulled over into these trees. He was going to park here and hike the rest of the way to the blast site like he always does. Now, he feels blindsided. That makes him mad.

He wasn't expecting Parker to be here. The tracker he planted on her Prius still shows her as being miles away. He recognized her colleague Agent Ramon Diaz when Diaz blew past him on the way in. He's guessing that Parker parked the Prius at Ramon's place and rode here with him. And now she decided to hitch a ride with Gunny? The hell is she up to now?

And who the fuck triggered his Claymore?

His tripwire booby trap went off a while ago, triggering the notification to his phone. It couldn't have been Parker or Diaz who set it off. They're still alive. Gunny's a pro so she wouldn't fall for that old silver eagle glinting in the dirt and the hidden tripwire.

But it can't be a coincidence that they were all here at the same time.

SAC Parker must have called a meeting at the site.

Why?

What's she onto now?

He doesn't like the smell of this shit. It stinks.

Time to go see what they were up to and figure out what happened.

A quick check and it starts to make sense.

Parker and Diaz must have gone out looking for it and found his hidey hole.

Somehow, they managed to evade triggering the Claymore and were able to figure out a way to set it off from a safe distance. Smart and resourceful, that SAC Parker. A gold star for her.

How Gunny Paula Contrera fits into this, the Saint doesn't know, but he doesn't like the idea of Parker speeding off with her. If Parker's talking to service members and vets, then he might need to up his game.

He glances over at the safe house site.

From a distance, the cluster of color and objects draws his eye.

He walks over to take a closer look.

The families of the dead have put up a small shrine.

Cute but pointless.

Dumb fucks shouldn't be mourning those people, they should be celebrating their deaths!

Fuck this shit.

He's going to kick down their shrine and trample their mementoes under his boots.

When he's done, he'll unzip and piss all over their shit.

He raises his foot and is about to bring it down hard on a framed photograph of the little Mexican girl, when his pocket starts singing that idiotic "Love Monkey" song.

Damn, he hates that song.

The boys must have gotten into his phone again and reset the ringtone.

This is the second time they've pulled that shit.

They'll deny it again, naturally, but this time he won't let it go.

They're going to feel the boom this time.

He still thinks it's nuts that parents aren't allowed to discipline their kids the right way. The old way: spare the rod and spoil the child.

No wonder the suicide rate among teenagers and young people is higher than it's ever been. This entire generation was brought up to be mollycoddled, shrinking snowflakes who outrage at everything and think being woke is all they need to get through life.

Yeah, right.

Get a job, get a partner, get a mortgage, have kids, raise a family. Then if you still have time and energy to stand in the street and protest whatever social media non-event you think is going to change the world (again), knock yourself the fuck out. But first, learn to be an American, brats!

The Saint's boys are gonna feel his wrath this time, though. He'll make sure of that. *"Love Monkey", my ass!*

He answers the call.

"Hey, dumbass," the Saint says. "Didn't I tell you not to call me on this number? You're supposed to leave an email at the drop like I told you."

"She's onto us!" says a panicked, on-the-verge of tears voice. "I told you she would piece it together! She's a smart investigator."

He sounds breathless, like he's been running, even though

the Saint knows he's probably just pacing the floor and hyper-ventilating. Pathetic fuck's a long way from the combat-ready fitness he used to be back when he was on tour.

"The fuck you talking about?" says the Saint.

"Agent Susan Parker. The FBI agent I told you about. She's asking about the pickup truck and Santos's stuff."

"So what? She already went to the church and questioned Monroe. Probably just a follow-up."

"I'm telling you, she's onto us. She's figured it out. You, me, Santos, everything."

"Listen to me, dumbass. First of all, box breathing exercise. Do it now."

Idiot doesn't have sense enough to hold the phone away while he does the breathing exercise. He's practically slobbering in the Saint's ear.

"Okay, now, calm the fuck down. Tell me exactly what she said and what you said back to her when she questioned you."

"She didn't."

"Didn't what?"

"Question me. Not yet anyway."

"Then what the fuck you worked up over?"

"She called Monroe. Asking about Santos's stuff. Monroe doesn't know a thing, so he went to ask someone who did. That's how I found out."

"What else?"

"That's it. Monroe said she's expecting a call back."

"That's it? That's the whole story?"

"Yes! For the love of Christ, what're we gonna do if she comes back with a search warrant?"

"There's nothing to do because there's nothing to find. The pickup truck doesn't matter, none of Santos's stuff matters."

"Yeah, but it means that she knows. She must know. Why else would she be asking about his stuff?"

He thinks for a minute. He has walked back into the tree

cover while he's been talking and is halfway back to his ride already.

"Where you at right now?" he asks.

"Same place I'm always at."

"Stay there. I'll see you in five." He pauses as a thought comes to him. "Make that fifteen. I gotta pick up something from my place first."

"Maybe I should come to you," the other man says, sounding uncertain now.

"No. Stay put. State you're in, you'll probably wrap yourself around a tree if you drive. Take your pills. Keep doing the box breathing. I'll see you."

He disconnects and hikes the rest of the way back to the spot where he parked the pickup truck. The door creaks when he opens it and he pauses, taking a minute to consider his options.

Nervous ninny's probably just panicking as usual.

SAC Parker can't already be on to them.

Not without the Saint seeing her coming from a mile away.

She's good and she's smart, but she's not that good and not that smart.

Nobody is.

But she did avoid getting her head blown off by his booby trap.

And she's on her way someplace with Gunny Contreras.

And she is calling about Santos's stuff.

That's three in a row.

Time to make sure she doesn't get a fourth.

TWENTY-EIGHT

Marge has a coffee pot in her hand as usual as she chats with a pair of beefy guys at a table. She looks up as the bells over the door jangle to announce our entrance. "Welcome!"

Paula and I take a corner table at the far end.

Despite its name, Gold Medal Coffee is basically a classic American diner, red upholstered booth seating, barstools lined up against the counter, and all. It used to be Gold Medal Diner until Marge's husband Bill passed away, and she spruced up the place, changed the name and updated the menu to cater to the new upscale clientele from the city that were moving to the suburbs to raise families. It's been known as Marge's ever since.

"Nice to see you again, Susan," Marge says politely as she comes over, pouring both of us complimentary cups of her trademark house coffee as always.

I asked her once why she gave it away free instead of selling it and she winked at me and said most people were nice enough that they felt obligated to then order a coffee off her menu and since all the menu coffees were gourmet brands priced at a premium, it helped cut out the loafers who would have other- wise just ordered the house coffee and sat nursing a dollar cup for hours. She makes an exception for locals she knows well, which apparently includes me now.

Marge acts as a barometer for me in SCV. I can usually gauge how the townsfolk feel about me by her reception. Right now, I'd say it's lukewarm. That's probably McD's doing.

"Who do we have here?" she says, looking Paula over. "I know you from somewhere, don't I, dear?"

Before Paula can answer, Marge holds up a beautifully manicured finger, tapping the long, lustrous painted fingernail on her cheek. "Don't tell me, I've got it. Nate. Nate Sanderson. He brought you to the Boots in the Park concert, didn't he? And the Cowboy Festival at the old ranch. We line danced together, as I recall. You cut a rug nicely. You two are an item, ain't you?"

Paula shrugs. "We date from time to time. Nothing exclusive."

"Well, good for you, girl. A girl needs to get laid. How about you, darling, you shacked up with anyone new?"

I just smile up at her without answering.

She bends down, her big head of blonde hair staying perfectly intact, and says in a conspiratorial tone, "Darling, I'm a widow, too, as you know. When my Bill died, I thought the earth might as well open up and swallow me whole. But I got over it. You wanna know how? Well, honey, here's my two cents. The best way to get *over* a man is to get *under* another man. Take it from someone with a lot more mileage than both you young fillies put together!"

Luckily for me, right after we place our orders, someone else comes in and Marge is off to greet the new customers.

"She's a force of nature," I say.

Paula nods, apparently unflustered by Marge's brassy manner. "I looked you up, Agent Susan Parker. You're quite the shitkicker."

"Just doing my job. Speaking of which, what you were saying out there, about that being a sniper's nest and him covering his retreat with the Claymore. You sounded pretty sure of it."

She shrugs. "It's how I'd do it."

"Why not someone from the demolition corps?"

She frowns. "I don't see that."

"Why not?"

The server brings us the water we asked for. I take a sip, then gulp down some more, suddenly aware of my thirst.

Paula uses a spoon to fish out ice chips from her water, and pops them in her mouth, crunching them. "Demo guys don't usually bother covering their retreats with Claymores. When they go in to do a job, they're already planting explosives. They've got bigger fish to fry. That set-up out there? That says sniper to me."

This is why I wanted to talk to Paula.

"We're looking at demo guys specifically," I say.

She nods. "I can see that. Because of the way he set the safe house charges, right? Clinical precision?"

"Exactly. You were the one who pointed it out to me that day. That's what sent me down this path. Now you're saying he couldn't have been demo, he's a sniper?"

She raises her palms. "Whoa. I never said he had to be a demo guy. That's what you took away. A lot of soldiers work with explosives and Claymores, not just demo corps."

I frown, thinking.

"What?" she asks.

"There's something that made me think he could be demo corps. They have this symbol, right?"

I describe the crossed cannons.

"Sure, that's their flag," Paula says. "But that's just a symbol. My boyfriend Nate has one."

"Your boyfriend is Nate Sanderson," I say then hesitate.

"Hold on. Are you looking at him as a suspect for this?" She laughs.

"Why is that funny?" I ask.

"He's a teddy bear!" she says. "You obviously haven't met Nate, or you wouldn't even be thinking about him."

"Look, Paula, I don't mean to offend you but, in my line, I've come across a lot of bad guys who also happen to be wonderful dads, husbands, brothers, whatever. It doesn't mean they didn't do it."

"You don't have to explain it to me, Agent Parker," she says. "I've been part of operations where we've caught or taken down bad players who are on a list, some real mean, vicious guys. But to their people, they're like role models or heroes. I get it. I'm just saying that Nate is not your guy. It's literally impossible."

"Okay," I say, knowing better than to argue the point. "Let's forget about Nate. Moving on. How about the local veteran community? Anyone local that you know of who might fit the bill?"

She frowns, thinking. "Well, there's these bars where a lot of vets hang out."

"I've heard. Planning to hit them up tonight. Apart from those?"

"There's this shooting range out on Bouquet, about ten minutes past Plum Canyon Road. The Gun Club."

"I've heard of it."

"It gets a lot of traffic from vets. You might want to try there."

I nod, seeing what she means. "That's a great tip. Thanks."

Our breakfast orders arrive, and we continue chatting as we eat.

"You're welcome. I want you to get the bastard. And I don't want you wasting your time on Nate! You really should meet him for a drink sometime. You'll laugh at the thought that you ever considered him as the Saint!"

"That would be great," I say. "How about tonight? Schooner Bay?"

She offers her fist for a bump. "You got it."

My phone begins dancing on the table, rattling the plates. I grab it to make it stop.

Unknown number calling.

"Hello, Special Agent in Charge Susan Parker?" I say. "Who is this?"

"Agent Parker, this is Father Monroe."

"Hello, Father. I was expecting a call from your colleague, Father Angelo."

"Yes, well, it's in that regard that I'm calling you, Miss Parker. I mean Agent Parker, excuse me."

He sounds flustered, completely unlike the charming, jovial man I met. He's fumbling his words, pausing at odd places and clearly experiencing some kind of emotional upset.

"That's all right, you can call me Susan if you like," I say gently. "Is everything all right, Father?"

"Susan, allow me a moment, please."

There's a pause during which I can hear someone else's voice in the background, asking him a question. I hear Father Monroe answering the man, then some noises that sound like he's just handed over his mobile phone to someone else.

"SAC Parker," says a man's gravelly voice.

"Who is this?"

"St. Katherine's. The pastor's quarters. Ten minutes. Come alone. Don't call anyone, especially your team. If you do, I'll know."

I slide out of the booth, pull some cash from my jeans, and toss it on the table as I walk to the door and exit.

"Where's Father Monroe and Father Angelo?" I ask calmly. "I'd like to speak to them."

"They're busy right now, but alive. They won't be if you're not here in ten or if you bring backup."

"Hold on a second. What is this about? Are you threatening to hurt them?"

A deep chuckle. "They won't feel a thing. They'll be on their way to beatification."

"You don't have to kill them."

"Why? You worried they'll be canonized?" he asks mockingly.

"Who is this?"

"The devil."

I laugh without humor. "I've met the devil. I've danced the dance of death with him. Compared to him, you're an amateur."

That shuts him up for a second.

"You're right. I'm not the devil. I'm something worse," he says.

"Oh yeah? Like what?"

"I'm the last thing you'll see before the lights go out."

"Not if I see you first," I say, taking out my service weapon and checking the clip.

Paula puts down her fork and raises her eyebrows.

"Ten minutes and we'll settle this shit," he says in my ear.

"I still don't know who you are, asshole," I say.

"They call me the Saint. But to you, I'm the end times."

He hangs up.

I look at Paula. "I need a ride."

TWENTY-NINE

The priest's quarters behind the church are quiet when I enter through the garden door, my Glock in my hand. It's peaceful out there. Flowers and sunshine, birdsong, the distant yells of children playing in the playground and the park below.

Inside, it's as silent and still as a tomb.

I stand and listen as precious seconds tick by.

Nothing.

I know it's stupid to go in like this, alone, not knowing what's waiting for me in there, without waiting for backup.

But he as much as promised to kill the two priests if I did, and I believe him.

The bravado I showed on the phone is gone now, chastened by the knowledge that he's somewhere in here, waiting, armed without a doubt. Possibly with explosives.

I work my way into the silent quarters.

The first floor, the same sitting room where we had tea with the two priests.

Clear.

The kitchen.

Clear.

A half-bathroom, just a toilet, no bath.

Clear.

A laundry room.

Clear.

The laundry room leads into a two-car garage.

Clear.

There's an old Ford Fusion and a minivan.

I check them both out.

Clear and clear.

I go back through the garage, the laundry room, the kitchen, to the stairs by the front door. I left it open for SCVPD when they arrive. I didn't call them. I did exactly as the Saint ordered. But I asked Paula to wait four minutes and call. By then, this will probably all be over, but I need that call on record, just in case.

I take the stairs a step at a time, listening and checking every angle.

The second floor.

A hallway leading in two directions, curving to the right, straight down to the left.

Both hallways clear.

I take the left first.

Two doors, one on either side.

The first is a supply closet.

Clear.

The second is a small bedroom.

Clear.

Single wooden bed, cotton mattress, crucifix on the wall, a cassock on a hanger dangling like a hung man from a nail. Sparse, spartan, bare. Probably the younger priest's room. Framed photograph on the dresser confirms it: a picture of a younger version of him with an older man and woman, both with the same flaming red hair as Father Angelo. His parents.

I'm about to turn away when I see the second picture.

Angelo in camo fatigues and a priest collar, crucifix around his neck, Bible in hand, posing with a squad of soldiers in some hot, dusty country.

A military chaplain.

I peer closer at the other faces.

They're all of a type, cut from the same cloth.

Big, brawny men. Hard muscled, hard faced, tattoos and empty eyes.

Men who've seen too much, done too much, for too long.

I don't recognize any at first, and then I see it on one man's forearm.

The crossed cannons with the cannonball and the fire symbol.

Nate Sanderson.

The dad picking up his kids after drama club at Natalie's elementary school.

Paula's boyfriend.

Alleged model citizen and teddy bear.

A sound pulls me from my thoughts.

It comes from the other side of the house.

I exit Angelo's room, go back up the straight hallway, past the head of the stairs, around the curve of the other hallway, which loops back around to the other side of the little building.

Three more doors.

The first is another closet.

Clear.

The second is a full bathroom.

Clear.

The third is the last door to check.

There are only two floors, so this has to be it.

I turn the knob and nudge open the door with the toe of my boot.

It swings open smoothly and silently, without a squeak.

A bedroom. As sparse as the first one but bigger, with a

prettier bedspread and matching curtains on the wall. Orchids on a pastel background.

A priest is sitting on the bed, holding something.

Because I know it's Father Monroe's room, I'm expecting to see him.

Instead, I see it's the other, younger priest, Father Angelo, mouth duct taped.

I swing the Glock around, checking every corner.

I see the body in a cossack by the bed, face down, lying in a pool of blood.

I go over carefully, squat, check the body. It's Father Monroe, I'm guessing with his throat cut from the blood, his body still warm.

I straighten up, my gun still held out, and rip the tape off Father Angelo's mouth. He gasps.

"Where is he?" I ask.

Father Angelo shakes his head. Tears spill from his eyes.

"I don't know," he says in a wail.

He holds out his hands, in a pleading gesture.

"Help me," he says. "I don't want to die."

I look at the object he's holding.

It's a bomb.

Duct taped to his forearms. It's so tightly taped to his arms that I'd have to cut him in order to get it off, and there's no surety that doing that won't set it off.

A small light blinks on the front of the bomb.

I don't know enough about bombs to identify what kind it is or if it's on a timer, but I'm betting it's got enough C4 in it to bring down half the building.

Sweat pops out on my forehead, rolling down into my left eye. It stings.

I dab at my eye with the back of my hand.

He's crying openly now, hitching in great, panicked breaths.

"Remote... detonator," he says.

Shit. That's as good as a death sentence.

This is just another booby trap, like the Claymore with the tripwire.

I walked into it like an amateur.

Hell did you expect, Susan?

Think!

"Okay," I say. "Okay, okay. Stay calm. I'm going to call for help, okay? We're going to try to get you out of here."

He bends over, his face touching the device as he breaks down. Crying in great gasping gouts, snot streaming from his nostrils and dripping.

"Father Angelo," I say, trying to get through his despair. "I need to know. Is it Nate Sanderson?"

Father Angelo raises his head, staring at me with shining eyes. "Nate... Sanderson."

A sprig of hope flowers inside me.

"You served together, didn't you? I saw the picture on your dresser. You're the connection. You met Santos, you knew he was the Saint, about the secret railroad. Maybe you helped him at the safe house a few times, bringing supplies to the refugees? And then, after he died, you took over his task. But somehow Nate Sanderson found out, didn't he? Maybe he didn't like your helping illegal immigrants enter the country. So he followed you out there, saw the location of the safe house, and killed those poor people."

Father Angelo stares at me, still weeping desolately.

"Is that what happened?" I ask. "Please tell me, I need to know."

He opens his mouth to say something.

Just then, the light on the front of the device changes color.

It blinks faster and faster.

A beeping sound, urgent, accelerating.

Father Angelo tries to stand but his feet are duct taped together. He does a bunny hop toward me. Then another.

He moans, the sound turning into a plaintive wail.

I start to back away.

"I'm going to call for help now," I say, even though I know it's already too late. Paula must be dialing 911 already but they're never going to get here in time. The Saint intended for me to die in here.

The best I can do now is try to defy him.

"I'm so sorry!" I say to Angelo.

Then I start to run.

I feel like such a coward, but I know there's nothing I can do to help that poor doomed man.

I have to try to save myself.

I throw myself down the stairs, stumbling, tumbling, hitting my shoulder, my head, banging my ear hard enough to make me cry out.

I land at the bottom of the stairs, in a heap.

Somehow, I manage to pick myself up and lurch forward just as the house explodes around me in a deafening thunderclap.

THIRTY

I'm lying on my face in a bed of flowers.

My ears are ringing.

My hair feels filthy, full of crud.

I spit out dirt, pushing myself up off the ground as I try to sit up.

The best I can manage is to rest on my elbows for a minute.

Bright colors dance in front of my eyes as I struggle to regain consciousness. Sirens are blaring. Some of the bright colors are flowers, others are lights on the tops of emergency vehicles in the parking lot of the church. Men in uniform are getting out of vehicles, yelling to each other.

A familiar figure in a motorcycle jacket comes running up. "Susan!"

Paula crouches next to me. "Are you hurt?"

I try to sit up.

She reaches out but I swat her hand away.

I can do this.

I just need to take it one breath at a time.

I sit up, then rise to my haunches, and then I'm on my feet.

Dirt and debris fall off my back, and I leave a trail of it as I walk over to the side of the church. There's a small fountain there. I can sit on the edge.

The world swims once, then settles and resolves.

I lurch, then regain my sense of balance, and make it to the fountain.

I turn and look back at the pastor's quarters.

The little building looks nothing like the charming little two-story building it was just a few minutes ago. The top is caved in, and a huge hole gapes on the side, revealing what's left of the second floor. The back wall is still mostly intact, and I recognize a picture of the Sacred Heart that was at the back of Father Monroe's room. There's no sign of the bodies or any other recognizable details. Firefighters and other first responders are standing around, pointing up and talking urgently. Nobody seems to care much about Paula and me.

"I'm going to get the EMTs," Paula tells me.

I grab her elbow to stop her. "No."

I feel around for my phone. It was in my back pocket when I went in. I always slip it in there when I have to draw my weapon. It's gone now.

"Your phone?" Paula asks. "Did you drop it?"

I look back at the flower beds. It looks like a long walk right now. Maybe in a minute or two. My throat feels parched, raw. I still have dirt and grit in my mouth. And my poor hair!

"I'll go look," Paula says.

I watch as she goes over and searches the flower bed. One of the firefighters barks at her. She says something back to him.

Someone comes up on my right, moving fast.

My gun is in my hand before I even know I'm drawing.

"Whoa. Just bringing you some water, Agent Parker," he says.

An EMT, young, male. Small bottle of water in his hand.

I squint at him. The sun's too bright.

"Do I know you?" I ask. My voice comes out hoarse and ragged.

"Joaquim Almeida. I know you, SAC Susan Parker. You look out for the small people. You're trying to catch the bastard who smoked the folks in the safe house. I have folks who came up here through that safe house."

I take the bottle of water, twist open the cap, and rinse with the first mouthful, then spit. I do it twice more, until my mouth finally feels cleaner. Then I drink greedily. The water feels like a benediction in hell.

"Thanks, Joaquim," I say, my voice sounding a little better.

"He do this?" He points at the pastor's quarters. "The Saint?"

I nod. "I think so. Gone by the time I got here. Killed both priests."

He mutters a curse in a language I vaguely recognize from my childhood in Goa. It's Portuguese. The name Almeida is a familiar one, too.

"Brazil?" I ask him.

He nods. "From the favelas to the barrio, to SCV."

I indicate the EMT uniform and kit. "You're doing good. Saving lives."

"Thanks. You going to get this guy?"

"You bet," I say as Paula comes back with a triumphant look on her face, holding up my phone.

"You're a lifesaver," I tell her, checking it.

Wonder of wonders. It still works.

I ignore the usual explosion of missed calls and unread text messages and dial Kayla.

Kayla answers on the first ring. "That's you, innit? The explosion at St. Kat's?"

"Very loud, very close."

"Damn it, Suse. We're a team. That means we back each other up. Not fly solo!"

"He said to come alone. He was very insistent. Where are you?"

"On our way from Toppings. ETA less than two. You okay? Sound frazzled."

"Copacetic," I say. "Did Ramon pass on my messages?"

"Mancini's at the sniper's nest. She said to tell you next time try to leave her some evidence to work with."

"I'll keep that in mind. I've got to go. I think an old friend wants to have words with me."

"If it's McD, tell him to go—"

I cut off her last words as I stand to greet Chief McDougall. He looks like he's ready to punch me out.

He points at me, bulldog cheeks rippling.

"You're responsible for this, Parker! You're a rogue agent! Running around my town, blowing up people!"

"This is the Saint's work. He called me here. Instructed me not to call for backup."

McD scoffs. "Saint! There is no Saint. I heard about your obsession with this fictional mad bomber. You're chasing ghosts."

I'm tempted to ask him how he 'heard' about my case, then realize it isn't worth getting into. The safe house bombing isn't a secret around town, neither is the steady inflow of immigrants that provide cheap labor for local businesses, and people talk.

Instead, I say, "Check my call log. He would have used a burner, probably tossed it somewhere around here, but the GPS will confirm the location. This guy's on a spree, chief. We need to work together on this."

"On what? Some kind of gas explosion in a pastor's quarters? There's no case here, Parker."

I struggle to keep my temper. "Chief, he killed twenty-nine people in that safe house. You don't want to acknowledge that, that's your problem. But now he's killed two priests. And he used a Claymore to try to blow up me and my partner. He's escalating."

"Go home, Parker. Oh, wait. You don't have a home. Why? Because a crazy killer burned it down, you say. Except you lured the killer into your own house, endangered your own family. The fire report confirms it was arson. Maybe you set the fire yourself to try and claim the insurance."

That stuns me. "Why the hell would I do that, chief? It's my house. I lived there with my family. My daughter!"

"You tell me. You're not fit to raise a kid. I should call child services on you!"

That pushes my trigger. It's a step too far and I won't take it. Not from McD or anyone else. "Fuck you, McDougall. You're not fit to be chief of police."

"You think you can do a better job than me, Parker? Is that what you want? My office? By the time I'm done with you, you won't even be able to get a job working security at the mall. This is my town. I run the show."

I struggle to keep from exploding and saying things I know I'll never be able to take back. Several first responders are watching us. For all I know, someone's got their camera out and is recording this.

"Look, chief, I don't want to waste valuable time arguing with you. You need to bring Nate Sanderson in right now. That's the important thing. Let's work together on this before this madman blows up someone else."

THIRTY-ONE

McDougall stares at me. "Parker, you're talking through your hat. Where does Nate Sanderson come into this?"

"Father Angelo named him before he died. There's a picture... was a picture of Angelo and Sanderson on his dresser. Both of them when they were serving. Sanderson is a demolitions guy. There's other evidence connecting them both to the safe house. I think there's a pretty good chance Sanderson is the bomber. At the very least, he's a person of interest."

McD looks torn between yelling at me again and actually doing his job. He looks at the ruins of the pastor's quarters.

"You telling me it was Sanderson did this? Are you completely out of your mind, Parker?"

"Let my forensics expert examine the scene. I'm fairly certain she'll find it was C4."

McD scoffs. "We don't need your fancy Italian American whiz telling us what we already know. Of course this was C4. Even I could have told you that. That's the difference between us honest folk who served our country, unlike you college-educated young snappers who think you can come into this country and take over our jobs."

"I thought you said it was a gas explosion."

He bristles. "I'm this close to having you placed under arrest, Parker. If I were you, I'd watch my mouth when speaking to my superiors."

"Look, chief. I'm just trying to catch a killer before he strikes again. Bring Nate Sanderson in for questioning. You can ask the questions if you like. Start by asking him where he was this past hour. Check his residence for C4, Claymores, anything suspicious."

McD shakes his head, laughing. "Based on what evidence? Your wild imagination? No go, Parker. No judge in his right mind will issue a search warrant based on what you have. You're wasting your time. Nate Sanderson's one of the finest members of this community. A lot of folk are going to be mighty upset if you start going around slandering him and making wild accusations you can't prove."

I'm about to say something back that will really sting. I'm at the limit of my patience. Just then, Kayla appears out of nowhere and grabs my arm.

"Excuse me, chief, I need a word with my boss here."

She leads me away. McDougall returns to the group of first responders loosely gathered around. I see the fire chief among them. They both exchange words and glance over at me. I feel a stab of irrational rage. That's the man whose report caused the insurance company to deny my payout.

"What are you doing?" Kayla asks me in a low but intense tone when we're in an arched alcove away from inquisitive ears. I see David and Brine coming over to join us.

I break away from watching McD and the fire chief to look at Kayla. Her dark eyes are fiery. "We need to get Nate Sanderson in for questioning right now. Ten to one he's our guy."

She stares at me. "This is about the tattoo? The caduceus?

Ramon caught us up on your talks with Ahmed and the old abuelita."

"Father Angelo had a caduceus tattoo. He served as a military chaplain. I saw a picture of him with Nate Sanderson, who has the demolition corps tattoo, crossed cannons with a cannonball. I'm pretty sure that's the connection." I look around. "Where's Paula?"

Kayla and the others look at me quizzically.

I see Ramon and wave to him.

Ramon finishes talking on his phone and rejoins the discussion.

"The Claymore-C4 extraction thing, jefe? It's doable. Thing is, tracking Claymore supplies is a lot tougher. There's a lot of military surplus that's been sold on the black market over time. There's tons of it out there. He could have gotten the Claymores from anywhere."

"Good work, Ramon, but right now, I want Paula. Where'd she go? She was right here."

"Contreras? She took off. Got a call."

That sets off alarm bells. She is Nate Sanderson's girlfriend, after all.

"We need to get to Nate Sanderson," I say, starting to move.

Brine says, "Whoa. Hold up a minute. I'm still playing catch up here. You're saying that Father Angelo was the Saint, he took over after Santos died?"

I'm itching to get moving but force myself to answer. "Yes. He was there when Santos passed away. It makes sense that he would have helped him. Santos was ailing in those last months, probably too sick to take the supplies out to the safe house each night. I think Angelo helped him and after Santos died, he took over. That's why Ahmed and Husain's statements about the Saint's age differed."

"Because Ahmed saw Angelo, who's much younger, and Husain saw Santos, who was older," David says, putting it together. "Probably when they were taking turns bringing supplies from the truck down to the safe house."

"Yes, it could have been on the same night or different nights. They didn't always get a close look at his face, but when they did, they each saw a different man."

"Okay," Kayla says. "And both the priests had the caduceus tattoos?"

I nod. "They both served as chaplains, different decades, different wars, same tattoos."

"And how does Sanderson come into it?" Brine asks.

"Nate Sanderson knew Angelo. The picture confirms it. If we look closer, I'm sure we'll find that they kept in touch once they were stateside. Somehow, Sanderson got wind of the fact that Angelo was acting as the Saint after Santos's death, or maybe Angelo tried to bring him in to help and Sanderson betrayed him. Either way, Sanderson blew up the safe house, planted the Claymore, and when I called Monroe this morning to ask him about Santos's truck and belongings, he got worried I was getting too close and so he killed Monroe and used Angelo to lure me to my death."

Kayla frowns. "Wait. Even if he killed you, how could he know that we weren't in the loop? You're FBI, not some lone wolf detective. Though you act like it sometimes! How could Nate Sanderson know that we didn't know about his involvement, too?"

I shrug. "Maybe he didn't. This smacks of a desperate man reacting. Maybe he just needed to slow us down long enough for him to get away. That's why we need to bring him in if we still can. We need answers, and we need to get him off the streets before he blows up someone else."

"And you're sure it's Nate Sanderson?"

The last question comes from behind me.

I turn to see Naved.

Emotion stabs me in the chest. "I'm not sure of anything but yeah, I have a pretty good feeling about this. I think Sanderson's probably our guy."

He looks at the others, then back at me, considering.

I can't read what's going through his mind. This isn't the time or place to ask him why he reacted so oddly when we talked about Amit the other day, but I'm worried about the tension between us. Right now, Naved is the only friend I have on the local PD, and I need his help badly to bring in this mad bomber.

"Okay," he says at last. "I'm going to go talk to him. Me, alone. Just a talk, mind you, not an interrogation. If he cooperates, and I find reason to be suspicious, I'll consider taking it further."

I stare at him in disbelief. "You've got to be kidding! This guy is a mass murderer. You're going to handle him with kid gloves, he's going to lie to your face! If he's even at his home. Hundred to one says he's taken a powder already. If you're going, I'm coming with."

Naved gives me a cold look. "You want to try pressing your luck with the chief again? Go ahead."

He turns and starts to walk away.

"Okay," I say, going after him, and tugging at his sleeve. "Okay. We'll do it your way. But I'll ride with you. I need to see his face when you talk to him."

He stares at me. "Just as an observer. No questions, no talking at all. Agreed?"

"Agreed."

He looks at the others, then nods to me. "Okay, let's go."

THIRTY-TWO

Nate Sanderson's house is a pretty two-story single-family home. The front lawn has a tire swing hanging from a branch of an oak tree. A bright red plastic slide, the kind Natalie had when she was a toddler, and several toddler toys lie about nearby. The sprinklers are on and some of the water spills onto the sidewalk and the driveway as we walk up to the front door.

I don't see any sign of Paula's distinctive ride anywhere, but then, she could be parked around the corner, or in the garage. I'm struck by a mental image of them riding away together on her low rider, Sanderson turning to give me the finger as he grins.

Naved pauses on the porch, looking at me.

He hasn't spoken a word since we left St. Katherine's. It's only a two-minute drive, but I still feel stressed that I can't get a read on him. Now, he looks at me with the same stern look he had back at the church.

"Silent observer," he says.

I nod, miming zipping my mouth shut, locking it, and tossing away the key.

He rings the doorbell. I can hear music, laughter and voices —both children and adults—from inside. I'm overcome by the conviction that Nate Sanderson is long gone and that we're too late.

A man opens the door, wearing a tank top and an apron with the words "Bakers Gotta Bake" embroidered on the front. He's carrying a toddler on his hip, a tow-headed two-year-old girl with a binky in her mouth and looking over his shoulder as he finishes saying something to someone inside the house. It's the same guy I saw at Natalie's school's parking lot. Nate Sanderson in the flesh.

"—Sharon won't take no for an answer!"

He turns to us with a grin. "Hey, what's up?"

"Mr. Sanderson, I don't know if you remember me. We met at the—"

"Sure, sure. Naved, right? Good to see you again, man. How's it going?" He glances at me. "You're the big superstar local FBI Agent, Susan Parker, right? Saw you the other day with your sister-in-law. You're doing a great job. Do you have, like, a special magic lasso to catch all the bad guys? I was just talking to my sisters about you a while ago, comparing you to Wonder Woman!"

Naved interjects quickly, before I can answer. "Mr. Sanderson, I wonder if we might have a quick word."

"Sure. You want to come on in? Excuse the noise. My sisters are here. We're having a bit of a summer get-together. Summer, you know. Kids home from school. My nieces and nephews like our backyard pool better than the one they have back home in Bakersfield, even though theirs is twice the size and prettier. Kids! Go figure. We've got a barbecue going and I'm baking so there's hot dogs and sweet treats if you've got a hankering. Welcome to join."

Naved smiles politely. "Thanks, but maybe we can just talk out here for a minute?"

"Sure."

Nate pulls the front door shut behind him and steps out onto the porch. The toddler on his hip pulls the binky out of her mouth with a sucking sound and offers it to me. I smile at her, shaking my head.

"Sadie, are you offering the nice lady your binky? I don't think she wants it, right, Susan? You don't mind if I call you Susan, do you? I feel like we know each other already, you're like a local celebrity," Nate says.

I smile silently and glance at Naved who's stroking his chin the way he does when he's nervous about something. He's clearly flustered by Nate's apparent lack of awareness of why we're here.

Truth be told, so am I. It's hard to believe that this friendly, a dozen-words-a-second guy could possibly be the man who killed all those people, but I've been doing this job long enough to know never to let first appearances guide you. The truth always takes a little effort to uncover.

Then again, sometimes you *can* judge a book by its cover. I'm conflicted, and I don't even know the man. Naved must be having a hard time just finding the words.

"Sorry, Naved, you wanted to talk to me about something. Go ahead, man."

"Mr. Sanderson, did you know Father Angelo from St. Katherine's?" Naved asks.

"Bart? Hell, yeah. We go way back."

"You served together?"

"Not exactly. I mean, sure, we both served, but not in the same unit. I was demo corps, he was medical. Also, different generations. Bart's, like, twenty something years younger than me."

"You were close friends?"

"I wouldn't say close exactly, but sure, we knew each other well enough. We all try to stay in touch, you know. The community. That's the nice thing about being here. Everyone knows everyone, we kinda look out for one another."

"When was the last time you spoke to Father Angelo?"

Nate's forehead crinkles. "Dunno. Two, maybe three weeks? We met at Schooner Bay. You know, the bar. A lot of us hit up that place regular like."

"Nothing more recent?" Naved asks. "Today, maybe? He didn't call you earlier this morning?"

"Nope. Or if he did call, I might have missed it. I've been up and at it since the crack of dawn. Little kids and active duty, pretty much the same gig, wouldn't you say, Susan?"

I nod, smiling along, unable to help it. His good nature and bonhomie are contagious.

"And you haven't been up to St. Katherine's today either?" Naved asks.

"I went out last night for groceries. Waterproof diapers, too. Little Sadie here needed hers for the pool. Been here ever since. Probably not going to step out today. My nephews, they're teenagers, are at the mall. If they need me to come pick them up, I might go, otherwise, it's just fun in the sun all day long today. No, wait. I almost forgot drama club. My boys have rehearsals for the school play. I think your Natalie is in it, too, isn't she, Susan?"

I'm a little startled at his mention of my daughter's name and just manage to nod.

Naved and I exchange a look. Nate catches it, then frowns.

"Hold on a second. You said 'did' and 'were' and... you're talking about Bart in past tense. Is he... did something happen to him?" Nate asks after a glance at Sadie, who seems content to suck on her binky and stare off into the distance with that placid thousand-yard gaze little kids have.

Naved looks at Sadie, too. "Um. I can't really talk about it, Mr. Sanderson."

"Hold your horses," Nate says. "Don't go anywhere, be right back."

He goes back into the house and emerges a moment later without Sadie.

"He's dead, isn't he? Bart Angelo?" he asks both of us.

I glance at Naved who nods.

"I'm sorry," I say.

"Oh man," Nate says, running a hand through his graying hair. "Oh man, oh man. Another one bites the dust. He was so young! What was it? If you guys are here, it must have been something violent."

"You'll probably hear about it on the news anyway," I say. "There was an explosion at St. Katherine's about an hour ago."

He stares at me. "An explosion?" His expression changes. "Wait a sec. You didn't come here asking all these questions because I'm demo corps? Because I was an explosives guy back in the day? And all those questions? You can't be looking at me as the guy, right? I mean, seriously? You don't think I would off Bart Angelo? In a church?"

Naved puts his hand on Nate's shoulder. "We're just trying to figure out what happened, Nate. You know how it works. I can't give you any details, but I think it's safe to say that you're off the hook now. Right, Susan?"

I nod, not trusting myself to speak.

"Again, we're sorry for your loss. Hope you can enjoy the rest of your day," Naved says.

Nate nods, holding up a hand in goodbye as we turn and go back down the drive.

"You satisfied?" Naved asks me as we reach his Camry. "You need me to check his cellphone records and GPS? Question the rest of his family about his whereabouts over the past hour or two? Dig further into his service records? Get a search warrant?"

I shake my head, despondent. "Nate Sanderson is definitely not our guy."

If he's lying, it would take a minute to check with his family. But even without checking his alibi for today, my gut instinct refuses to believe that the man we just spoke to is the Saint.

Which leaves the question.

Who is?

THIRTY-THREE

The Saint is laughing as he watches SAC Parker and her partner walk back to his Camry.

Fooled ya good, didn't I? You never suspected for a minute. And I was right there in front of your face!

They stand by the car, talking for a minute.

Man, oh man, he really has her chasing her tail now.

It's such fun watching her and Seth chasing up blind alleys.

Seth glances back in the direction of the Saint once. Doesn't bother him. He knows they can't see him through the tinted glass of his side window.

If they could, the shit-eating grin on the Saint's face alone would give him away. Almost gotcha good that time, Parker!

It's too bad he couldn't get her with the two priests.

She came close to buying the farm. Really close.

He should have set the countdown to five seconds instead of ten.

But he'd figured, where'd have been the sport in that?

Sure, he wanted to blow the brunette FBI bitch to pieces, but she deserved a fighting chance. She's a veteran, just like he is. He's looked up her career history. She's racked up more deadly encounters than some soldiers he knows. Her wars are fought on homeland, not foreign soil, against domestic criminals rather than foreign enemies, but she's still a soldier, and a fellow soldier deserves a chance to take a shot.

Besides, there'll be other opportunities.

He's going to make sure of that.

THIRTY-FOUR

"I sent you three messages yesterday," I tell Naved as he drives. "Why didn't you reply?"

He keeps his eyes on the road.

"Are we still working together or not?" I ask.

Again, he doesn't reply.

"I thought we're partners," I say.

"I'm here, aren't I?" he says. "You wanted to talk to Nate Sanderson, I brought you here to talk to him. You're welcome, by the way."

"And I appreciate it. But I'm not talking about just doing one interview. I'm talking about the safe house bomber case. I thought you were working with us on this."

"I told you yesterday about what the chief said. He needs me to handle something else."

"So you can't even text me back? Sit and brainstorm with us? Participate?"

"It's complicated, Susan."

"Why? You've had run-ins with McD before. You've always fallen on our side of the line. What's changed?"

"Everything's changed," he says.

"You mean Amit's case."

He doesn't answer.

"Look, if you think I knew about this CBI investigation, then you need to hear me say it loud and clear. I did not know. A thing. About any of it."

He makes a sound, turning his head to glance out the window on his side, averting his face.

"What's that supposed to mean?"

He looks at me. "You admitted you got a call from Inspector Mahak Arora months ago."

"Yes, exactly, I admitted it."

"Yet you didn't feel the need to let me know about it when it happened? Back in... when was it, you said?"

"April sometime."

"Right. Four months ago. And you never said a word all this time."

"Because I had no idea it had anything to do with Amit's murder!"

He makes that scoffing sound again. "You seriously expect me to believe that?"

"Yes, I do. Because it's the truth."

"Susan, be realistic. You're a brilliant detective. One of the highest closing rates in the Bureau. And that's saying something since the Bureau has one of the highest closing rates in law enforcement, period. You expect me to believe that you got a call from this CBI inspector, and you didn't dig further into it?"

I stare at him, blinking. "Why would I?"

"Because it's what you do. You research everything. You cover every angle. You exhaust your team, work them night and day till you get the answers you're looking for. You're relentless. It's what makes you such a great detective."

"On a case I'm working, sure. But this wasn't a case, Naved. It was just a random call from some cop in India. For all I knew, she wanted to consult with me on a procedural matter. Who knows?"

"So you're saying you didn't look into it?"

"I did not. That's the honest truth."

He's silent for a long moment, before he continues, "And you had no idea that the CBI has been looking into your husband's family for years? Decades actually?"

"Not a clue. The first I heard of it was when you told me yesterday."

He's silent again, thinking.

"So now, at least, do you believe me?" I ask at last when the silence has stretched on unbearably long.

"I guess so," he says, but he doesn't sound convinced.

"Look, Naved, when I told you to look into Amit's murder, you asked me if I was willing to accept whatever you found out. No matter how shocking or disheartening. I said yes, I just wanted the truth. That's still my stand. I just want to know the truth, that's all. Why would I even ask you to look into it if I was lying myself?"

He sighs, exhaling loudly. "Okay."

"Okay, what? Okay, you'll trust me again and continue working with me and the team on the safe house?"

"We already talked about that. McD has me calling in almost every hour. For all I know, he's got someone checking my GPS. I have to stay away from you and the case otherwise he'll know it and he'll suspend me in a flash. And I can't afford that right now, Susan."

"Then how were you able to do the Nate Sanderson interview with me?"

"Because that was about the church bombing, remember? That's an SCVPD case now. Not the safe house. As far as McD is concerned, the two have nothing to do with each other."

It's my turn to make a scoffing sound now. "He's full of shit."

"Sure. But he's the sheriff of this town and he'll run his investigations any way he likes. Not a damn thing you or I can do about it. So stop butting horns with him and just let it go."

"I've let it go a hundred times, Naved. He's the one who keeps getting in my face every time I turn around."

"Well, you can't really blame him. You're always doing something flashy and loud that attracts national headlines. What do you want to bet that today's headline will be 'Church Bombed in LA Suburb: Two priests killed, motive unknown.' Now that's major news."

"Damn, you're right. I didn't think of that. It'll attract a lot of attention, won't it?" I say.

"Damn right it will. And somehow every time something like this happens, you're in the center of it. Can you blame him for being mad at you?"

"When you put it like that, I guess not. Maybe this time the national attention will get him off his ass and force him to acknowledge the safe house murders. Maybe it'll even get the press to cover it finally."

He shakes his head. "Don't go getting your hopes up. These days, even the most reliable media platforms are very resourceful. They know how to detach the truth from the facts without actually lying about them. It's all a matter of perspective and presentation."

I sigh. "You're right. They're going to do a McD on it, too. Pretend it's got nothing to do with the safe house."

"Now you're catching on. There may be hope for you yet, Susan Parker."

He pulls into the parking lot of Toppings.

I reach for the door handle then pause and turn around. "We friends again?"

He nods slowly. "Sure."

"Okay," I say. That's good enough for now.

THIRTY-FIVE

I stare out the window of Toppings.

There's a new protest going on across the street. Or maybe it's the same one as yesterday. I can't tell the difference. There're people with banners and handmade signs. A number of them are wearing military fatigues and look like vets. There are a lot of American flags, including on the couple of wheel-chairs. A table with a banner over it asks people to sign up to a petition to recall the governor and *Protect our 2nd Amendment Rights*.

A tattooed guy in a sleeveless tee shirt with bulging biceps is standing at the curb, practically in the street. He waves his sign at a passing car: *Guns don't kill people. Illegal immigrants do!*

The woman driving the car shoots him the finger.

Tattoo guy takes off his sunglasses and gives her the evil eye before tapping on the driver's side window and gesturing to her to roll it down.

The woman responds by flooring it, leaving him to choke on the fumes.

Smart woman.

He yells something at the departing car and glares after it as if he'd like to do more than just yell. I watch him for a moment, and I can almost see him mulling it over, then another car honks at him to get out of the way, and he raises his sign, doing his schtick again.

When did we fracture this badly as a country, dividing into all these camps of Us vs Them tribes?

My phone rings.

Lata calling.

I get up and walk to the back hallway to give myself some privacy. Back at our table, everyone's talking on the phone as they've been doing since we got back from the church. The lunch "rush" is in, which means a half dozen tables. Urduja and her other delivery driver colleagues are in and out every ten minutes, delivering orders.

"Hey, I just heard about the big explosion in SCV, at the church. Was that the same guy you're looking for?"

"Yup," I say.

"You weren't actually there, were you? Where it happened?"

"I can't talk about it, Lata. You know how it goes."

"Right, of course. Long as you're okay."

"I'm copacetic. What's up?"

"Listen, thanks for letting me sleep in this morning. I needed it."

"Of course. How was your hot date last night?"

"It was good," she says, then pauses. "Listen, I need to go meet the lawyer this afternoon. Can you handle picking up Nats?"

"Sure. I'll make it work. But, lawyer?"

"I told you, remember? To talk about our options for the insurance claim? It's possible we can get the fire department to reopen the investigation and file a new report."

"Fat chance," I say bitterly. "Not as long as McD's in charge."

"Well, this guy thinks we might have a shot."

"How would he know if you haven't met him yet?"

"I sent him the file, Suse," Lata says. "He looked it over and asked me to come in today. I think it's worth a conversation at least."

"Wait," I say, "this is the lawyer that Aishwarya offered to pay for?"

Lata scoffs. "Like I'd ever accept that favor from her," she says. "No, this is a different lawyer. Dad set it up. He does some legal work for Dad sometimes. Dad's coming with me, of course. That's why he can't pick up Natalie."

"Of course. It was cool of him to drop her off this morning. I had to go to work very early. I texted him at, like, five, and he replied in two minutes with 'Of course'. Your father is such a good grandpa."

"And a great dad, too," Lata says. "So, you're good to pick up Natalie? She has drama rehearsal after school, so same time as yesterday. And she would really love it if you could get there early to watch a bit of the rehearsal. She's so excited about being in the school play."

"I'll make sure I'm there."

"That's great. I should be there to pick her up pretty soon. I'll text you when we finish here."

"That's fine. We'll be at Toppings."

"Got it. And Suse, I hope you catch this guy you're after," she says. "He sounds scary AF. Madman with a bagful of bombs. Get him off the street fast."

"I'm working on it," I say as I end the call.

Urduja walks back in, carrying an empty delivery bag. Her face lights up when she catches sight of me. "Hey, Susan."

"Hey, Urduja. How's it going?"

"Whole town's talking about the church bombing. Such a

scary thing. Were you really in the pastor's house when it blew up?"

I shrug.

She covers her mouth with her hand. "OMG. For real?"

I smile at her. "I need a coffee. Badly."

"Sure," she says. "What kind should I get you?"

I hesitate. I don't want to tell her that their coffee isn't that great, which is why I've been getting my caffeine from diet cola for the past two days.

She leans in closer. "I don't mean *our* coffee. I know it sucks. I could go get you some from across the street."

She means the Starbucks across the street, inside the Barnes & Noble, the one and only chain bookstore in our little burgh.

"I don't want to put you out," I say. "You're on the job, right?"

"I have a break coming up anyway. And don't worry, I can pretty much come and go as I like. Quadros knows I'm a good worker."

"Okay," I say. "If you're sure it's all right, then across the street would be great." I hand her some cash. "And if you're going anyway, would you mind getting some for everyone? I can tell you what they like."

"Anything for you and your team, Susan," she says, beaming.

Everyone is absorbed in their phones, laptops, or tablets when I return to the table.

Ramon is pounding his keyboard with hard, angry strokes.

I raise a brow subtly at Kayla who twitches her eye in a very tiny shrug as if to say, *Yeah.*

"Anyone have an update?" I ask as I sit down.

David raises a finger. He's on the phone, talking earnestly to someone in his best lawyerly manner. Ramon pounds away angrily. Brine seems to be chatting with one person on his tablet while talking to another on his Bluetooth earpiece; how does he do that? My idea of multitasking is drinking wine and watching TV at once. Kayla seems to be on hold.

I'm tense with anticipation.

With the Nate Sanderson lead failing to pan out, the taggants are our best shot of tracking down the Saint. I put my team to work on it right away and we've been at it for hours.

"Yes?" Kayla says as the person on the other end says something. "All right, thank you so much."

Kayla puts down her phone and looks at me.

I lean forward, eager for some good news.

"Talk to me," I say.

Kayla checks off a name from a list. "Okay, first on the taggant, about half of those names are a no-go."

"By no-go, you mean...?"

"I mean all their C4 is present and accounted for or has been deployed."

"Deployed where?" I ask. "Be specific."

She glances at me. "Overseas. That's where most of this stuff goes, apparently."

"That makes sense, I suppose. None of it is being used in the US?"

"Not that we've found so far," she says. She indicates the others. "We're still checking and, in some cases, double checking like you insisted, but these guys are pretty tight when it comes to maintaining a secure inventory. We'll probably hear back from the remaining ones in a couple hours but Suse, I don't think we're going to find anything missing or stolen. It's impossible for anyone to just lift a few pounds of C4 and walk out of a depot."

I rub my temples again.

This can't be a dead end, damn it.

"What about the Claymores? Ramon?"

Ramon looks at me with an angry expression. "No go, boss. It's all over the place. Too much unaccounted-for military surplus, black market. It's impossible to track all this shit."

Another lead busted.

"Mancini?" I ask. "The sniper's nest forensics? I know it's too soon but anything yet?"

"I just got off the phone with her," Brine says. "She tried to reach you, but you weren't answering."

"I lost my phone for a while," I say, "back at the church. What'd she say? Please tell me she's got something? Anything?"

He bites his lip. "She says it was clean. Sorry, Susan."

"Damn it!" I say.

I drum my fingers on the tabletop.

"What about Santos's stuff?" I ask. "The pickup truck?"

David speaks up. "I looked into that just now. The truck was sold off to a parishioner. A Hispanic gentleman named Torres. He moved to Albuquerque last fall. He uses the truck to transport chickens."

"Chickens?"

"Poultry farm. There wasn't much else. The good pastor's clothes and books went to the local Goodwill. Nothing else that's traceable."

I can't believe it.

Everyone is silent for a long moment.

It happens on every case. You reach a dead end, a cul de sac. Leads don't pan out, witnesses retract their statements, or admit they lied or made a mistake. Evidence is contaminated. But this? This is a total disaster. None of our leads has led anywhere useful. I can't remember another case where so much has happened, so many people were killed, we had mountains of evidence, and still nothing to show for it. Not a single viable suspect.

"Okay," I say. "Okay, okay. Kayla, about the taggants. You said that none of the delivery points report anything missing or stolen. But for all we know, they could be lying or accomplices.

Let's not take them at their word. Let's go down there in person, eyeball the inventory, make sure every last piece of C_4 is where it's supposed to be."

There's a long moment of silence after I say this.

"That's it, boss," Ramon says. "Let's get off our asses and go out there. Maybe one of these supply officers is the Saint, lying to cover his own ass. Or maybe he's covering for a buddy. There're things we can spot when we do a physical check-in that we can't see online or on the phone. Right, guys?"

Nobody responds to his call for support.

I frown as I look around the table.

"Anyone have any problems with that?" I ask. "You guys don't look very enthusiastic."

David, Brine and Kayla all have different expressions and body language, but they're all saying the same thing: they disagree with my plan.

"Hey," I say, attempting a smile, "I'm not going to get mad, guys. I'm genuinely soliciting feedback here. You know we always work as a team. If you have a take on how to go about this, I want to hear it."

Brine and Kayla both glance at David, the eldest and most senior on our team. He clears his throat, uncomfortable at being put on the spot but accepting his role.

"I think these are all solid individuals, ranking officers who've been carefully vetted and given these positions for good reason," he says. "Ramon has run the data they provided us—or in some cases, which we, um, managed to peek at even though they wouldn't grant official access—and I've looked it over. Audited it, you might say. It holds up to scrutiny. I'd sign off on its veracity."

I nod. That means a lot. David is a highly qualified forensic accountant as well as a lawyer with experience in compliance, specializing in due diligence certification. If he says the data holds up to scrutiny, then it's authentic. That rules out tampering with stock inventory numbers to cover up any pilferage or misallocation.

"Okay," I say. "That's great. But I'd still like us to go down to each of those depots and do one-on-one interviews."

Kayla bites her lip, as if literally trying to bite back a comment.

"Something to add, Kay?" I ask.

"Susan, we're talking hundreds of miles, all over a tri-state area." She looks over at Brine who holds up two hands, showing seven fingers in all. "Correction, a seven-state area, so that's thousands of miles in all. We'd need a couple dozen agents at the very least, and local PD support, as well as military intelligence coordination, clearance from above, the OGC's approval, coordination with JAG, access to local judges and warrants, and that's not taking into consideration the problem of whether some of the bases will even grant us permission to enter."

I shake my head impatiently. "We're the FBI. Not a local sheriff. We have jurisdiction nationally. Worldwide actually if it involves US citizens."

Kayla exchanges a look with Brine and David. I can't help noticing that Brine is keeping quiet. He's clearly wary of being chewed out by me again.

David steps in. "That's just the thing, Susan. We're not the FBI. Not on this case. We're effectively functioning as rogue agents, acting without authority. We've still managed to get to all the supply officers on our list, despite those limitations, thanks in large part to Brine's excellent connections, but there's a limit to how far we can take this without the Bureau backing us."

I stare at him, then at all of them, in frustration. He's right. We're hamstrung, and we're up against a brick wall.

And yet, the Saint is out there, scot-free after killing all those people.

There *has* to be a way to get him.

I grit my teeth, resisting the urge to slam my fist down on the table to express the anger I'm feeling. Instead, I get up and turn around, intending to go to the soda fountain and draw myself a cup of water. I start walking without looking, just as Urduja approaches with a cardboard tray filled with our drinks with the familiar mermaid logo.

"Hi, I hope I got your orders right," Urduja starts to say, as I collide with her hand, knocking the tray to the ground.

The cups all pop open and the hot drinks spill out on the freshly mopped floor, spattering over Urduja's uniform, the next table and chairs, going everywhere.

THIRTY-SIX

I apologize to everyone, even help clean up the mess I made—Urduja and her colleagues say they can handle it, but I insist since it was entirely my fault—and then give myself a time out.

I head to the restroom to clean myself up and regroup. There's a coffee stain on one of my best shirts and I'm pretty sure it won't come out, but right now, that's the least of my concerns.

In the restroom, I splash water on my face, run my fingers through my hair, raking and combing it back.

I'm reminded of Winona Ryder in a 1990s movie.

I almost laugh at the comparison.

I'm no Hollywood star. I'm starting to doubt my ability to even be a good FBI agent. Right now, it feels like I'm a finger's width from being a total fuckup.

Then I think about it for a moment, and it strikes me.

"*Heathers*," I say to the Winona-Susan in the mirror. The classic black comedy.

I hit the restroom door with the heel of my palm on the way out, striding back to the restaurant.

Urduja is in the baking section, and she glances up at me with a smile as I pass.

I nod and call out, "Sorry again for the mess!" as I walk back to our table.

Everyone looks up at me.

Brine and Kayla stepped out while I was gone and have brought us fresh coffees. Brine offers me my favorite and I take it gratefully.

"Ramon, your friends at the safe house the other day. The ones with the construction equipment. They probably have a lot of contacts in the biz, right?"

He stares at me. "The construction biz?"

"Yup. Don't construction companies use explosives, too?"

He stares at me for a long moment, then snaps his fingers. His eyes brighten. "Gotcha, boss. Give me a sec. I'm on it."

He starts working his laptop as he uses his Bluetooth to simultaneously call someone. He pauses in his typing to grab his phone and thumb out a text.

When Ramon's firing on all cylinders, he is a force of nature. I'm lucky to have him. Hell, I'm lucky to have every single one of these guys.

"Kayla, you're a fan of old movies. Remember *Heathers*?"

She lights up. "Oh yeah. Cult classic. Christian Slater when he was young and hot. Winona Ryder and the three Heathers. Mad sick black comedy."

"You remember Slater's character, JD?" I say. "His dad in the movie owned a construction company, didn't he? He's obsessed with explosives."

Kayla nods slowly.

"Could be that's how he got hold of the C4," I say.

"From a construction company he owns?" she asks.

"Owns or works for, or maybe he just stole it from one. The point is, we need to look at other avenues."

"Construction companies that use C4?" David says doubtfully.

Brine shakes his head slowly.

"Brine, you have something to add?"

"Susan, we went over this already. All the C4 is under military control. The end user doesn't matter. The source is always US military. We already checked the C4 stocks. There's no other way that anyone could have gotten hold of C4."

My head throbs.

Kayla's asked me more than once if I'm feeling all right, if I need to get myself checked out in a hospital. I lied to her that an EMT looked me over at the church and said I was fine.

"Yes, and I know that, Brine, thank you for reminding me. What I'm saying now is that we look for the C4 from the other end. The receiver, not the distributor. Construction companies, anyone who sells or resells Claymores, anything that handles C4 at any stage. We check *them* out."

Nobody looks convinced.

Even I know I'm reaching. Ramon is jumping at the idea because he's ready to buy into any idea that will put him within striking distance of a viable suspect. He's hurting and wants justice. But the rest of them aren't buying it.

"Let's look into it, people," I say, sounding unconvinced myself. "We need to keep at it. Otherwise, we're never going to find this guy."

And that, I'm starting to fear, is a real possibility.

THIRTY-SEVEN

My Prius doesn't start on the first try. That's not unusual, so I wait a few seconds then try again. When it doesn't start on the fourth and fifth tries, I realize I've just been sitting in the parking lot of Toppings for almost fifteen minutes and finally admit defeat.

By now, everyone else has left in their own vehicles. Once Carlotta spat out a list of possible construction companies, and we called around, we found a half dozen worth checking out. I split up the assignments and sent my team off. It's better than sitting here and going around in circles. Now, it's time for me to get to Natalie's elementary school. Since I suddenly seem to have a little time, I'd like to get there early enough to watch her rehearse. Except, my Prius doesn't want to cooperate.

I get out of the car and slam the door hard. It creaks open again slowly. I slam it shut again, whacking it once more for good measure.

"Are you okay?" a voice asks.

I turn my head to see Urduja, still in her black and red Toppings uniform. She's looking at me with concern. I realize how I must look, wild-haired and evidently upset, pacing to and fro in the parking lot. So much for acting 'normal'.

I force out a smile.

"My car won't start."

Urduja looks around the parking lot. Apart from my Prius up here and the row of Toppings delivery cars at the back of the parking lot, each with its triangular light box and logo on the roof, there's no other vehicle.

"My team already left," I add. "I don't want to make them turn around and come back for me. I was just about to call a friend to come pick me up."

"I can drop you off," she says. "I'm about to go make a delivery."

I notice the pizza box in her hand.

"I don't want to make you go out of your way."

"My delivery's only, like, two miles away. I could just drop it off and then take you where you need to go. Are you going home?" she asks.

I offer an ironic smile.

Urduja slaps her forehead, remembering. "I'm sorry. I forgot. The fire."

"It's fine," I say.

"So I can totally drop you wherever you need to go," she says.

I hesitate.

I was about to call Naved but that won't work because, as he said, McD's probably keeping tabs on him and two trips to Toppings in one day will be hard to explain away.

Urduja raises up the box.

"Pizza's getting cold," she says. "Come on. It's no biggie."

She starts walking toward the back of the lot. I follow her.

Her delivery takes barely a minute. She gets back in the car, and we start back down Miracle Mountain Parkway, heading in the direction of Natalie's school.

Urduja is texting as she drives which makes me cringe when she negotiates the intersection and turns right onto Bouquet Canyon, merging with the oncoming traffic with the careless ease of the very young.

It's always hard for me to sit up front with someone else driving and the texting makes me doubly nervous, so I turn my head to look out the passenger side window. The painted face of the large sign on top of Dapper Don's Car Wash grins at me, inviting me to "treat my car". I'd like to treat my car, all right— treat it to a flying leap off a hundred-foot cliff!

My phone buzzes. I answer without looking at the screen, thinking it's one of the team.

"Miss Parker, please don't hang up," says a crisp voice. It's vaguely familiar but in my distracted state, I can't place it.

"Who is this?" I ask.

"Leland Chivers-Hall, we spoke the other day."

"Mr. Hall, I'm sorry but I really don't have the time or the bandwidth to deal with anything new right now. I have too much on my plate already."

"I understand completely, Miss Parker. Losing one's house is a terrible thing. I understand that your insurance claim has also been rejected, consequent to the investigation report being inconclusive as to the origin of the fire."

That takes me by surprise. It also makes me mad.

"I don't know where you're getting your information, sir, but that is a personal matter."

"Miss Parker, what if I told you that you needn't worry about your insurance claim being denied? That being able to afford to rebuild your house or buy an entirely new one if you prefer, is entirely within your means? What would you say to that?"

"Mr. Hall, I don't know what kind of mortgage or finance scheme you're selling, and I'm not interested. Please stop calling me."

I disconnect even as he starts to object.

Just the cherry I needed to top off a really bad day! Who is this guy? Is it some kind of scam? Probably. But he's suave, and polite, and has a lovely British accent that reminds me of my Nana. And what was that line about being able to afford to buy a new house? Some days, I just want to scream my lungs out.

Urduja pulls over.

A curly-haired young man in a tank top and cut-offs is standing on the curb, busy texting. His floppy hair almost covers his face. What little of it is visible makes him look too young to be with Urduja. She's only nineteen but looks mature for her age. He looks barely old enough to be out of high school. Unsurprisingly, he has a skateboard tucked under his arm.

Without looking up from his phone, he gets into the back seat, still texting like his life depends on it. Urduja takes off before he's even had time to get his seatbelt on. I feel him bump his head on the back of my seat.

"Yo!" he says.

"Sorry, Fry, but Susan's on an important case and needs to get back, stat," Urduja says. "And say hi to Susan. Susan, this is Fry."

"Hello," I say politely.

The young man leans forward excitedly. "Agent Parker, I'm a superfan! You're like the local guardian angel of Santa Carina!"

"Thank you," I say, a little overwhelmed by his enthusiasm. Fry? I assume it's a nickname. "Nice to meet you too. Urduja was kind enough to give me a ride when my Camry wouldn't start."

"I could take a look at it for you," he offers. "I'm good with cars."

"He's great with cars," Urduja adds. "His dad and brothers run the best body shop in town."

She makes what I'm pretty sure is an illegal U-turn and accelerates up to the speed limit and beyond.

"Um," I say, "a minute here or there isn't going to kill us." Urduja takes my request to heart and slows down abruptly. A pickup truck speeding behind us blares his horn in complaint. He overtakes us from the right and shoots Urduja the finger.

Both she and her boyfriend return the favor.

"Asswipe," says the boy from the back seat. "Peeps can be mad rude when they get behind the wheel!"

My phone rings.

Naved calling.

"Hey," I say, hopefully.

"I can't talk," he says quickly. "Just want to give you a heads up. It'll be a while before they close it out officially, but unofficially, McD is concluding that the explosion at the church was a murder-suicide."

"*What?*"

"Father Angelo had a history of mental health issues. Had a breakdown a couple years ago, in front of the congregation. That's when the church sent in Father Monroe to take over the parish. Angelo was supposed to succeed Santos, but he couldn't cut it."

"What does that have to do with today's bombing?"

"McD thinks that Angelo went off the reservation, killed Monroe and then offed himself. That's why he did it in Monroe's room."

"That's not what happened."

"They have your statement. You said that when you arrived, Monroe was already dead. You have no way of knowing who actually killed him."

"Okay, but the way Angelo was duct taped. He couldn't have done that to himself."

"The C4 pretty much blew all that evidence to shreds, so there's no way to confirm what you said. McD believes that the duct tape was for show. Your statement says he tried to grab you when you started backing away."

"He was trying to get away, not grab me!"

"Again, your word, no corroboration."

"What about the call the Saint made to me? Did they find the burner?"

"Not a burner. Angelo's phone. We only have your word that it wasn't Angelo speaking. It's easy to mistake one man's voice for another, especially with modulation apps."

"This is bullshit, Naved."

"It's a done deal. McD is going to announce it in a press conference, pending further investigation. He wants to shut down the speculation before it gets out of hand."

"Damn it!"

"I gotta go."

He disconnects.

I want to throw the phone out of the car.

I'm hopping mad.

I can see how neatly this works for McD. Take credit for the case. Close down speculation before some outlet puts the church bombing together with the safe house and starts a panic about a mad bomber in Santa Carina Valley.

All tied up neatly in a bow.

Except for the fact that Angelo wasn't the bomber.

It was the Saint.

And he's still out there.

Waiting to do it again.

THIRTY-EIGHT

Natalie is the Viking goddess Freyja. Decked out in golden battle armor with winged helmet and a sword, she appears in a vision to a bald, middle-aged man in the middle of the night. The startled man repents his wrongful ways and promises to change. Freyja is pleased by his promise but warns him that she will be watching closely and if he strays, he will feel her wrath. Then, she boards her chariot drawn by cats and is spirited away.

Since all the parts are played by seven- and eight-year-olds, the armor and weapons and most of the props are painted cardboard. When Natalie is required to speak, she uses American Sign Language to communicate while an interpreter recites her dialogue aloud from the side of the stage. Somehow, this only adds to Freyja's mystique and drama, and Natalie plays it up to the hilt, exaggerating her expressions and actions to appear suitably godlike and fierce. The highlight is when she struts to her chariot, also made of painted cardboard, and gestures imperiously to her cats—kids in cat makeup with stuck on tails—to hit the road!

There's a handful of parents in the auditorium watching along with me and we all clap as the scene ends. I'm a little more enthusiastic than the others, feeling a burst of pride at seeing my daughter holding her own among other able-bodied kids.

There was a time when Amit and I were pressured to put Natalie in a special school for the disabled. We insisted on keeping her in a regular school even though it presented many issues at first. This is one of those moments when I feel very happy and vindicated.

I wish Amit could be here to see her now. Our daughter, growing up so confident and beautiful.

Natalie sees me from the stage and waves, dropping out of character. She goes to the tall, blond man who has been instructing the kids and correcting them for the past several minutes that I've been watching. She signs to him, asking permission to go to her mother, who has just arrived. He turns and glances in my direction. I raise my hand and offer a smile. He smiles back, nods and signs back to Natalie that she can go, but to wait a moment as he would like to speak to her mother.

She starts to climb down from the stage, then remembers and runs back to take off her cardboard armor and hands it to him, along with her helmet and sword. He takes it, smiling at her eagerness.

She clambers down and comes running to me, signing as she runs.

"Mom! Mom! Why didn't you tell me you were coming? How long have you been here? Did you see the whole rehearsal? How was I, Mom? Did you like it?" Her questions fly rapid-fire at me.

I laugh and hold up my palms in surrender, signing back: "You were great, sweetie. Awesome sauce! Best goddess ever!"

She beams, basking in my approval.

"Where's Lata?" she asks, looking around.

"She had something to take care of. You'll be coming with me. I have to work still but you can have pizza."

She does her signature elbow dance, jigging her hips. "Yay! Pizza!"

Some of the parents pass us by, smiling at us, and waving at Natalie. "She's brilliant," says one dad. "You must be so proud."

"Thank you," I say.

I take Natalie's hand and turn to go, but she tugs, holding me back.

"Mom," she says, looking back over her shoulder. "Kelby wants to speak to you."

I frown, looking around. Who's Kelby? The only other parent still around is a grizzled, white-haired guy with a muscular neck crawling with tattoos. He's standing on the far side of the auditorium, powerful arms crossed across a weightlifter's chest. Our eyes meet briefly, and he nods at me with a mild smile, then makes a circle with his thumb and fore-finger, pointing at Natalie. I nod in acknowledgment, offering a smile.

"Mrs. Parker?" says a voice.

Natalie tugs at my arm hard to attract my attention.

I look down at her just as another person enters my frame of vision, and I raise my eyes to see the drama teacher who was instructing the kids on stage standing before me.

He has deep blue eyes and a scraggly growth that accentu-ates his heart-shaped face. Floppy hair and a general unkempt appearance give him a laid back, surfer dude kind of vibe. The tee shirt with the rainbow-colored legend "Kindness Will Save The World" and baggy, distressed jeans complete the image. Hiding inside that loose tee shirt are broad, tight shoulders and a lean, athletic physique tapering from a V-neck down to narrow, slender hips. Because I'm looking at Natalie when he approaches, my first view of him are those hips, and my eyes naturally travel upwards, across his body, ending at his face.

His eyes look amused when they finally meet mine.

"Hi, I'm Kelby, I teach drama here," he says. His voice is

low-pitched with a promise of a deep rumble which is belied by his friendly tone.

"How nice to meet you. I'm Natalie, Susan's mom," I say.

Natalie punches me in the hip with her fist, glaring up.

My hand flies to my mouth. "I'm sorry. I mean, I'm Susan, of course. Her mom. Natalie's mom."

He laughs. "I kinda figured that. It's very nice to meet you. You've got a great kid there. The absolute best."

I grin. "Thanks! We think so, too."

He looks around. "I think this is the first time we've actually met. Usually, she gets picked up by your sister."

"In law," I say. "Sister-in-law. I call her my sislaw. Lata."

He makes a face at his mistake. "Sister-in-law, sorry. So, she's your brother's wife?"

"Husband's, actually," I say. Then add quickly: "Husband's sister, I mean. Not his wife. That would be weird! I'm sorry, I'm really distracted right now."

He raises his hands. "One of those days, huh? I know the feeling."

When he lifts up his hand, I notice the ink peeking out from under his half sleeve.

"Did you serve?"

He follows my gaze to his upper arm. "Yes, I did. Four tours. But teaching drama to elementary school is so much better."

"Say, a lot of you vets hang around at the local bars, don't you?"

He rubs the back of his head, tousling his hair. "Sure. Not that I'm much of a drinker but I hang out sometimes, just for the company. Why? Are you looking for a recommendation?"

"Do you know if the demolition corps vets have a favorite place they hang out?"

He frowns. "Oddly specific question. Let me see. I'd try Schooner Bay. Or Mabel's Big House. They're right across the street from each other. You planning on going?"

"Maybe. I'm looking to hook up with some of the demo vets." I cover my mouth with my hand. "I mean, not *hook up* hook up. Talk. Just want to talk to some of them. God, I'm such a hot mess today."

"It's cool," he says, grinning. "I'll probably drop in at Schooner Bay around eight-ish tonight. Buy you a drink if you're there."

I give him a thumbs up. "It's a date. I mean. *Not* a date. I'll... see you if I happen to drop in."

Natalie tugs at my jacket. *Let's go, Mom,* she signs. *You're embarrassing me!*

"Well, we have to be going but it was nice to meet you, Kelby."

"Nice to meet you, too, Susan. You have a really special kid there. Natalie's a star."

He signs it out as he says it to make sure she understands it. Despite what people believe, English is only partially lip-readable.

Natalie blushes and yanks my hand, pulling me away.

"Bye, Natalie. I'll see you next Monday at dress rehearsal!"

Natalie signs bye to him. It's pretty obvious she has a crush on him. She probably isn't the only one. I noticed a couple of the teenage stagehands talking together and giggling as they stole looks at him. I'm betting that for Kelby, student crushes are an occupational hazard.

Outside, Natalie frowns at the sight of the pizza delivery car.

"Hey, look, Mom! Isn't that funny? We're going to eat pizza and there's a pizza delivery car right there! What a coincidence!"

"Actually, that's our ride, sweetie," I say, opening the rear door for Natalie. "Urduja here was nice enough to give us a lift."

I request Urduja's boyfriend—Fry, was it?—to move to the

front so I can sit behind with Natalie. He does it without taking his eyes off his phone and as he gets out, I see that he's playing a video game on it. Natalie signs "Hi" and he takes one hand off his game to offer her a fist bump. That wins him some points in my book.

"Mom, there's no booster seat," Natalie points out as I ask her to get into the back.

"I know, sweetie but you're going to be eight in just a few weeks and Mommy's with you, so it's all right to travel without one just this time."

She hops in happily, looking very pleased to be strapped in like an adult. As I buckle her seatbelt, I plant a kiss on her forehead. I want to smother her with kisses, but am conscious of Urduja and her boyfriend and the long detour I've made her take already.

"Urduja, I'm really sorry to make you go so far out of your way?" I say as we get rolling.

"No! It's fine, honestly. It's not like it's rush hour. That'll be later. Late afternoons and evenings are crazy busy."

"So, Fry?" I say. "Is that short for something?"

They both laugh.

"It's short for Small Fry," Urduja says. "He has four older brothers, and they're all, like, hulks. So that's their nickname for him."

"Runt of the litter," Fry murmurs, still absorbed in his mobile game.

Natalie can't hear any of this conversation from the back seat but she's looking from me to Fry in the shotgun seat. She's attracted to the video game he's playing and signs to me.

"Mom, can I play a video game on your phone?" she asks. Natalie has her own cellphone, but internet access is disabled for her own protection. As an FBI agent, I know far too much about online predators and how easily they dupe and lure and groom children through various ruses.

"Sweetie, I need my phone for work," I start to explain when it buzzes in my hand again. I show her the screen by way of explanation.

David Muskovitch calling.

"Back to the parlor, right?" Urduja asks from the front seat as she turn onto Bouquet Canyon. "I mean, I can drop you anywhere you like, I just have to go back to the parlor to pick up a couple more deliveries."

"Hold on, Urduja," I say as I take the call. "This is my colleague."

"Susan?" David says when I pick up. "Where are you?"

He sounds frantic. David is the coolest, calmest agent on our team, maybe in the entire LA field office. He never gets frantic.

"On my way to Toppings," I say. "What's up?"

"Susan," he says. "Ramon is going after the Saint. We need to stop him."

THIRTY-NINE

Naved and I are racing up Canyon Boulevard.

David's on the phone with me. He's enroute, too, Brine driving them both, but they're coming via the freeway and are still a good fifteen minutes away at best. We're much closer and stand the best chance of getting to Ramon first.

After disconnecting David's call, I called Naved and told him I need him to come pick me up *now*. He said he'd meet me at the corner of Canyon and Bouquet. He didn't ask any questions or offer an argument. This being Santa Carina Valley, he was barely a minute away, and so were we.

I told Natalie that Urduja and Fry would take her to Toppings and feed her pizza until I got back. She was totally cool with it, as were Fry and Urduja. Thank God for them. There's no way on earth I'm taking my daughter into an active shooter situation again. I did it once because I had no choice at the time and even though I stayed outside, it still came that close to ending badly. Never again.

I check my Sig Sauer clip and rack it again.

"The hell happened?" I ask David. I've put him on speaker-phone so Naved can participate, too.

David explains that they were running down the list of companies that had taken delivery of the C4 stock marked with the taggant, trying to confirm if their inventories were up to date and tallied with the stocks actually on the shelves.

I'm double checking my weapons and ammo while I listen. Glock, check. Sig Sauer, check. Both with full clips, check. Two extra clips for each, check.

"We were crossing the t's and dotting the i's," David says. "Brine and I were following the batch to try to see if any of the C4 had gone missing or if one of the buyers was trying to cover up something, using his family contacts to get their cooperation, while Kayla and Ramon were looking closer at the actual buyers themselves, their deep backgrounds, criminal history if any, even juvenile records, anything they could get access to, to see if they might be our unsub."

Impatiently, I say, "David, I know all this. Tell me about what happened here. Why did Ramon take off to go after this particular guy?"

"I heard it from Kayla, so it's second hand but she said that he was using Carlotta as usual to check out multiple sources, some of them on the dark web, she thinks, when he saw something that made him react. Before she knew it, he was out the door and gone. He took off on his Harley like a bat out of hell, she said. Kayla's following him in the van but she knew there was no way she could catch up to him, so she called me and told me to get everyone to haul ass while she talks to SCVPD to make sure if they get to the scene that they don't shoot Ramon. She thinks this guy might have bought up a stock of Claymores, and you remember one of our working theories was that the Saint might have repurposed the C4 from multiple Claymores to make his bombs? That's all I know."

"You did good, David, just tell Brine to drive safe and get there. We'll reach it before you guys or Kayla so don't break any speed records trying."

I look at my phone, wondering why Kayla didn't call me first. Then I see she did. I must have missed her call when I was talking to Natalie's drama teacher. Damn.

"Stop beating yourself up. It wouldn't have made a difference of more than a few seconds," Naved says, sensing what I'm fretting about even without my having to spell it out. He's checking his Smith & Wesson as he drives, keeping the heels of his palms on the steering while working the clip out with his fingers, then snapping it back in.

"Sometimes, a few seconds can be the difference between life and death," I say grimly as I pull on my vest. "Hang a right here, I know a short cut through this side street."

He does as I ask, the Camry's tires screeching in protest as he takes the left turn while doing ninety-five.

Some asshole in an Audi has the audacity to hit his horn in protest as we cut him off. Does the idiot not see the lights and the siren? Does he not know that you're supposed to pull over and wait till an emergency vehicle passes you by?

I shoot him the bird as we swing by, too quickly for me to catch his license plate. I'd have liked to take him in for obstruction but there's no time for that.

The location David gave me is a shopping center that claims to house more than a hundred stores. It's a concrete cell block in an elongated U-shape. I direct Naved to the delivery entrance at the rear of the building. As he pulls the Camry into the back lot, I spot Ramon's Harley out in the open.

"There!" I point.

I'm out of the car before the car comes to a complete halt, snapping the last Velcro strap into place and unholstering my Sig again. I spot the rear entrance to the store.

MATT'S ARMY SURPLUS & HUNTING SUPPLIES Delivery Entrance.

A wooden crate props the door open. There's a pile of similar wooden crates, all empty, stacked nearby, and a pile of butts on the ground. I'm guessing employees probably use the crate to keep the door open while on a smoke break out here. Ramon got lucky and didn't even need to ring the bell to request entrance. Damn it.

"I'm going in," I tell Naved softly.

"Susan, wait for backup," Naved says, keeping his voice low, too. "SCVPD's already on their way, ETA three minutes."

"The hell I am," I say. "Ramon's one of us."

The service hallway is cool despite the August heat. I make my way to the end, then go through an open doorway, past a unisex toilet, and a rear storage room stacked with boxes and crates. There's a closed door across the hall. The odor of cordite is pungent in the air. I'm guessing there's a small shooting gallery in there, for customers to check out the product before buying. I ignore it and continue.

The hallway turns a corner and then expands to become the main store. I hang back a moment, craning my head to look out and scan both sides. The store itself is a large open-space rectangular area lined with glass counters running along three sides, and shelves stacked with merchandise on the wall behind it. The merchandise is pretty much what you'd expect in a gun store: guns of every shape and size, ammo, munitions, camo wear, accessories, assorted stuff intended for the sole purpose of killing, maiming, blowing up, tearing apart, sustaining or destroying human beings.

I hear voices ahead and glimpse a trio of figures.

Ramon is one of them, his squat, short but powerfully built physique unmistakable. He's pointing a .38 police special at the head of a man who's down on his knees, hands locked behind his head. A single glance at his silhouette tells me that it's the eponymous Matt, owner of this establishment.

I've actually been in this store a time or two: once with Lata, the other time on my own. I recognize Matt's trademark Dodgers ball cap turned backwards and his distinctive profile, the result of an encounter with a Claymore that took a part of his jawbone. He was lucky to survive at all, and to retain most of his face, but that truncated jaw makes him impossible to forget.

He can't be the Saint.

If he was, then at least one of the relatives we interviewed at the safe house site would have mentioned the broken jaw, wouldn't they?

Unless...

"Ramon, it's me, Susan," I say clearly enough to be heard. "I'm coming in."

I move out of the hallway into the main store.

There's a display of camping equipment partially blocking my view of the three figures in the open space at the center of the store. I can only see Matt himself clearly. As I come out slowly, taking it one step at a time, I see Ramon's tattooed, muscular arms and then the side of his face. He looks worked up. His arm is loosely extended, finger on the trigger of the gun.

The third figure still isn't visible. To see the person, I'd have to step around the display and that would put me directly in Ramon's line of sight. I don't want that just yet. I want him to have to turn his head slightly to look in my direction, while being able to hear me perfectly well without moving at all.

"Ramon. This isn't our guy," I say softly.

He still hasn't said a word.

Ramon's face is a tight, unyielding mask revealing nothing. To survive in the gangs of East LA, you have to be able to show nothing at all times: no pain, no reaction, nada. Any sign of emotion is an admission of weakness that can get you killed at any moment. Ramon is a sculpted wooden statue. Yet I know he can hear me and is listening.

The sound of approaching sirens becomes audible.

"SCVPD will be here in another minute. Let's de-escalate this before they arrive on scene," I say.

I sense movement at the periphery of my vision. It's the

third person in the store, the one concealed by the display. I itch to take three more steps so I can see them clearly, but I don't want to do anything to startle either Ramon or Matt. The store owner is a veteran but he's also getting on in years, and has had his tussles with PTSD. It's heartbreaking how quickly and easily a situation where guns are involved can suddenly deteriorate into a shot exchange. I don't want any shots fired here today, no casualties.

"Ramon, goddammit," I say, raising the tone rather than the volume of my voice. "Quit fucking around here and let's get back to work to nail the real sonofabitch who put your people in the ground."

There's a tense pause as the sirens continue getting closer. Out the front windows of the store, I see movement. It looks like people running across the front parking lot, bent over.

I'm guessing that's probably the security guards ordering the customers and employees from the other stores to exit the lot. Hopefully, it isn't another gun-slinging local. Our Golden State has more than twenty million guns among its forty million residents, with over half the state either owning or sharing a roof with someone who owns a gun. The state average of five guns per gun-owning household goes up considerably in places like SCV.

To my relief, Ramon's arm goes slack, and the gun hand drops down to his side. I come out from behind the counter, lowering my own weapon but staying alert. The irritating display stand falls behind me and I'm finally able to see the third person in the store. It turns out to be Mirabelle, a middle-aged veteran whom I know from around town, and has a half-share in a local dive bar, named after her by her ex-husband.

"Mirabelle, I almost—" I start to say.

The matronly white-haired woman shrieks as she snatches up a long dark object from a counter and brings it down hard on the back of Ramon's head. It lands with a sickening sound that will probably haunt my dreams and Ramon collapses like an empty sack.

The next thing I know, I'm pointing my Sig at her, and someone is yelling. That someone is me, of course, ordering her to drop the weapon and raise her hands. She ignores me and charges at Ramon's prone body, both arms raised over her head to strike again. If she hits him a second time with that much force, she'll almost certainly kill him. And she's in no mood to listen.

I squeeze off two quick shots, loud and resounding in the quiet store, and then sirens are bleating outside and lights flashing as men in tan uniforms enter the store with guns drawn and voices raised.

FORTY

Hours later, I'm sitting in the rear of an LA deputy sheriff's Interceptor. I'm alone in the black and white SUV, looking out at the parking lot of the shopping center. The place is crawling with emergency vehicles, cruisers, cops, FBI. I'm not hand-cuffed, which is something, but I'm in deep trouble. There's no question about that.

I left Natalie with Urduja and Fry who said they'd be happy to take her to Toppings and keep her occupied and fed until Lata came to pick her up. That would have been a while ago. I'm desperate to call Lata and make sure she picked up Natalie and that she's okay.

I try to catch the attention of a passing cop but either he fails to notice my arm waving or pretends to ignore it.

I can see Kayla, David, Brine, and Naved about fifty meters away, talking to one of McDougall's bulls, a senior detective who's notorious for his temper and his aggressive methods. The last of the old school Irish, they call him.

I can understand that they're prohibited from talking to me until the FBI team handling the agent-involved shooting inquiry has had a chance to interview me. My phone was confiscated when I was placed in custody on McD's orders, which is also routine. All in all, SCVPD is going by the book but there's no particular show of aggression or gloating so far, which is a relief. Our law enforcement processes are impersonal and dehumanizing enough without adding toxicity.

I still remember the sickening crunch of that object connecting with Ramon's skull as he went down.

And the sound of my two gunshots as I fired at Mirabelle before she could strike him again.

Is Ramon okay? Nobody will tell me. I did see the EMTs come out carrying two people on stretchers. Both were spirited away in ambulances, lights and sirens going. That suggests both Ramon and Mirabelle were alive when rushed to hospital. Did they make it there alive? Are they in surgery? Recovery? Or... what?

It's the not knowing that's crippling.

A trio of new vehicles arrive. I can only glimpse the dark vehicles as they enter the lot, but they have lights on, so they're law enforcement. That must be the shooting team come to interview me.

To my surprise, Deputy Director Zimal Bukhari emerges from one, dressed as usual in a dark suit, looking authoritative and in control. I'm simultaneously overjoyed and deeply ashamed to see her. Overjoyed because she's the closest thing to a friend I have in the maddening senior bureaucracy of the FBI. Ashamed because I feel like I've let her down by allowing myself to get into this mess.

She speaks briefly to Chief McDougall who seems surprisingly calm and relaxed.

He nods and jerks his head in my direction.

My pulse quickens.

Deputy Director Zimal Bukhari walks over to the Interceptor I'm in.

She looks at me through the rear window, then walks

around to the other side, pops open the door, and gets in. Not in the front passenger seat, as protocol would usually recommend, but in the rear, alongside me.

There's a long moment of silence which I feel compelled to break.

"Deputy Director," I say, keeping my tone level but low to convey my contriteness at the circumstances.

"SAC Parker," she says in a neutral tone.

Tense seconds pass.

Finally, she breaks the silence with a sigh.

"How the fuck did we get here, Susan?" she says.

I take a long breath before replying. "I had no choice. She assaulted Ramon from behind and was going to hit him again. I'm pretty sure she would have killed him if the second blow landed."

She makes a dismissive gesture with her hand. "The shoot was clean. It's all on store cameras. The shooting team will still need a statement from you but it's a formality."

"What about Ramon? Is he okay?"

She sighs. "They're still working on him. There's a lot of blood loss and trauma, they say. That lady sure put a lot into that blow."

My heart sinks. "He's going to make it, right? Please tell me he's going to make it."

"I don't know, Susan. They say it was bad, that's all I know right now."

I send up a silent prayer for Ramon to be all right. "And Mirabelle?"

"That's the woman who brained him?" she asks. "She's not expected to make it. They're still operating on her but it's not looking good. Both your shots went in her chest, and she already had multiple complications from long Covid, a heart issue, kidney and liver problems..." She looks up at me. "How the hell did you let this get away from you? This is your team. You already knew Ramon was too close to this. You should have been watching him more closely."

I shake my head. "It was so sudden. None of us expected it. He ran out, jumped on his Harley, and took off. I came in barely a couple of minutes after him."

"A couple of minutes too late, looks like," she says. "And you're absolutely sure that this Matthew Brewer, the store owner, isn't the unsub?"

"He can't be," I say, feeling miserable. "He's disfigured from an old service wound. It's the first thing anyone notices about him. We have multiple wits who saw the unsub, the one they call the Saint, on more than one occasion, face to face. None of their statements mention any such disfiguration."

"There's no way he could have covered it up with prosthetics or makeup or something?" she asks. "I'm just spitballing here, Susan. Help me out. It would really make a big difference if this guy is, in fact, your unsub. That wouldn't erase the shitshow that's coming down on us, but it would go a long way in alleviating certain major concerns. Give me something I can use to counter all the allegations against you."

That makes me feel even worse. "I don't know what to say, ma'am. I could do a deep search of him with my team but I'm pretty sure that Matt Brewer isn't the Saint. Even if we discount the facial disfiguration, he also has a bum leg, which is the result of the same service injury. For all the wits to fail to mention both the face and the leg, that's not likely. So yeah, even without looking any further, I'd say there's almost no chance that he's our guy."

Zimal shakes her head again, placing her hand on the back of the driver's headrest. "So how the hell did Ramon go running off half-cocked?"

"He didn't know about the disfiguration and the leg, ma'am. He was only looking at the data. He saw evidence confirming that Matthew Brewer acquired C4 from the same batch that we've identified as being responsible for the safe house implosion. That made him believe Matt was the Saint. When he came face to face with him, he probably saw the face and leg and realized his mistake. I'm pretty sure he was about to say so to me when I came in and ordered him to stand down."

Zimal nods. "Why did you wait until then? If you were looking at the data together, you should have corrected him at once. Told him why Matt Brewer couldn't be the unsub. You should have been on top of this, SAC."

I feel a deep sense of shame. "Ma'am, I wasn't with Agent Ramon Diaz at the time. Agent David Muskovitch and he were working on one angle, while Agent Brine Thomas and Agent Kayla Givens were looking at another angle."

She groans. "And where were you?"

"Ma'am, we have no PD support. No boots on the ground to do door-to-doors or assist. We're working out of a pizza parlor, our cars, the mobile unit. We're doing the best we can with what we have."

She shakes her head. "No, SAC Parker. You're not doing anything more on this case. Consider yourself shut down as of this instant. You're off the case, permanently."

I start to answer, but she's already getting out of the Interceptor. She shuts the door in my face.

FORTY-ONE

It's almost closing time when I return to Toppings with Naved. Kayla and David are with us. It's a very subdued team that occupies the same window corner table we sat in at the start of the day.

We talk about the specifics, discussing the different companies that they were looking into and eliminating, and why. Hard as it is to deal with the fact that one of us is lying in a hospital bed with an uncertain future, we all understand that the only thing in our control right now, is catching the Saint. Despite what Bukhari said, I have no intention of giving up. Besides, she can't stop me from talking about it with my team, which is all we're really doing right now. Frustrating as it feels, talking is all we have left. For now, at least.

We're deep in discussion when I feel someone in my peripheral vision. After the day I've had, I'm jumpy enough to shoot at shadows. I look up to see Urduja and her floppy-haired boyfriend, both changed back into their street clothes again. She gives me a shy little wave, keeping her distance. It's obvious they don't want to interrupt what they can see is a serious discussion.

I excuse myself to go over to talk to them.

"We heard about the shooting at Canyon Country," Urduja says. "It's all over town. Everyone's talking about it. Are you okay?"

That figures. The smaller the town, the bigger the gossip. "I'm fine, thanks for asking. Listen, I meant to thank you for taking care of Natalie earlier, till my sislaw came by to pick her up. I really appreciate your doing that."

"It was our pleasure, Susan. Natalie's such an amazing kid. She was telling us all about her play. We promised her we'd come see it."

"Hell, yeah," Fry says. "I hear the new drama teacher is a really great guy. Did you know he was on a bigtime TV show? It was, like, the next *Criminal Minds* or something. Got cancelled after one season but still. Everyone says he's going to break out and be really big. School's lucky to have him even part-time."

The last thing I want is to talk about my daughter's drama teacher's career prospects.

"Thanks," I say, changing the topic. "When you said people are talking, what are they saying?"

Urduja's gaze cuts left to Fry. He looks like he's about to say something but closes his mouth when Urduja looks at him.

"You know how people are here," she says evasively. "They say all kinds of stuff."

I nod. "That bad, huh?"

She looks at me and shrugs. "A lot of people like Mirabelle Macpherson. She has her issues but who doesn't, right? She's a mom and a grandmom, and she knows a lot of people. Even the people who fought with her over the years kinda like her, if you know what I mean?"

"They must be really pissed that I shot her," I say wearily.

She shrugs, which I take to mean *yes*.

Fry just stands by her side, looking like he'd like to be anywhere else but here.

"If that's it, I need to get back to my team," I say as I turn away.

"Actually, I just needed to ask if it's still okay for Fry to take a look at your car," Urduja asks.

I stop and look back. "Oh. Right. You have the keys. Didn't you already do that earlier?"

Fry makes an apologetic face. "I was on shift and one of the other guys called in sick, so I had to take his shift, too. Just got off."

"I decided to stay on and work a double shift as well," Urduja says. "We're trying to save up to get our own place."

"That's a really smart idea," I say. "It's cool, though. You guys must be exhausted after a double shift. I can get someone to look at the engine."

"It's really no bother, Miss Parker," Fry says. "I know cars. And ninety-nine percent it's either your battery or the valve inflow."

"Are you sure?" I say, impatient to get back to the discussion. "I don't want to keep you guys."

"No, it's all good," Urduja says. "Just let Fry take a quick look. If he can't get it started in, like, five minutes, I'll come back and give you your keys." She thinks about that then adds, "I mean, I'll give you back your keys either way. But I bet he can get it started in five minutes. He's a genius with engines."

I shrug. "Okay. Knock yourselves out! Do you need me to come out with you or..."

"No, you just get back to work," Urduja says. "He'll handle it. You need to catch that guy, the Saint. I heard what he did to those poor people. He's a monster."

"Oh, we'll get him all right," I say. "Count on it."

"Yeah. 'Cause, you know," she says, "that's the only way you can make the townsfolk shut up."

"I know," I say. "One misstep cancels out two good deeds."

"Exactly, and you guys are like the nicest cops I've ever met in my life. That's why I want to be like you someday, Miss Parker."

"Yeah," Fry says, nodding his head vigorously. "Hell, yeah."

I smile at them. "Thanks, guys. I appreciate the vote of confidence."

They head out the front door, and I return to the table.

"Where are you guys at?" I ask as I retake my seat.

Naved says, "I had my doubts about how things were going. But now, after catching up on everything that David and Kayla were doing, I think you might be on the right track after all."

"Seriously?" I say. "Explain to me how. No, wait, I really need to get hydrated. Give me a second to refill my cup."

I walk over to the soda dispenser. All the staff now know me by sight as well as by name, and the three Toppings employees working in the open kitchen look at me and instantly start talking to each other. I can't hear what they're saying but I have a pretty good idea. I sense a couple of customers, an older man and a younger one, possibly a father-son duo, also glancing in my direction. *She's the FBI agent that shot Mirabelle McPherson at Matt Brewer's gun shop.*

I refill my large cup with sparkling water and remember I haven't eaten anything since this morning's pasta. I don't feel hungry even now, but I should probably get some food in me. It looks like being a long night. I also make a note to check my messages and let Lata know that I'll be pulling an all-nighter. And I really should make sure the rest of the team gets something to eat, especially Brine. He's always so great at making sure we're all fed and hydrated, I must bring him some dinner. Kayla will know what he'd like.

I start back to the table, looking out the large windows. Bouquet intersection is quiet at this late hour, with almost no traffic. The grassy verge across the street, in front of the courthouse and public library, is almost empty now, but there are still a handful of protestors with their sign boards standing around. Looks like they're almost done for the night.

The Toppings parking lot is to my left as I walk back, clearly visible through the black tinted glass windows, and my Prius is right there, in plain sight.

It's still in my field of sight when it explodes in a fireball of heat, light, and noise.

FORTY-TWO

Sirens are blaring all around me. Flames rage high above my head. Smoke billows, dense with the stink of burning rubber, oil, gas, and assorted chemicals.

Several cars are double parked on the street or have pulled into the Toppings driveway as the drivers stop to see what's going on. People have their phones out and are recording the fires. Fires, plural. The bomb was almost certainly in my Prius, but the fire it ignited has spread to the three other cars parked alongside it.

The owners of the cars are all out on the parking lot around me, talking in panicked voices and recording their burning vehicles with their smartphones.

Kayla, Naved, and David are with me, all talking at once, into phones and to each other.

Only I'm silent.

I don't have my phone out.

I'm not interested in recording this on video.

I left the task of calling 911 to someone else—we hardly need to since the nearest fire station is literally across the street in the municipal complex, just behind the courthouse and the old sheriff's station. They almost certainly heard the explosion.

It was loud.

Even through the sealed glass windows of the pizza parlor, everyone heard it. Kids screamed through mouthfuls of pizza. The windows rattled. Stuff fell off the tables. Someone in the kitchen dropped a pizza dish and the sound was drowned out by the second explosion, which I'm guessing was the gas in the tank of the Prius blowing up.

There couldn't have been more than a half-gallon or so, since the Prius is a hybrid electric-gas vehicle, but apparently that was enough to produce a fairly loud bang. Not as loud as the first explosion: that first one was C4, no doubt about it. Nothing else makes quite that big an impact.

It's been less than thirty seconds since I dropped my cup of sparkling water, splashing it on the floor, and ran out of the entrance door of Toppings. It took just that long for all these people to gather around, most indulging in the timeless human fascination with violence and death.

My first thought when I ran out was Urduja and Fry.

I assumed they must have been in the Prius when it blew up.

But now, looking at the raging inferno that my poor beat-up car has become, I see that the front seats are empty. The windshield exploded outwards when the C4 ignited and is lying in one large, crumpled heap nearby. I can see the front seats clearly, burning merrily away. If Urduja and Fry had been seated there, surely there would be some remains visible? Or would they have been flung out, too?

Then it strikes me: Why would they be in the car at all? Fry was supposed to take a look at the engine. Urduja would have been standing nearby, most likely.

Which means...

I turn around in a full circle, trying to take in the entire parking lot at once.

Kayla stops in mid-conversation to look at my face, reacting to my expression.

I don't know what it looks like, but I feel a mix of half-horror and half-hope.

"They must have been blown back by the explosion," I say.

She frowns at me, then takes a step closer.

"Urduja and Fry," I croak, my throat dry with fear.

Kayla's eyes widen.

She swings around, her eyes scanning the parking lot, too.

David and Naved both pause their phone conversations to look at us.

Naved gets it and tells David, who nods and joins in the search.

I frantically try to make my way through the lot, trying to see around the crowd of scattered people that are still coming in to rubberneck at the burning cars. Someone is saying, "There's been a terrorist attack, I think," on their phone.

"It wasn't a terrorist attack," I say to them, before moving past to continue my search.

At the far end of the lot, back by the building itself, against the wall, I see something. It looks like a crumpled-up broadsheet newspaper, like a windblown spread from the *LA Times* that caught itself on the wall.

As I get closer, starting to run, it resolves into what appears to be a pile of laundry instead.

People block my way, trying to record the fires.

"Coming through!" I warn before pushing them aside.

"Hey!" someone complains.

I ignore them.

Urduja.

She's lying against the bottom of the wall, her head twisted to one side, her body from the hip downwards twisted the other way. A carelessly discarded, soiled mannequin.

I bend down and check for a pulse.

Red lights wash over me, turning and blinking.

Out on the street, a ladder truck is trying to get into the Toppings lot but is finding its way obstructed by the rubber-neckers who've left their vehicles on the street and in the driveway and gotten out to record video on their smartphones.

The fire truck driver uses the PA system to ask the vehicle owners to get back in their vehicles and clear the scene to give first responders access. When some are slow to respond, he reminds them that obstructing first responders at a crime scene is a crime and that their license plate numbers will be recorded.

That gets the crowd to clear in a hurry.

Kayla comes up behind me.

"Oh god," she says, "oh god, oh god, oh god."

"There's a pulse," I say, standing up slowly. "Very faint but it's there. Where are the EMTs?"

She points at the gate.

"Don't touch her," I call back over my shoulder as I start walking. "Her spine might be damaged."

It's an unnecessary warning. Kayla knows better than to move an obviously injured person, but I felt the need to say it anyway.

That's another person I failed today.

Urduja.

Sweet, innocent nineteen-year-old Urduja.

And Fry.

Where is Fry?

I come out of the gate onto the street. The ladder truck is turning into the driveway, a firefighter standing outside on the street and guiding the driver through the awkward turn.

"Where are the EMTs?" I ask the firefighter directing the truck. "I have an injured girl."

He points behind me without speaking.

I turn to see an ambulance, lights flashing, waiting to follow the ladder truck in. I can see a man and a woman in the front. I run to it.

"Injured girl in there," I tell them. "I think she was standing by the car when the C4 went off and got thrown across the lot. She might have head and spinal injuries. Very faint pulse. My colleague's with her right now."

They get out of the ambulance, safety kits in hand, and start jogging into the lot, slipping through the gap between the guy directing the truck and the truck itself.

I'm about to follow them in when something catches my attention.

Across the street.

The grassy verge where the protestors were standing earlier today.

A handful of people have collected there and are staring across at the Toppings parking lot. At the burning cars.

Except for one man.

He's staring directly at me, from across the street and across eight lanes.

He's dressed in camo fatigues and is built like a brick. Hippy long gray hair, clean chin and cheeks, a pepper-salt moustache. An older guy, fifties, maybe sixties, maybe even older. Hard to tell from twenty-five meters away.

A recent memory stirs.

This afternoon, when I was leaving Toppings with Naved.

Both of us in the Camry, exiting the parking lot, turning onto Bouquet.

A man, one of the protestors across the street, standing and staring directly at me like he knew me.

The same man.

Same clothes, 'stache, hair.

Same crazy grin on his face.

It's the Saint.

I know it.

I start across the street, ignoring traffic, and start running.

My hand is already reaching for my gun and drawing it as I go.

FORTY-THREE

I'm sprinting across the street.

Horns blare as I cut across traffic.

A few minutes ago, before the explosion, there were hardly two or three cars on the street. Now, all of a sudden, there are a few dozen. Where did they all come from? The Regal Cineplex up the street, most likely. The last shows must have just let out. Ditto for the bars and restaurants in the town center. Most establishments shut down by 10 p.m. in SCV. Only a handful stay open till midnight or just after. This is what qualifies as a late-night rush hour here.

I ignore the blaring horns, yells, and raised fingers, and sprint all the way to the grassy verge.

Where is he?

I had him in my sights just a moment ago, right before an SUV cut between us, blocking my view briefly.

I run to and fro, then see a figure in camo fatigues and point my Sig.

"Whoa," says a gravelly voice. "Don't shoot, lady. I'm just trying to git to my car is all."

He indicates the parking lot of the public library behind me.

I squint, moving to one side to get him in the light. He's not the person I saw across the street. This guy is an elderly man, with steel-rim spectacles and a long white beard that reaches down to his gut. He's in a floral pattern half sleeve shirt and long shorts.

"Show me your hands," I bark.

I try to keep my eyes swiveling, to watch my surroundings, even as I keep the Sig trained on him. This is a shitty situation. Too many people, too many cars, chaos, the fires across the street, emergency vehicles, sirens, lights, yelling, horns. Too easy for another shooter to pick me off from behind, or from my blind spots. I'd be face down in the grass before I even knew what hit me.

The old man fumbles in his back pocket and comes up with what looks like a tan color wallet, beaten up and misshapen. He holds it up and lets it drop open, reaching out to show me.

"Barney Buffett, originally from Florida," he says. "No relation."

I don't know what he means by the last bit, but even at a glance, in this light, the driver's license pic looks pretty much like him. He has that timeless look of some older men. It's hard to tell if he's sixty, seventy, eighty, or even older.

He points a finger at me, grinning. "And you're the pretty little local FBI Agent. Special Agent in Charge Sarah Parker, am I right? Pleasure to make your acquaintance. You been stirring up this burgh of late, ain't you?"

I don't bother correcting him or answering his clearly rhetorical question.

"You a vet, Barney?" I ask sharply.

"Yes, ma'am."

"What branch did you serve in?"

"Paratroopers."

He names a regiment and unit but I'm already talking over him.

"You handle explosives in your time of service?"

He looks at me with a crafty expression, then nods his head sideways in the direction of the Toppings lot across the street. "C4, from the sound of it, am I right or am I right? You got yourselves a mad bomber on your hands, looks like?"

"Who else was out here with you today, Barney?" I ask.

"Buncha folks. Angeline Cordova was waving Old Glory. She drapes it around herself, sticks out her chest. Makes the stars pop real nice. She gets a lotta horns honking. Geddit? Horns? Horny? Honking?"

He laughs and his laughter devolves instantly into a coughing fit.

"Who else?" I ask impatiently. "Any demo corps guys?"

Footsteps come hammering across the street, pursued by irate honking.

Naved appears beside me. I see Kayla following close behind. Both have their guns drawn. Naved's face is filmed with sweat. I'm guessing it's from the heat of the fires, not the exertion.

"This him?" Naved asks.

I shake my head.

Barney laughs again. "Detective Seth. I know you. You guys are pardners, ain't cha?"

Naved frowns. "Who is this?"

"Nobody," I say, lowering my gun. "False alarm."

I turn a full 360 as Kayla comes hammering up to me. I shake my head at her, indicating that she can stand down.

"He was here," I tell Kayla and Naved. "I saw him across the street. I think I saw him earlier today, too. He was watching us the whole time. It's like a glass box in there. He could see us at all times. That's how he knew when to slip into the lot and fiddle with my Prius."

Kayla and Naved look across the street at Toppings. Painted

black with red trim, from top to bottom, it does look like a glass box. Or a glass cage.

"What about this guy?" Naved asks, his gun still pointed in Barney's direction.

"Let him go, he's useless," I say.

"If you looking for a vet, you looking in the wrong places," Barney says.

Naved waves at him. "You can go now, sir. Thank you for your cooperation."

Barney turns and shuffles away.

"Wait a second," I say. I run after Barney. "What did you mean just now? What places should I be looking in?"

He keeps walking, turning his head to look back at me.

"Them demo guys are rats. You don't find rats out in the open, do you? Goodnight, Sarah Parker. Good luck finding the mad bomber. You're gonna need it!"

He laughs as he keeps walking, shuffling into the public library parking lot.

I stand for a minute, trying to make sense of what he said.

You don't find rats out in the open, do you?

A scream rings out from across the street, shrill, sharp, and terrified.

"The hell is that?" I say.

Naved holsters his gun, looking downcast. "We found Urduja's boyfriend," he says in an unhappy tone. "What was left of him. He must have been standing right in front of the Prius when it blew. Poor guy."

I am mortified. Before I can even think of what to say, a second scream rings out, sharper and harsher than the one before.

"What is that?" I say again.

Naved scrubs a hand across his face. "Looks like someone found the rest of him."

FORTY-FOUR

It's early the next morning. I'm at the FBI field office at 11000 Wilshire in Los Angeles.

Deputy Director Zimal Bukhari waits patiently as I use her tablet to read the Saint's message. It's on a social media website and I already know its origin will be untraceable or end up somewhere in some remote foreign location. He'd have used multiple VPNs to reroute it around the world a dozen times in addition to using an encrypted dark web browser to post it. He's too smart to be tripped up by a technicality.

The message says simply:

Start deporting illegals or I keep blowing them up —The Saint

I look up at Bukhari.

"Are we sure it's really him? I mean, this could have been posted by any random crazy—"

She raises a hand. "Let me stop you right there. Do you see the signoff? Where it says 'The Saint'? It doesn't show up as a link even when you hover over it, don't ask me why, but go ahead and double tap on it."

I do as she asks. The click opens the direct messenger app connected to the social media platform. There's a message from an account which identifies itself as 'The Saint'. The message itself is blank.

"Go ahead and tap on—"

"The profile," I finish for her. "Got it."

The profile page is completely blank except for the name 'The Saint', the profile picture and a banner image. The picture is an image of a face. At first, I can't quite make out who it is but when I tap on it and the image expands to full size, I'm taken aback.

It's a picture of me. Taken in the parking lot of Toppings just after the car bomb went off. The Prius as well as the cars beside it are all in flames and my face is lit by the garish orange-red glare of the fires. Seeing the look on my face frozen in the picture takes me back to the moment, and I think again of poor Urduja and the even more unfortunate Fry. I can smell the gasoline from the burning cars even now. I swallow, using my decade of professional discipline to keep from getting sucked into the dark despair that threatens to overwhelm me.

The background image is a picture of the safe house. I'm in this one, too. My entire team and all the relatives of the survivors are standing around, watching as Ramon's construction friends bring up the bodies. The picture is of the moment the little girl's body came up in the bucket of the electric shovel. From the angle, it had to have been taken from not more than twenty yards away.

I'm tempted to pound my fist into the tablet but it's not mine.

"He's been watching me," I say through gritted teeth. "The bastard has been stalking me since I started on this case."

"Yes," Bukhari says. "That's evident. I spoke to Regan and Prodorutti over at BAO, Quantico. Separately, of course. They have differing views on his possible motivation, but both concur on one thing quite affirmatively: He's formed a predator-prey fixation with you."

I shake my head. "We don't know that for sure."

Bukhari gives me a look. "Samuel Regan and Genelia Prodorutti are the two top profilers in the country, which means they're the best in the world. Would you like to tell them yourself that they don't know what they're talking about?"

I tilt my head to one side, but before I can answer, she sighs and holds up her hand again.

"Don't answer that. I keep having to remind myself of your tendency to push back against authority figures. Anyway, *I* believe them. That's the point."

"Okay," I say. "I'll concede that he does seem to have been stalking me."

She nods several times. "I went over your and your team's debriefings. You said you actually saw him at the site of the second detonation."

"I'm sure of it. He was grinning at me. I went after him, but traffic got between us and—"

"This was across the street from the pizza place?" Bukhari interrupts. "At the protest in front of the courthouse?"

"Yes," I say. "I think I might have seen him a few times earlier, too, but I just didn't believe it could be the Saint."

"Yes, I noted that, too. Your team's already running down the list of people who attended the protest, as well as everyone who signed the petition, on the off chance that he could have been either a protestor or a signer, or both."

I like the sound of the words "your team".

That, and the fact that I'm sitting here at all in Bukhari's office are good signs, but to be sure, I ask, "Ma'am, last night you said I was off the case."

She nods. Getting up from the small round conference table where we're seated, she returns to her desk by the window. She picks up her phone and brings it over, tapping and scrolling to find what she's looking for.

When she finds it, she holds the phone out so I can read the text message. It's from the governor of California, and it says simply:

Put Parker back on it.

It feels so strange that the governor knows my name. And that he personally asked that I be put back on the Saint investigation. Strange, but in a good way.

"I... don't know what to say, ma'am."

She looks at me. "No need to say a thing. Just get back to work."

I nod slowly. "You got it, deputy director."

I get up and start toward the door.

"SAC Parker?"

I turn to look at her.

"Get the son of a bitch."

FORTY-FIVE

The Santa Carina Valley Town Hall auditorium is packed. It has a seating capacity of only eighty which has been exceeded by almost double. There are as many or more people standing as seated. I would worry about the fire code regulations but the fire chief himself is present and he doesn't seem concerned, so I guess it's okay.

For a moment, the sight of the fire chief reminds me of his report on our house, and I'm tempted to call him out on it, but then better sense prevails. I may be the victim of my mother-in-law and her brother's corrupt influence on local SCV politics and business, but that's a personal matter. Like the video Kundan showed me this morning. Those are both personal matters that I intend to deal with once this case is put to bed. Right now, I'm here only as the lead investigator on the Saint bombings and that's all I'm interested in.

Kayla crooks a finger at me, gesturing. I nod and move through the crowd. Naved is behind me. Brine and David have just arrived, and both are busy tapping and typing on their devices and phones, multi-tasking. I go up to the front of the space, standing to one side of and just behind Chief

McDougall. Naved stands beside me, while Kayla, David, and Brine stay close at hand.

McD, for his part, has what looks like his entire roster of senior detectives. There's more white hair on display here than you'd find in an SCV senior living community, but to be fair, they're all veteran detectives with decades' worth of successful investigations behind them. Some of those investigations might have been botched and McD's political views and methods might not be palatable to me, but there's still a lot of great police work on display there and I acknowledge it. Whatever it takes to catch the Saint.

McD makes a speech. I don't pay attention to it, especially the parts where he uses his platform to take several potshots at his favorite punching bag, the governor. His quips all land well, judging by the response of the crowd.

Then he gets to it.

Talking about the "senseless tragedy" of the parking lot explosion, the death of a "promising young man with a bright future ahead". There's a lot more blather in that vein, which is all good, because it's true. Fry is the catalyst that has gotten this community off its butt and actually caring about this madman among us.

About halfway through McD's de facto eulogy, I see Fry's brothers in the audience. They're accompanied by an even taller, even larger man with a shock of white hair, and a large blonde woman. The family resemblance is unmistakable as is their red hair.

As I half-listen to McD's rambling, I scan the audience closely.

This is one of those times when I really miss Ramon.

David, Brine and Kayla are all pitching in, and the several dozen uniformed cops that are present in the hall have all been briefed and are also looking out for anyone fitting my description of the Saint, but Ramon would have simply hacked into the town hall cameras and used Carlotta, his AI companion, to run every single person's face against an AI-rendered composite based on my description, then run the possible matches against federal and state databases. Since everyone here is either serving or has previously served in the armed forces, first responder services or law enforcement, they should all be in the databases. Ramon would be able to get Carlotta to give us names, IDs, addresses, contacts, within minutes.

But we can still do this the old-fashioned way. And we will.

When it's my turn to speak, I start by thanking McD and tread safe ground by offering my own eulogy to the victims of the Saint, starting with the immigrants killed at the safe house, which McD conveniently brushed over with only a single vague reference to "dozens of other human lives".

Stony silence greets this part of my speech but the minute I touch on Fry, I see his father get to his feet. He's swaying and red-faced and from the way the woman seated in the row ahead of him wrinkles her nose, it's pretty obvious that he's stinking drunk but that doesn't really matter under the circumstances.

"Keep my son's name out of your fucking mouth!" Mr. Logue yells across the town hall. "You're the one got him killed!"

Not surprisingly, this gets a round of ragged, uncertain applause. I'd bet it would be louder and more enthusiastic but to his credit, McD cuts it short by stepping in and uses my mic to say, "We're so sorry for your loss, buddy, now please sit down and allow Miss Parker to continue."

I nod at him in appreciation and as I go on, Fry's brothers pulling at their dad's arms to make him retake his seat. He does so, grumbling audibly, but doesn't rise again or harangue me anymore. I guess that means I got through to the boys.

"Thank you, chief. Folks, my colleagues here are going to show you some slides we just made up based on the profile generated by two of our seniormost profilers at the Behavioral

Analysis Unit at the FBI's headquarters in Quantico, Virgina. If you'll just take a look at this first slide..."

As I turn to look at the screen set up behind me, a man stands up in the audience.

For a moment, I assume it's Fry's dad again.

But it's not. This man speaks loudly enough to carry across the hall even without a microphone.

"You won't be needing all that FBI mumbo jumbo," he says.

A heckler, I think. Another fine upstanding citizen of Santa Carina Valley who objects to my handling of the case, maybe? Or just someone who hates the federal government.

I know better than to ask him the question. That's exactly what he wants, to justify airing what's probably a lifetime of grievances, real as well as imagined.

"Sir, please sit down and allow us to continue," I say politely. I gesture to David, urging him to put on the first slide.

David nods and taps his tablet.

A slide appears on the screen.

Before I can read the words aloud, the heckler says, "No, *you* sit down, federal bitch."

Without turning to the man, I gesture at Brine and Kayla, both of whom are already taking action. They use their sleeve mics to instruct the fellow FBI agents here today to take the man into custody. We anticipated something like this, of course. We were even hoping for it. Agents start moving down the aisles and into the row where the man is located, converging from both sides.

I turn to look at him.

My heart stops for a moment.

It's the old protestor who was across the street last night. The guy from Florida. Barney. He grins at me with a sense of familiarity that makes my stomach flip.

"Hello again, honeybuns. Remember me? Order your

people to stop where they are, or we all go to blazes in hellfire," he says to me.

Everyone's looking at him now. Even McD is frowning and speaking to Captain Hogarth who's nodding and gesturing at the uniformed cops at the back. They start to move forward, hands on their holsters. If this were a federal facility, we would have passed everyone through a metal detector as well as hands on security check to keep any weapons out. But this is Santa Carina Valley, a historic red zone in an otherwise blue state, and the right to bear arms is a sacred right.

"Sir, I think you need to leave," I say calmly.

"Oh, you bet I will, federal bitch," he says, "But I'll be taking some of you with me. And if those federal goons don't stop where they are, they're coming with me, too."

That only brings down more heat on him. My backup agents continue inching forward, their hands already reaching for their guns. The uniformed cops draw their weapons, pointing at the heckler. The audience is restless, several wanting to leave but scared to move for fear of startling the troublemaker.

Barney notices the movement converging on him and shakes his head. "You people think this is a joke? Back the fuck up *now*!"

Then he tears open his flak jacket and screams, "I am a bomb."

FORTY-SIX

Pandemonium breaks out.

People are leaving their seats and filling the aisles, rushing for the exits. My FBI agents are shoved aside by panicking people. The cops in the aisles are pushed back like deadwood caught in a flash flood.

These people may have been soldiers once, or cops, firefighters, EMTs, even SWAT, but for most of these folks, that was decades ago. They're middle-aged, porch rockers now, some of them old enough to be grandparents and great-grandparents. They came here to help, not to be heroes.

And even the relatively younger ones in their thirties and forties, the ones who still have some kick in their engines, know one thing from long, bitter experience: you can't fight a bomb.

You can't even argue with it.

The only ones not being swept away by the tide of panicking people are those of us in the front, away from the exits. Several of the detectives near me pull out their guns and point them at the heckler.

"No," I say sharply, making a gesture with my hand. "He

might have a dead man's trigger. Nobody shoots unless I give the order."

And I won't be giving that order today.

Because if anyone's going to take this bastard down, it's going to be me.

Even though I should be scared witless, like the other good people gathered here today, I feel exactly the opposite.

I lose sight of the heckler as the crowd fills my view.

Then I'm pushing my way through, using my relatively shorter height and smaller size to my advantage, slipping through the gaps, feeling my way into the rows of seats.

I climb onto the seats themselves and over them, going from row to row, heading toward the target.

I see Barney then.

He's exactly where he was when he started speaking.

The crowd flows around him like a river around a rock.

On either side, I see my agents, guns drawn, zeroing in.

"Hold your fire!" I shout above the hubbub.

The agents hear me and react, their training and my seniority enough to make them lower their weapons.

The uniformed cops in the aisles hear me, too, but they're not trained or interested in taking orders from me.

Instead, they react to McD shouting from behind, "Stand down, goddammit. SAC Parker is on point here!"

I'm surprised but grateful.

McD actually backing me up?

That's a first!

Then I get it.

He thinks this is going to be another disaster.

There's no good ending to this nightmare scenario.

And when it does go south, as it almost surely will, McDougall has no desire to be splattered by the mudsplash.

He's happy to let me take all of it.

So yeah.

Thank you, but also fuck you, McDougall. I do appreciate your backing me up even if you only did it to leave me holding the can.

By the time I reach the heckler, most of the audience has left their seats and are crowding the aisles or already out of the hall. I'd like it if the SCVPD cops left as well, but I don't have time to waste trying to convince them or my agents.

My entire attention is focused on the man with the C4 strapped to him.

I'm standing on the chairs two rows in front of him, barely six feet away from him.

I can see the beads of sweat on his balding scalp, and the vein pulsing in his left temple.

Is this the Saint?

I saw Barney up close last night. I remember writing him off on sight.

Could I have been wrong?

Are my instincts all screwed up on this case?

Right now, it doesn't matter.

All that matters is the bomb he's rigged with.

From this close, there's no mistaking the distinctive clay-like texture of C4, or the wiring, neatly and precisely arranged, clipped, stripped, and laid out.

Or the detonator that he's holding in his left fist, taped to his wrist, thumb pressing down the trigger to keep the circuit open.

A classic dead man's switch.

If we shoot him and he goes down, releasing the trigger, the circuit closes and the C4 detonates.

If he chooses to release it himself, the C4 detonates.

If I throw myself at him, wrestling him to the ground, and try to rip the tape off and pull the detonator away, the C4 detonates.

There's no good ending to this predicament, as McD saw in an instant.

Yet here I am, close enough to the man to be blasted into little bits when his bomb goes off.

Just like Fry.

Barney's looking at me now.

His eyes scan my hands, tongue flicking out nervously as he looks for the gun, or guns.

I open my fists to show him they're both empty.

"What we have here," I say to him in a calm, even voice, "is what's called a Mexican standoff."

He shakes his head slightly, then repeats the gesture with more confidence. "No. You're wrong, federal tool. I've got all the power here. You've got nothing. You do as I say, or I let go of this and take all these people with me. Including you."

I pretend to think about that for a moment, then shrug.

"Okay," I say, "go ahead, make my day."

He stares at me, licking his lips again. "What the fuck did you just say?"

"I said 'go ahead, make my day,' or pick whatever movie line you like. Because if you set that off, sure, you'll take out a few federal agents, including me, and a few cops, and that's sad, it's a tragedy, too, but it's our job to put ourselves in harm's way, and our families will grieve and be devastated, but at least then you won't be around anymore to take out any more young innocents like Christopher Logue, or hurt the likes of Urduja Tikaram, or massacre twenty-nine poor, desperate immigrants seeking only a chance at a better life. You'll be done forever, and your mad bombing spree will be done, and you won't be able to kill anyone else. And if the price of achieving that is a half dozen federal agents, and about a dozen cops, then so be it. Better us than them."

He stares at me for a long minute, then shakes his head again, as if he can't believe what I just said.

"No, no, no. You listen to me, bitch. You get your boss on the phone, and you tell him that I have demands. And if I don't get what I want right now, I will blow up this whole building and everyone in it. You understand? I am not fucking around here. This is serious shit. You see what I have strapped to my chest? It's six pounds of plastic explosive, rigged to a dead man's trigger. That means—"

"I know what that means," I say curtly, cutting him off. "And the building will have been evacuated by now. So, like I said before, you can go ahead and blow yourself up and take out all of us cops here. Blow up a municipal building, too, why not? They're planning to tear it down and rebuild it next year anyway, in case you hadn't heard. It's part of the new downtown redevelopment plan. You'll just move the date forward and save them the cost of demolition."

He stares at me again, licking his lips constantly now. Sweat is pouring down his forehead and scalp in little rivulets, the vein pulsing twice as fast.

"I have demands!" he screams. "I want—"

"I don't care what you want!" I yell back at him, crouching forward to put my face on the same level as his own. "You're not getting it. So if you're going to blow us all up, then go ahead and do it. Kill yourself, why don't you? Because it's the only thing you're going to get today. And like I said, good riddance to you, asshole. If this is the price to take you out, then I'm willing to pay it. Look! I'm signing the invoice. Approved! Now, stop talking and do what you're gonna do!"

When I make the gesture, like I'm signing an invisible voucher in the air, he flinches so hard, he trips and falls back onto his chair. It yields under his weight, breaking and dropping him to the floor.

Before he can so much as regain his breath, I'm on him, leaping across the chair between us to land on his chest, straddling him and pinning both his hands down. I grab the detonator just as he lets go involuntarily, reacting to the one-two shock of the fall as well as my weight landing on his chest.

There's a moment when we both fumble on the ground, his breath sour and stinking against the side of my face, before I slam his wrist down with a force hard enough to snap the bones and grab the detonator with my other hand—just in the nick of time before the circuit closes.

He screams in my ear at the pain from the broken wrist as I tense for the obliterating explosion.

FORTY-SEVEN

"You took a helluva risk, Parker!" McDougall says.

He's taken off his trademark cowboy hat and is pressing an already damp handkerchief to his thinning hairline. From the looks of it, he's going to need new hair plugs.

We're on a bench in the open-air cafeteria downstairs, behind the town hall. The place is swarming with cops and federal agents. I can glimpse the satellite broadcast vans of the networks out in the street as well as the crowd of local reporters, true crime podcasters, influencers, and who knows what else. My phone has been blowing up nonstop for the past hour, and I've been stubbornly ignoring it.

"That whole thing could have gone south in a hurry," McD continues. He's parked his large butt on the edge of a picnic table and is in a half-standing, half-seated position that makes his beer paunch bulge in an unsightly way. He's too frazzled to worry about how he looks right now, and what he looks like in this off-guard off-camera moment is very much an aging suburban man in his late sixties.

"He could have blown us all to kingdom come," he says. "You were provoking him, egging him on, like you had a death wish. Were you trying to get him to detonate that device? What were you thinking?"

I shrug. "What I said."

He stares at me. "Hell does that mean?"

"Like I told him. We were all LEOs up there."

I'm deliberately using the inclusive term, law enforcement officers, which includes federal as well as local cops.

I go on: "The civilians had evacuated. Better he blow us up and end his spree. Better that than continue killing innocent civilians like Christopher Logue."

McD stares at me for another long moment. He brings his handkerchief down from his forehead and looks at it. It's sopping wet. He looks around and tosses it in the general direction of a trash can. It falls short by three feet and lands wetly on the stone floor.

"You're a crazy one, Parker," he says. "I knew there was something wrong with you the minute I laid eyes on you. Never seen an FBI agent the likes of you before in my life. It's like you read the manual on how an FBI agent is supposed to talk and behave and act and follow protocol and then you go and do the opposite."

I brace myself for another McD tirade.

Instead, he surprises me.

"But goddammit, you sure as hell stopped him in a hurry. I thought my heart was going to give out when you jumped on him. I once saw a wild mountain lion jump on a kid up in the Santa Carina mountains. That's what you reminded me of. You took him down like a sack of potatoes. Six pounds of C4 and all! Goddammit, woman. I've never seen anything like it. Even my oldest detectives are impressed. What a takedown!"

It penetrates through my shield that McD's tone has changed. He isn't hectoring and badgering me anymore.

If I didn't know better, I'd think he's actually trying to compliment me!

I look up at him.

He's staring at me with a big shit-eating grin on his florid face.

Holding his thick hand out.

I look at his face, then at his hand.

I realize he expects me to take it.

I take it.

And shake it.

He laughs, clapping me on the back hard enough to make me cough.

The contrast between our physical sizes is like a well-fed bear with a season's worth of salmon in his belly and a coyote lean from a hard winter.

"I never thought I'd say this, Parker. But you earned my respect today. All this time I took you for one of those woke federal do-gooder types. Turns out, under all that jurisdiction bullshit camouflage, you're just a goddamn cop after all. A damn good one at that. Next time you take your family out for dinner in this town, or you and your gals are out drinking, you tell them the tab's on me. In my book, after what you did today, you're a goddamn local hero!"

McD's executive assistant, Sergeant Gormley, comes up and informs the chief that the media want him to say a few words. He mentions that they have not just national live coverage but international live coverage as well. McD makes an honest attempt to get me to agree to join him, but when I demure he doesn't press too hard. I know he loves his time in the limelight, and I'm always happy to avoid putting my face out in front of the world. I'd rather face a suicidal mad bomber than a roomful of cameras any day.

As he goes off to address the press corps, Naved, David, Kayla, and Brine come up, asking how I am. Naved was outside the town hall at the time of the incident and missed the excitement, and is the most concerned.

"Girl, you *are* a hero. I thought we were all goners when you started ranting at him. What were you thinking?" Kayla says, giving me a hug and a squeeze.

"Are you all right?" Brine asks anxiously. "Can I get you something to eat? A Boston Crème from Dunkin'? In-N-Out Double-Double Animal-Style?"

I laugh at his listing of several of my favorite comfort foods. "Thanks, Brine."

"Incredible," David says. "How did you know he wouldn't have the courage to detonate the device?"

"I didn't!" I say.

"McD's taking a victory lap out there," Naved says. "You're the one deserves all the credit."

I shake my head again. "No, I don't."

Kayla makes a face at me. "You took down the Saint! Own it!"

I smile at her. "I did not."

"What are you talking about?" she asks.

I look at each of them, my partners in crime prevention, my found fam. "I didn't take down the Saint."

David frowns. "He's in custody, Susan. There's no way he's going to get out of this. We have him dead to rights. Even if we can't prove he was responsible for the safe house and the pizza parlor bombings, and whatever previous crimes he probably committed that we don't know about yet, there's no escaping this rap. He's going away for a very long time. Guaranteed."

I run my hands through my hair, which still desperately needs a wash. It feels like jute strands. Disgusting! "Sure, that poor bozo is done for good. But it doesn't change anything. The case is still wide open, and we have a mad bomber to catch."

Everyone looks at each other then at me as if I'm crazy.

"Don't you get it, guys?" I say. "That man in custody? The old veteran, Barney? He's not the Saint. He was a fall guy, most likely set up by the Saint himself to throw us off. The Saint is still out there! And he's laughing at all of us right now because he thinks he's gotten away with it clean and left poor crazy old Barney taking the blame."

"How can you be so sure?" David asks.

"Because I saw him and spoke to him, remember? I caught a glimpse of the real Saint last night, at the protest across the street. And earlier, when he called me from Father Angelo's phone, I heard him speak. It's not a voice I'll forget in a hurry. That voice, that face, they were not Barney. I'm sure of it. Besides, I had Naved look up Barney last night, just to be sure. Tell them what you found, Naved?"

"Barney Buffett was in Florida the past three years," Naved says. "He only came to Santa Carina Valley three months ago. But more importantly, the day the safe house explosion took place, he was at a demonstration way over in Agua Dulce for two whole days, protesting. There are multiple witnesses who confirm he was with them throughout, and videos from the protest on YouTube."

"And we know from Mancini's report that the safe house explosion was triggered by a device that required the Saint to be on-site when he set it off," I add.

Naved continues, "And he's no sniper. He was at the bottom of his class and his unit when it came to sharpshooting. The Saint was using a sniper's nest, we know that. And left a Claymore. Classic sniper moves. And lastly, at the time of the church bombing and the shooting, Barney was right out there across the street from Toppings, protesting. His phone GPS confirms it, too. There's no way he could have been at St. Katherine's which is where Father Angelo's phone was when Susan received the call."

Their shocked faces give way to understanding.

"So, what now?" David asks.

"Now," I say, "we're well and truly bamboozled. There's no hard physical or DNA evidence to tie the actual bomber to any of the explosions, and with Barney in custody, there's no way we could convince anyone that the Saint is still at large. Besides which, we have no real leads left. We're tapped out, guys. This is the one that got away."

"That can't be," Kayla says, looking like she's on the verge of tears. "The son of a bitch can't get away with this."

"Sometimes, the bad guys win," I say. "This looks like one of those times."

Everyone looks depressed.

"What now?" Naved asks. "I can't believe you're just going to lie down and quit."

I shrug. "You have any concrete ideas on what we can do next?"

"No, but—"

"Well, in that case, I think I'm just going to get some shots."

"Shots?" David asks. "We just failed to catch one of the worst mad bombers in the history of the United States, and you want to do shots?"

"Yes, David. I'd like to do some shots. In fact, I think we should all do shots."

They look at me like I've lost my mind.

I allow myself a sneaky, sly grin.

Kayla wags a finger at me. "You're up to something, girl. I know you, you don't give up easy. Hell, you don't give up at all. Fess up. What's on your mind?"

I shrug. "Just what I said. Shots. First the kind you shoot, then the kind you drink."

"Huh?" Brine says.

"You mean, like a shooting range?" Naved asks.

"Yup," I say. "And then we hit the bars. I promised Paula Contreras I'd buy her a round for saving Ramon's and my lives the other day. I intend to keep that promise."

FORTY-EIGHT

The Saint squeezes off another round, then uses the scope to check the target.

Right through the center.

The bullseye is so frayed, he's shooting through his own previous shots. That's three in a row he's put through the bullseye. Dead center.

He always shoots well when he's had a good day.

And man, oh man, has he had a good day!

A whole run of them, in fact.

He's grinning as he carries his gear back to the shed.

His grin slips when he sees a familiar face talking to Olafson, the owner of the shooting range.

It's that Mexican jarhead, Contreras. The one with the low rider tricked out in pink who gave Parker the ride the other day.

Hell is she doing here? At *his* shooting range?

He pretends not to see her, going about his usual routine, but out the corner of his eye, he watches as another woman joins Contreras who seems to be introducing her to Olafson.

It's Parker.

That almost makes the Saint's hand slip, tipping over the

squeeze bottle of cleaning fluid. He has to bend to pick it up, and when he does, he feels a prickling on the top of his head, like someone has set the crosshairs of their target right there.

From around the range, the sound of shots being fired rings out from time to time as various patrons go through their routines. The Saint is in the long-range area, which is away from the main building and handgun ranges, and right now, there's only a handful of other long gun shooters like himself. There's nobody else in sight except for Olafson and the two women visitors. But the feeling of being targeted is powerful and unshakable, and he feels convinced someone is about to take a shot at him.

When he straightens up, nobody seems to be looking at him.

The Contreras woman and Agent Susan Parker are nodding at Olafson again, then they turn and walk away, back to the main building.

The Saint knows better than to just go over and start grilling Olafson.

He's been so careful in his everyday life not to draw suspicion to himself by refusing to do a single thing out of the ordinary.

But right now, he's willing to risk it all just to get Olafson to tell him what the hell's going on. What did Susan Parker and her jarhead friend want?

Should he be nervous? Are federal agents going to come pouring out from the parking lot? Is SWAT on the way? Are they here to arrest him?

He wracks his brains, trying to think of any way he might have slipped up.

He's pretty sure the stunt that good ole Barney pulled at the town hall meeting threw them off his trail good and proper. He knows McDougall and the rest of his force are convinced that Barney was the one responsible for the bombings.

The Saint even planted the C4, the Claymores, and a

cassock in Barney's garage. The house is a sub-rental Barney's staying in temporarily and the secreted items won't have Barney's prints on them. They won't have anyone's prints on them, since the Saint made damn sure to clean his own prints and DNA off so they wouldn't lead back to him. But just finding those items in Barney's possession should be enough to hang him.

So what is she doing here at *his* range?

Out the corner of his eye, he sees Olafson coming over, sauntering with his slow gait. Olafson, the owner of the gun range, is an elderly vet, and very large. He also had hip replacement surgery not long ago, and still complains about not being able to walk right.

Olafson asks his permission to pick up his scope, which is on the table along with the rest of the disassembled rifle parts. The Saint nods brusquely. He gets the sense that Olafson wants to say something and is looking for an opening.

"Good shooting," Olafson says after he uses the Saint's scope to look at the target. "Maybe your best ever."

The Saint says nothing, not even acknowledging the compliment. Right now, he's thinking that maybe he'll use his hunting knife to make Olafson spit out whatever it was he told the FBI agent and jarhead. He's starting to feel itchy and restless. He feels violated that she would come here, to his range of all places. It's Olafson's range, but the Saint has been coming here as long as he can remember. The number of rounds he's shot here, he's probably paid a sizable percentage of the range's income over the years.

"FBI was here a minute ago," Olafson says with deceptive casualness. "Wanted to know about sharpshooters, snipers."

"Why?" the Saint asks bluntly.

"Wouldn't say. Probably some new case. Can't be the bomber. They caught that guy. You hear? Crazy old Barney from Florida, the one living in Gerry's garage."

The Saint reassembles his rifle in short, compact motions.

"What'd you tell 'em?" he asks.

Olafson scratches his butt, taking his time and pleasure doing it. "The truth. Ain't gonna lie to no federal agent. That's a federal crime, you know. So I told her there were a few. She asked me for names and details, I said I'd email those over right away. But I did say that the best shooter I'd ever seen was right here. Pointed you out."

That must have been when the Saint bent over to retrieve the fallen cleaning fluid. That explains the sensation of being watched.

Olafson adds with an apologetic tone, "I mean, you are the best. Around here anyways. Just thought I'd let you know. In case."

"In case what?"

"I dunno. I mean, who knows what bug that FBI lady has up her ass? Must be something big. She's making quite a name for herself. Rep for closing out big cases. Big game hunter. Whoever she's after, he might have to watch his six."

The Saint finishes reassembling and lays the rifle down carefully.

"You trying to tell me something?" he asks Olafson bluntly.

Olafson raises his hands, the heavy wads of flesh on his upper arms jiggling loosely. "Hey, I'm just trying to warn an old friend. I run a clean operation here. No illegal gun sales or any funny business like some other ranges I know. Everything by the book. Whatever you're into here, Cartright, you should be more careful is all I'm saying. No offense."

Sweat breaks out on Olafson's ample face. The Saint weighs his options. Finally, he turns away, packing the rest of his gear into his duffel bag.

"What else she say?" he asks with his back turned.

Olafson lowers his hands, sounding relieved. "That's it. She and the Marine were talking about hitting up a bar, getting some shots in when they walked away. Schooner Bay, I think."

The Saint zips up his bag and turns to look at Olafson one last time.

"That's it?"

Olafson nods. "That's it, buddy. I didn't say anything about you knowing Barney or what I overheard you guys talking about the other day when you brought him up here to shoot. The thing you were saying about illegal immigrants and doing something to make everyone wake up. I covered for you, man. I don't want any trouble—"

He breaks off as he sees the hunting knife in the Saint's hand, blade gleaming in the late afternoon sun.

The radio in his pickup truck turns on when the Saint twists the key in the ignition, playing a Morgan Wallen song. He hits the radio with the heel of his palm, killing the music. His good mood has turned sour, as has the day.

SAC Parker has her sights set on him.

At least that's how it looks now.

It's only a matter of time before Olafson's body is found, and before she connects it to him directly.

Things are escalating.

Time for him to do some escalating of his own.

For starters, he needs to do something that will throw her off her game.

Take out one of her team?

No, it needs to be more personal than that.

A low body blow.

Something that will hurt her badly enough to cripple her emotionally. It's common knowledge on the internet and around town that she fell apart after her husband's death. Almost flushed her life and career down the toilet.

Imagine what losing someone else close to her would do.

Her partner, maybe? Detective Seth.

He has access to the SCVPD parking lot where Seth parks his Camry.

That's a start.

Now, think escalation.

Keep the hits coming, nonstop.

Seth for starters.

Who else?

Her sister-in-law? What's her name? Lata?

She drives a Jeep.

That will take a little more effort but it's not impossible either.

What else?

It comes to him then.

So fucking obvious and so fucking perfect.

Her daughter.

Natalie.

Yes.

That would be the perfect coup de grace.

It would finish her off.

Okay then, he thinks.

You came for me, SAC Parker? Dropping by my friendly neighborhood shooting range? Forced me to kill Olafson and lose my main source for explosives and ammo? Olafson is *your* fault. I had to kill him because of you.

Now it's time for you to feel the burn.

I'm coming for you and yours.

Boom. Boom. Boom.

FORTY-NINE

My team and I get a lot of looks and head turns the minute we walk into Schooner Bay.

I know that coming here is a long shot but right now, a long shot is the best shot we have of catching the Saint, and possibly, the only shot.

The bar is divided into three areas: several tables and booths on one side with the bar at one end and the entrance at the other end, an open area that's used for dancing, or to accommodate the standing room only crowd as it is right now, and a third area with several pool tables and a row of dart boards against one wall. All three areas are packed with people and there's even a short line by the hallway that leads to the restrooms and the back exit.

I've only been here a couple times, both occasions with Lata, once with a girlfriend of hers named Ariana whom I thought (and Lata thought) was going to amount to something serious, and it wasn't even half as crowded as it is tonight.

"Woman of the hour!" someone calls out from one of the back tables.

He's echoed by a woman cheering and a spontaneous round

of applause breaks out. Soon, every pair of eyes in the joint is upon us.

Kayla gives me a look that conveys: *Are you seeing this?*

I shrug and grin, accepting the applause good-naturedly.

"Thanks, folks," I say when the applause dies down. "Just doing my job."

"*You kicked ass!*" another man's voice calls out from the pool area.

"And her own ass ain't so bad either!" yells another wise guy.

This last comment is greeted with a chorus of wolf whistles from both men and women, and a lusty round of cheers and laughter from the crowd in general. A lot of beer mugs and shot glasses are raised to me as we navigate our way through the crowd and to the bar.

"Looks like we're late to the party," Kayla mutters under her breath to me.

Brine takes that as his cue to break out in song.

"What is that song?" David asks.

"Kacey Musgraves," I inform him. "'Late to the Party'."

There are two bartenders at work, both busy pouring drinks. The most popular items are clearly shots and beer, so when Brine optimistically asks for a cocktail, he's greeted with blank stares.

Kayla pats him on the head affectionately. "Shots all around tonight, Briney boy. You, too."

Brine rolls his eyes. "What is this, high school?"

A guy with salt-and-pepper hair and a goatee at the bar says, "Did you say you're still in high school? What are you, kid? Seventeen? Are you even allowed to be in here?"

Brine sighs and ignores him. As the baby of the team, he's used to cracks about his age. He's only recently turned twenty-five but looks years younger, and still gets carded every single time as he loves to remind us.

"Go find us a table," I tell him and Kayla. "I'll get the drinks."

One of the bartenders is a young Hispanic woman with her hair done up in twin braids, ink wrapped around every patch of visible skin, and more metal on her face than a John Deere tractor.

She looks at me knowingly as she sets our shots and beers down on a round tray. "You the sister of the ex-Marine lesbian."

"Sislaw, actually," I say. "If you mean Lata."

"That's it. Pretty sure she's going around with one of my homies."

She names a woman that I can't recall Lata mentioning even in passing. Then again, Lata has been going around with a lot of women since she and Ariana broke up. I've tried to talk to her about it but somehow, she keeps avoiding the conversation.

I don't want to tell the pretty bartender that her homie was probably just one of several passing fancies in a long list. Instead, I smile and nod, thanking her for the drinks and making sure I leave a good tip.

Naved has magically managed to find us a table. Kayla, Brine, and David are already in occupancy, while Naved stands nearby, in conversation with a short, skinny guy with a thick moustache that I think is a senior detective in McD's bullpen.

We wait for Naved.

When he comes over, I hand him a shot glass and raise my own.

"For those we lost and those still with us," I say.

We all drink.

"Isn't that McCaffrey?" I ask Naved.

"Jim. He retired last fall."

"You guys looked pretty pally."

Naved takes a sip of his beer. "He's ex-NYPD, too. New Yorker most of his life until he came over here twelve years ago.

Gave me a few tips on surviving SCVPD. He was just on his way out at the time so could be frank."

I nod. "So just two NYPD bulls exchanging war stories."

"Right now, you mean? He was telling me about how McD is on top of the world. He's so kicked about the publicity he's been getting today that he's planning to toss his hat in the ring for governor this fall."

I raise my eyebrows. "Are you kidding me? McDougall as governor of California?"

"Stranger things have happened."

Over the next hour, each of us drifts apart, engaging in conversation with other people. The place has the feel of a private party. Everyone knows each other or knows someone in common. A lot of alcohol was probably consumed before we got here and a lot more is consumed after we arrive, and the volume level is high, the buzz drowning out the jukebox music at times. A few dozen people are managing to dance despite the noise, although it's more like swaying while in conversation rather than actual line dancing or swing.

We're popular tonight, especially me.

Even though I've lived here for eight years, I've never really felt accepted into the community. The last year or so, as my most recent cases happened to be right here in SCV, the general attitude went from indifferent to actively hostile.

But today, after the incident at the town hall, the tide has clearly turned. McD's ringing endorsement of me has altered their perception. Instead of the meddling federal government tool poking her nose into town affairs, I've suddenly become the town's guardian angel. I've never had so many people compliment me in one evening, and not just about my professional achievements. There're open flirtations, and a few cross the boundary into blatantly sexual invitations.

I play along, getting into the role of a cop enjoying a much-deserved blowout after a long, hard case successfully put to bed, and at some moments, I'll admit I even let my imagination run wild at the possibilities. It's been almost twenty months since Amit died, and I'm a young woman with needs and wants.

But that's as far as I'm willing to let it go.

Amit may be dead, but the questions about his death aren't. And after what Naved told me about the CBI case, I know I have a lot more investigating to do to find out the truth about Amit's murder. I intend to take care of that once I'm done with this case.

And then there's the question of where we're going to live. Not under a roof owned by Aishwarya, that's for sure. I've had a small taste of what that would be like at the Bel Air condo, even though that's owned by Kundan. God alone knows how she'll treat me and Natalie if I take her up on her offer and live in a house she's paid for.

I end up disappointing a lot of guys, some of whom are not bad looking and a much younger, not-married me might have even considered sharing a bed with. But not this Susan.

I manage to pass the evening mostly sipping on a couple of beers. No hard liquor after that first shot. After that first round, which we had had to play the part, the bartender with the braids brings us another round, compliments of someone or other, and even returns my money to me, saying that my money's no good here. She gives me a wink and taps the shot glass in a not-so-subtle message: tap, as in tap water!

The rounds keep coming after that, and I keep tossing back shots of tap water. The rest of the team will be doing the same.

At some point, I become aware that I'm being watched.

It's not the ubiquitous 'hey, it's the hero of the hour, the cute FBI chick' look that the guys and girls have been giving me all evening. Schooner Bay is as notorious for being a pickup joint as it is for attracting cops and vets and being checked out is a professional hazard here.

This is different.

Someone is watching me and being sneaky about it.

I turn my head, pretending to laugh several times at something someone or other says, tossing my hair, looking around as if seeking out one of my buddies, but I'm unable to spot him every time.

Whoever this guy is, he's good at surveilling.

The only reason I even sense him is because of the hunter-prey connection: that sixth sense we all have that warns us when someone is watching us with wicked intent. It's a sense as old as survival itself.

"Hey there," says a male voice while I'm looking around again.

I turn to see an older guy standing in front of me, holding a long neck beer in one hand. He's wearing a corduroy jacket over a red plaid shirt with a lumberjack pattern, and matching corduroy pants. He's in his late forties or early fifties, and has spent a lot of time out in the sun, judging by his deeply baked-in tan and the leathery skin.

Suddenly, I'm tired of being hit on and having to repel all comers with a smile and a friendly laugh to avoid giving offence.

"Hi," I say, continuing to look around, "I'm actually looking for a friend. I think she's over there."

I point in the direction of the pool tables, even though I can glimpse Kayla's hair to my right, over by the bar. My destination is actually the rear hallway, and through there, the back exit.

I start to walk away as I feel the guy move in closer, grabbing hold of my elbow and touching my ribs.

I turn to slap him down. It's one thing to be hit on verbally, and a totally different thing to be touched physically. That's a line I don't allow any guy to cross.

He grins at me and jerks his chin down, pointing to his hand.

The hand holding the gun that he's pressing to my ribs, using his corduroy jacket to shield it from view.

"Let's get some fresh air," he says.

FIFTY

The August air feels warm as toast after the bar.

The older guy in the corduroy jacket hustles me out the back door and across the parking lot of Schooner Bay. It's a small lot, barely space for a couple of dozen vehicles. Most of the patrons inside have parked out on the street. But not this guy. He points to a pickup truck that looks like it's seen better days.

Inside, I didn't want to make a scene to avoid unnecessary bloodshed. There are a *lot* of guns in that bar right now, and one shot could have drawn down a firestorm. It would have been a massacre, and in that mess, the guy himself might even have gotten away. Alcohol, guns, and gung-ho cops and vets don't mix well.

But out here, it's different. I only have to worry about my own life.

But just as I'm about to make my move, he says, "Think about Natalie."

My head jerks back. My heart thumps.

"What about Natalie?" I ask, trying to look back at his face.

He stays behind me, his face out of sight. Only the gun in my back gives me a clue to his presence.

"You wouldn't want her to end up the way the Logue kid did, would you?" he says quietly.

Across the parking lot, a Ford is swaying from side to side in that telltale motion that can only mean that someone inside is hooking up and couldn't wait to get home or to a motel. Other than that, the lot is deserted. All the action is inside.

I feel a white-hot rush of anger fill my chest.

"You touch a hair on my daughter's head, you fucker, and I'll gut you like a fish," I snarl.

He chuckles. "Sure, sure. Talk big, why don't you? I've got you by the hairy balls, federal tool. And there ain't nothing you can do about it."

That phrase—'federal tool'—stirs something in me. It kills my anger quicker than a bucket of ice water dousing a stove.

The wannabe bomber at the town hall used the same phrase.

He said a few other choice things, too, but that particular one was among them.

"Climb up into the truck," he says. "Door's unlocked."

I look at the black Ram.

"No," I say.

He jabs me in the back with the gun. "What'd you say?"

"I said no. I'm not getting in that truck."

Behind me, I hear the sound of the back door of Schooner Bay pop open. Music and the hubbub of a hundred drunk voices spills out as the door stays open. I hear boots and shoes scrape the concrete as more than one person exits before the door is allowed to swing shut again, squeaking noisily as it grinds its way back.

"Susan!" Kayla's voice calls out.

"That's my team," I say quietly to the man with the gun at my back. "Their weapons are drawn and they're surrounding you. They've already called for backup and in another minute, this place will be crawling with cops. That's not including the couple dozen back there in the bar who would love to shoot themselves a bad guy tonight."

When he doesn't answer, I turn my head slowly, expecting to feel the whiplash of a blow on my jaw or head at any minute, or to see the muzzle of the gun aimed at my face instead.

Neither comes.

I'm allowed to turn all the way around to face him.

Behind him, I can see Kayla, David, Brine and Naved all spread out across the parking lot, guns drawn and sighted, using cover where possible to give themselves a shooting advantage.

"We were expecting this, you asshole," I say. "Did you think we came here to have a good time? We came looking for you!"

He's still holding the gun, but it no longer scares me. I haven't drawn my gun yet because once I do, then this will end only once one of us fires their weapon. I'm still hoping to be able to talk him down. He's just a man with a gun. I've talked down harder cases than him before.

Then I see what he's holding in his other hand and my heart stops.

"Well, you struck pay dirt. I'm the guy you've been looking for all this time."

He switches to a deeper, more gravelly tone, altering his voice just enough to make it sound different from his everyday speaking voice. "*Pastor's quarters at St. Katherine's. Ten minutes.*"

He's the Saint.

Even though I came here tonight, fairly certain he was shadowing me and would attempt something, the sound of his voice still brings a chill to my bones.

He grins as he holds up the electronic remote keypad.

"You know what this is, don't you, federal tool?"

I nod, swallowing.

"EIS. Electronic initiation system," I say.

He chuckles. "Your generation loves your short forms. I just call it a good ole remote detonator. You see the keypad here? It allows for multiple detonations. Theoretically, you can set it for almost any number of explosions. I won't tell you how many I've set it for tonight, but let's just say, it's a heck of a lot!" He laughs, throwing his head back. "Didja get that? A heck of a *lot*, as in a parking lot!"

Over his shoulder, I can see Kayla and Naved moving in on the guy, converging in a pincer movement. Naved is barely twenty feet away now.

"You can tell your guys to stop right where they are," the Saint says.

"You won't get away this time," I say, "so you might as well hand over that device and your weapon. It's over."

He smiles at me.

It's a smug, supremely confident smile.

The smile of the very arrogant and narcissistic, convinced of their own immortality.

He raises the detonator and his voice as well. "Guys! I hope you have your safeties on because this party is about to get loud!"

He presses a number on the keypad.

And the night explodes with fire.

A car on the street rises a dozen meters or more in the air, flipping to land on its side in a blazing heap. Debris rains down everywhere, reaching all the way to the far side of the street and into this lot, drumming on the tops of parked vehicles, smashing a rear windshield. A piece of twisted, smoking metal lands only a few feet away from me.

All of us react. Except for the man with the detonator.

I see his eyes light up, twin flames gleaming in his pupils, reflecting the explosion.

Behind him, I see Kayla and Naved turn and point their

guns instinctively at the sound of the explosion, then stare open-mouthed as they see the car on the street go up.

The Saint smiles at me and glances at the detonator held up high in his left hand, drawing my attention back to it.

He keys another number on the keypad.

Another car goes up, this one in the parking lot, only a few cars away from the spot where Brine is crouched, gun aimed.

Brine yelps, throwing himself to the asphalt, as the car rises and falls, upside down this time, onto the hood of another nearby parked vehicle. The sound of metal clattering and glass shattering fills the parking lot as debris rains down again. David reacts as something falls almost on his left shoulder, missing it narrowly.

The Ford that was swaying earlier pops open both doors and a trio of naked people spills out, falling on the asphalt in their desperation and fear. They scream as they see the burning car nearby and start running in the direction of the bar's back door. Why there? Who knows? Any port in a storm.

The Saint makes sure I'm watching again as he keys the detonator a third time.

This time, the car is in the adjoining lot, just over the dividing wall.

Instead of going up, this one shifts horizontally, demolishing the wall and bringing it down onto the boot of a Tesla.

Bricks from the wall fly across the parking lot like bullets.

One of them smashes into the side of the Ford near which I'm standing, thumping with a loud, echoing clang.

Something, either another brick or a chip from one, strikes Naved on the thigh and he goes down without a sound, grabbing the injured leg.

"Enough!" I shout over the roaring of the triple fires and clattering debris. "You made your point! I'll get in the truck."

He grins at me.

Then he jerks his head wordlessly.

I nod silently and climb up into the truck. The driver's side, of course, because he's no dummy. He may be young and look like a kid fresh out of high school, but he knows that you can't keep a gun on a hostage and drive at the same time. The only way to do it is to make the hostage drive.

That also comes with certain risks, though.

He gets in the passenger side of the truck.

He looks at the gun in his right hand.

"Guess I don't need this anymore, do I?"

He stuffs it into his jacket pocket.

He's right.

He doesn't need the gun anymore.

Just as he knows that both my weapons are useless right now.

The only one of us who has the power here is him.

That power is in his other hand.

And in his evil heart.

"Drive."

I do as he says.

FIFTY-ONE

We're out by the safe house again, right where this all began.

"Here's good enough," he says.

I bring the Ram to a halt.

We sit quietly in the darkness.

There's an almost full moon out tonight but it hasn't risen yet. There are no lights anywhere for miles around. We're in a darkness so deep, so true, I can see every star in the sky.

There are always more than I could ever think were possible.

We're so isolated out here, it feels like we're the only two people left in the world.

"Who are you?" I ask softly.

I let the question lie between us, in the darkness.

He shifts in his seat, turning to face me.

He still hasn't taken the gun out of his jacket pocket.

He hasn't asked me to remove my guns from their holsters and hand them over or throw them away.

If I move suddenly, quickly, using all my training and speed, I could probably shoot him at least once before he can get his gun out. Maybe even kill him.

But he still has that evil black thing in his left hand.

And the words he said back at the Schooner Bay parking lot, when he threatened Natalie, burn in my head like a slow burning fuse.

Where else has he placed his explosives?

Suddenly, I'm on the verge of panic. I need to contact Lata, tell her to make sure that she and Natalie are safe!

How far can that remote detonator work?

Usually, they have a very limited range.

But there are ways to rig them up with a cellphone chip, enabling a key or a key combination to trigger a speed dial call to a cellphone any conceivable distance away, and that in turn would trigger an explosion.

I can't take any chances.

Whatever happens here tonight, it has to end here.

No comebacks, no blowbacks, no sequels.

Endgame.

"I came through that same safe house, you know," he says suddenly, surprising me.

I wasn't expecting that.

He looks at me. I can feel his eyes on me in the darkness.

"You didn't think of that, did you?" he says softly. "Another immigrant? A refugee? Starving, persecuted, on the run, barely one step ahead of survival. Father Santos fed me, clothed me, found me shelter, a home, family, a job. I'm alive thanks to him."

"Then what happened?" I ask, keeping my voice low, gentle, unchallenging.

I sense him shrug.

"I thought I had it made. I had survived. I was in America. I had my whole life ahead of me. I could do anything, be anyone. The American fucking dream."

"It's not just a dream," I say. "What happened to you was real. You said so yourself. You're alive today because you're here. That's the real American dream. A better life."

"Sure," he says, agreeing. "I thought so, too, at first. But as I grew up, saw more of life, I saw the underside. The bottom of the rock, where all the creepy crawly things live. I saw illegal immigrants pouring in, forming gangs, selling drugs, human trafficking, every kind of crime imaginable. They used a pipeline meant to lift people up, and they abused it. They commercialized the shit out of it. Turned it into a goddamn *enterprise*!"

On the far horizon, I see the sky glowing dully.

The moon is about to rise.

Is that why we're sitting here waiting?

Does he have a bomb in Kundan's house? Or Lata's car? Or maybe even... in Natalie's backpack?

I shudder, unable to even think about it.

"Santos was the last of the good ones. He did it for the right reasons, true reasons. But he got old, sick, he died. After he was gone, the cartels started to move in, to take over. It was a pipeline, see? Like any other. They wanted to use it to move their product and their people. Like everything else in America, what started with the best intentions got perverted and abused over time. Then they were going to turn it into a money railroad, the sick bastards."

I speak quietly, keeping my tone neutral, non-judgmental.

"But all those people you killed, they weren't cartel mules. They were just ordinary refugees and immigrants like yourself, they just wanted a better life. They didn't deserve to die like that."

He shrugs. "Maybe one or two of them were mules. Maybe not. I didn't have any way to tell for sure. I had to send a message. Tell the cartels and traffickers that this pipeline was closed forever. The safe house was the message."

I close my eyes, thinking of the little girl, Consuela. Dying in the dark, crushed by tons of concrete and rock, suffocating on a mouthful of dirt.

"They'll just send more. They'll keep sending them, the

mules. And they're smart enough to make sure they blend in with the real refugees and immigrants. To stop them permanently, you'd have to kill maybe twenty innocent people to get one mule. And even the poor mules aren't actually cartel. They're acting under duress or out of desperation for their families."

"Sure."

"So what did you actually achieve?"

"I sent a message to the refugees and immigrants out there, too."

"What message is that?"

"Don't come. The American Dream is dead. It was never real to begin with. Just an illusion. A fucking commercial to sell credit card debt and mortgages. Whatever you're looking for, it doesn't exist anymore, if it ever did. Stay where you are. Survive or don't survive. But come here and you will die."

I swallow. "That's a hard line to take."

"It's the only line. Have you seen what they do to most refugees and immigrants these days? It's worse than what the lowest of the low in this country have to suffer. Worse than poverty and racism and bigotry. These people are product. They get turned into prostitutes, indentured slaves in all but name, lower than minimum wage workers, forced to do jobs that nobody else will do for any rate. They're exploited and squeezed dry. When they're all used up, they're tossed in the trash, and replaced with new ones. There's a never-ending supply. The whole world wants to come to America to be used and abused. They're lining up at the borders. Ready to crawl over or under barbed wire, climb walls, run shooting gauntlets, do whatever it takes. It's a pipeline to breed inhumanity."

"And for that, they deserve to die?" I ask.

"It's the only way," he says sadly.

"But—" I start to say, and he cuts me off.

"Get out," he says.

I open the door of the truck and climb down.
It's cooler out here than in town.
He climbs out after me.
"Walk," he says.
I walk.

FIFTY-TWO

The moon is rising now, almost halfway over the horizon.

I can actually see the globe moving, like a groundhog emerging from a hole. It's amazing how fast it seems to travel, the velocity of the earth spinning on its own axis, hurtling through space, toward infinity.

We walk for what feels like a mile or more but it's hard to tell without any landmarks and without my phone, which he made me leave in the pickup truck.

"Why did you bring me here?" I ask.

He's silent for so long, I think he isn't going to answer.

Then he sighs, a low, sad sigh.

"I want to send another message," he says.

My stomach flips.

"Haven't you already killed enough people?" I say. "First the safe house. Then the priests. The pizza parlor parking lot."

"The pizza parlor message was to tell you to stop," he says. "I thought that was pretty obvious. Instead, you did the opposite. You went and called a goddamn town hall meeting!"

"What about the priests? What message was that?"

He chuckles. "Bart Angelo lost his nerve. I recruited him

after Santos died, to help me keep the safe house active, the pipeline flowing. He helped me out at first. But at the end, he panicked. He thought you were onto us. Maybe you were, maybe you weren't. The things you were asking about, Santos's pickup truck and stuff, they didn't matter. But I knew that when you talked to Angelo, you would know that he was somehow involved."

"Did he know what you planned to do to those people in the safe house?"

"You're asking if he was an accomplice? How could he be? Back when we started, right after Santos died, I didn't know myself. I started out thinking I'd continue Santos's work. I would become the Saint in his place. I *was* the Saint for a while."

"Then what changed?"

"Everything. The world. People. The people coming in, the people exploiting them. Maybe they were always there, but somehow it seemed to have gotten worse. Out of control. There was no way to stop it or contain it anymore."

"So you decided to shut it down. Send a message. By taking innocent lives."

"I don't expect you to understand. You're an idealist. Dreamer. You still think you can save the world."

"Not the world, no. But a few good people maybe."

"It's not enough."

"Those people who are saved would beg to differ."

"I used to be like you, you know. That's why I served my country, went on foreign tours, did what I was ordered to do. Nothing made a difference. It's all so fucked up. The politicians and corporations run the whole show. Private military contractors, drones, mind manipulation algorithms. It's all working for commercial gain. Fake truths spun like cotton candy for kids."

"And bombs are better?"

"A bomb is a perfect thing, like a gun. It exists for one purpose only. To destroy. Wipe clean."

"To kill."

"Sure. You're half-Indian, aren't you? I read that online. Your country has a Sanskrit epic, *Mahabharata*, the longest poem ever written. It starts with a big bang, exactly like the scientists say started the universe. That's how everything began. With a bomb."

I know better than to argue with a pseudo-scientific worldview.

I focus on what I can control.

The moon is up now, lighting the night, the terrain around us.

We're probably visible for quite a distance out here, the only upright, two-legged, mobile animals in this empty landscape.

Is the light good enough?

It'll have to be.

"And me?" I ask. "Tonight? Why do this now, when your ruse at the town hall meeting worked so well? McD's already declared the Saint is in custody, the crisis is over, the manhunt called off. Why take such a huge risk by abducting me?"

"Because you're Susan fucking Parker. You just don't quit. You keep at it, no matter what happens. You're unstoppable."

I stop.

I turn slowly to face him.

He stops, holding up the gun and the detonator again to show me.

"Careful, SAC Parker," he says. "I still hold all the cards."

"No," I say. "You don't."

I raise my right hand, hold it steady for a moment.

He stares at it, frowning.

I clench my raised right fist.

"I hold the ace, asshole," I say.

FIFTY-THREE

The shot comes out of nowhere.

It smashes the Saint's right hand into a puff of blood spray, the hand holding the gun.

The second shot is aimed at his left hand.

It hits barely a fraction of a second after the first, but the son of a bitch is too quick, too experienced, too seasoned at combat. He's already lowering the left hand and throwing himself to the ground as the second shot strikes.

It gouges out a chunk of flesh. I see it hitting and blood spattering, silhouetted against the moon.

I'm throwing myself to the ground at the same time, rolling over and over in the dirt, trying to put as much distance between us as possible.

My heart is pounding like a jackhammer.

Crazy as my plan was, I only half-believed it would actually work.

Thank God for Paula. Third best in her regiment? She deserves the gold medal for that shot.

I come to a halt, hitting my elbow and head against a rock. It stuns me for a moment.

When I look around, he's nowhere to be seen.

The ground looks empty, but there's still chaparral, rocks, natural ditches and levees, enough cover for an experienced combat vet to hide behind from a sniper for a while. Eventually, Paula will get him, but meanwhile, he still has the detonator.

"Did you think I was just there to get drunk and celebrate?" I call out. "I knew you were watching me. You've been stalking me since this started, haven't you? Once I realized that, I knew you wouldn't end with the town hall ruse. You would come after me. You had to. Because if you didn't, I'd have found you first. Sooner or later."

A dry chuckle comes from somewhere to my right. Ten, maybe fifty meters? It's hard to judge distance from sound out here.

"You're a smart one, Susan Parker. Was that Gunny Contreras? She's a pretty decent shot, isn't she? I should have known to expect that. Color me slow to figure it out."

"Nah," I call back, crawling slowly in the direction of his voice while trying to pitch my own voice the other way. "You're good. I'm just better than you, that's all. I anticipated something like this and kept Paula on standby, just in case. She was shadowing me at the bar all evening and followed us. You just made the mistake of bringing me out here, where she could get a nice, clean shot without worrying about any background or collateral damage. Thanks for that."

He laughs, the laugh turning into a choked cough. "You're... fucking welcome. But you haven't won the round, Parker. I still have the detonator. And guess where I planted the explosives this time?"

"I don't give a fuck. It's over, asshole. Give yourself up and I'll take you in alive. Otherwise, I'll just walk away and leave you to Paula. You can't stay down forever with that wound. You'll bleed out. Sooner or later, she'll get the drop on you."

"Not going to happen," he calls back. "Tell you what. I'll

give you three guesses and the count of three. You guess correctly before I reach one and I'll turn myself in."

"And if I don't?"

He chuckles harshly. "Then you find out the hard way what three pounds of C4 can do to someone you care about."

That almost makes me stand up and come running at him, which is exactly what he's hoping for.

It takes every ounce of patience for me to lie still in the dirt and keep watching.

I glimpse something that looks like a human head.

Or is it a rock?

Damn this gibbous moon.

It's enough light to see shapes and silhouettes by, but not details.

Every time I think I see him, a cloud drifts over the moon, veiling it just enough to obscure.

"First guess for the count of three!" he calls out.

I clench my teeth and play along to buy myself time.

"Lata's Jeep!" I call out.

"Second guess for the count of two!"

"My partner Naved's Camry?"

"Last and final guess, SAC Parker. Make it count."

"My daughter's backpack," I say, as I rise above him and bring down the rock on his face.

I feel flesh, cartilage, and bone all yield beneath the force of the blow, and see his hand jerk, thumb leaving the detonator.

I bring down the rock again to be sure.

Until his face is nothing but a dark mask in the moonlight, and his breathing is barely a thin, faint rasp from an exposed windpipe.

His left hand, striped in blood above the elbow, is raised just enough for him to keep it off the ground. It's still holding the detonator. His thumb is too close to the detonator.

I grip his forearm in one hand, ignoring the sticky blood,

take hold of his thumb and yank it back, breaking it with a sound like a twig snapping.

Then I slowly take the detonator out of his hand.

And fall back on my ass, still clutching it.

I find the activation switch and turn it off, watching as the light changes.

A long, shuddering breath forces its way out of me.

I drop the detonator and try to get up, only to fall to my knees.

My head dips and a deep, low wailing sound startles me, coming from seemingly nowhere.

It takes me a minute to understand that I'm the source.

A primal, animal scream rips its way loose from my soul, as I raise my face to the empty skies and roar my emotions out.

The sound of my pain ripples across the landscape.

Tears spill out of me as I weep my guts out.

That's how Paula finds me several minutes later. She uses her foot to nudge the body, making sure of him.

She stares down at the obliterated face.

"Who is he?" she asks.

I swipe the tears off my cheeks with the backs of my hands.

"An immigrant who forgot why he came here," I say.

FIFTY-FOUR

After the service, the old abuelita comes to me, accompanied by Paula.

She starts speaking in rapid-Fire Panamanian Spanish to me. Paula manages to translate.

"She says her heart is very full today. She has great gratitude to you for everything. For catching the man who killed her Consuela and all those other people. And for making the world become aware of the deaths here at the safe house. She says that this memorial service was beyond her expectations. She never even dreamed that such a thing was possible. To have all these people here, joining us in remembering the death of Consuela and the others? The governor himself? All these media people? For the whole world to now know her little Consuela's name, see her picture on their television sets everywhere? It was unthinkable even a week ago. Yet you have achieved this miracle. She owes you a great debt."

I bow my head and take the old lady's withered hand in mine, saying softly, "Tell her that the debt is owed to her and all the immigrants like her who came to this country, worked hard, invested their sweat, tears, and blood to make it what it is today.

She and her Consuela deserve all this attention and much more."

The old lady listens, bows her head and kisses my hand before adding a few more words.

"She says that you are an angel descended from heaven. And your wrath is that of the angels. May you go on to have a fruitful career and life and may no one ever trouble you, on pain of death."

I hardly know what to say to that but manage a few final words.

As the old lady shuffles away, I see another familiar face approaching. This one much taller, more famous, and accompanied by the usual retinue of bodyguards.

"SAC Parker," says the governor of California, taking my hand. "Once again, thank you for your efforts."

"Just doing my job, sir. Thank you for gracing the occasion and spotlighting these people. It's a great thing you've done here."

"Just doing my job," he says, grinning. "Immigrants have made this country great. Sometimes, some of us try to pretend that isn't the case, but it is. Agent Parker, if you have a minute, do drop by my office someday. There's a proposition I'd like to discuss with you."

I blink, taken by surprise but manage to nod. "Sure."

As the governor walks away, to be whisked away in a waiting retinue of dark SUVs, Ramon grins at me. His head is still bandaged and he's a little pale and weak as yet, but he's on his feet again and claims to be doing a lot better.

"You did good, el capitan," he says. "I told them you always come through."

My eyes prickle with tears. "Thanks, Ramon. Couldn't have done it without you guys. You know that."

The rest of the team and I exchange hugs and a few words

before they leave. The feeling is upbeat and positive. The memorial service was a real coup, and the event has somehow managed to unite the entire community if only for a day. Even McD made eye contact with me and had a few good words. I suspect he'll always be skeptical of me and my way of doing my job, but he's not one to pass up a photo op and all said and done, at the end of the day, the safe house case left him with some of the biggest photo ops of his career. As always, I'm happy to let him hog the limelight. I'm content just to have taken one more monster off the streets.

A lot of people smile at me. Even the unfortunate incident with Elle MacPherson seems to have been forgiven. She survived surgery and is expected to make a full recovery. McD's statement reassuring people that my use of force was necessary at the time helped, too.

Urduja is the only one not smiling. But that's not because of me. She's having a hard time dealing with survivor's guilt after waking up to learn that she made it while Fry was blown to pieces, quite literally. But she does come and exchange a word or two with me.

"Thanks, Susan," she says. "For including him in the memorial. That was a really nice thing to do."

"Of course, Urduja. I feel terrible about what happened. He didn't deserve to die like that. The least we can do is remember him and honor his memory."

She nods. I suspect it will be a long time before she recovers from Fry's death. If ever. That kind of thing changes you, shapes the rest of your life.

I should know. Amit's death changed me forever.

"What's next for you?" I ask.

She looks at Naved, standing beside me.

"I'm thinking about a few things," she says.

"Whatever you need, you know I'm always just a call away," I say.

She nods, and finally allows herself a sliver of a smile. "Thanks, Susan."

After she leaves, I look at Naved. "What did she mean?"

Naved nods. "She talked to me about maybe joining SCVPD."

"That makes sense," I say. "She's always talked about becoming a cop."

"She wants to be you," Naved says. "I'm guessing at some point you told her that law enforcement experience would be good for her resume."

I sigh. "Probably. Though why she'd want to be me after what happened to Fry, I don't know. I'm not sure *I* want to be me anymore."

"Don't be too hard on yourself. That's on the Saint, not on you."

I nod gratefully. "Thanks, partner."

"So this guy, Donny Cartright, was the Saint?" he asks.

"He was one of the first immigrants Father Santos sheltered in the safe house," I say. "I guess his American dream turned sour over time."

"And he had kids in the same school as Natalie?"

"Yeah. One of them was in her drama club. In the annual play. I probably saw Cartright several times in passing, but he was just another parent. If I hadn't gotten hung up on Nate Sanderson, maybe I would have been more alert of other veterans who were also parents."

"Why would you? There was no reason to think he was a parent or that he was that close to you," Naved says. "And what you had on Nate Sanderson made sense at the time, especially since you didn't know the guy. Don't beat yourself up over this."

I sigh. "It's tough not to. I still can't believe I let him get close enough to slip a bomb into Natalie's backpack while she was rehearsing."

"You didn't *let* him do anything. He was insane and dangerous. He managed to slip bombs into your Prius and Lata's Jeep, too, didn't he? And my Camry? We had no reason to expect any of that. This guy was off the charts."

"Yeah," I say. "I know. I'm just glad he's finally in the ground."

He looks at me. "You okay?"

I nod. "I will be."

"If you need anything, you know where to find me," he says gently.

I smile up at him. "Thanks, Naved."

He nods. "We still need to talk, though. About the CBI case. I have an update about that we need to discuss as soon as possible."

I look at him, concerned and curious. "Is it about Amit?"

He looks around. "Yes, but not just him."

"Then tell me!"

"Not here, not now. We need to discuss this in private, Susan."

"Okay, okay," I say, frazzled but understanding the need for privacy. "I'll call you as soon as I'm done here."

He nods and walks away.

My mind is still racing with the possibility of what his "update" might consist of when I sense someone approaching me in my peripheral vision.

"Miss Parker!"

I turn to see a smartly turned-out man in an impeccably tailored suit.

"SAC Parker, we've spoken on the phone before," he says warmly.

"Mr. Hall?" I say, not very kindly. "The attorney?"

"I'm pleased that you remember me."

"I remember the accent. It's very, um, distinctive."

"I get that a lot. As they say, you can take the Englishman out of England, but you can't take the English out of him."

"I'm surprised to see you here, Mr. Hall." I don't try to hide my lack of enthusiasm. Him showing up here seems like the next worst thing to handing out visiting cards at funerals.

"I shan't deny that it was my only means of getting to you personally, Miss Parker. Since you seem to have blocked my number and won't take my calls."

I start to turn away. "Well, Mr. Hall, you'll excuse me, but—"

"Miss Parker, I'll come straight to the point. I specialize in estate law. In point of fact, I have only one client. A very wealthy client who recently passed away."

"I'm sorry to hear that, Mr. Hall, but what does that have to do with me?" I ask, looking around for someone to take me away before he launches into his spiel, whatever it is.

"Everything, Miss Parker. Because you see, he left his entire estate to you."

I turn back to look at him. "What?"

"That's what I've been trying to reach you to tell you, Miss Parker. This is not a scam or a scheme, it's simple estate law. You are the sole beneficiary of a very substantial fortune and estate. And we need to speak privately to discuss the details so we can proceed with the inheritance at the earliest."

I stare at him, trying to process what he's just said.

"This is my card," he says, handing me a visiting card. "This time, I trust you will take me seriously and do me the privilege of joining me at my offices on a day and time convenient? Thank you, I shall take your leave now. And may I add in parting that it is a great thing you've achieved here today. Good day, Miss Parker."

"Who was that?" Lata asks as she comes up with Natalie, who smiles and signs to me: "Cool memorial service. I met the governor, too! He thanked Lata Auntie for her service!"

I bend down and pick up my daughter. She's much too

heavy to carry but right now I need to feel her warmth, her love. She kisses me on my cheek happily.

"Someone who just gave me some news," I say, still a little dazed.

"What kind of news?" Lata asks.

"The kind that might just change our lives," I say.

I add after a moment. "For the better, I think."

A LETTER FROM THE AUTHOR

Hi!

I hope you enjoyed *The Safe House*.

If I did my job right, it was a rollercoaster of a ride, with enough chills, thrills, suspense, action, and shocks to keep you turning the pages late into the night. And if you enjoyed it as much as I enjoyed writing it, then I have a request: Hit the link below and sign up to my mailing list. That way, you can be sure of never missing the latest news and updates about Susan and her adventures.

www.stormpublishing.co/sam-baron

The only thing more wonderful than a great read is sharing it with another avid reader. I would really appreciate it if you could spare a few moments to leave a review. Even a short review of just a couple of lines and that all-important five-star rating can make a huge difference to an author and book. Sharing is caring, after all! Thank you so much!

From *The Therapy Room* to *The Murder Club* and now *The Safe House,* we've seen Susan put through the wringer. Each time she survived (barely) and lives to fight another day. She's also crept closer to the truth about her husband Amit Kapoor's murder, but she still has more questions than answers.

But here's the good news: Those questions are about to be

answered in full, closing out that very personal case with the most shocking twist!

So hold on to your hat—and your reading or listening device —because things are about to get really deadly for Susan and her fam, real as well as found.

To know more about the Susan Parker series and me, stay in touch with me at my website or social media links below.

Love, only love, and happy reading forever!

Sam

sambaronauthor.com

facebook.com/sambaronauthor

x.com/samkbaron

instagram.com/samkbaron

tiktok.com/@samkbaron

Made in United States
Cleveland, OH
06 December 2024

11419224R00184